PRAISE FOR RICHARD B. SCHWARTZ

Proof of Purchase

It's like this guy is just channeling Raymond Chandler on every page. . . . The ending . . . would make Mike Hammer proud.
— Jochem Steen, *Sons of Spade*

In this engaging hard-boiled mystery, one of three in Schwartz's Jack Grant series (Frozen Stare; The Last Voice You Hear), the seasoned California PI looks into the disappearance of an ex-girlfriend at the request of the woman's husband. When her mutilated body turns up in the woods, Grant makes it his mission to track down her murderer. With the assistance of Lt. Diana Craig, an attractive fast-riser in the San Bernardino police department, Grant follows leads that point to his client, as well as to a consortium of underworld bosses who are branching out into a mega-real estate project. The pair find time, between car chases and gun battles, to begin a relationship. . . . Fans of Robert Parker will enjoy encountering Grant . . . .
— *Publishers Weekly*

The Last Voice You Hear

It's not often that an author's second book is as good as the first, and even less frequent are the instances when an author . . . top[s] it with an extraordinary second . . . deliver[ing] a walloping good tale as well. Richard B. Schwartz has done just that. In *The Last Voice You Hear*, Mr. Schwartz places himself on par with our finest contemporary murder-mystery writers. This is a book you won't want to miss. . . .
— Alan Paul Curtis in *Who Dunnit*

The author . . . writes vividly, putting the reader right into the scene. Schwartz explores the meaning of right and wrong, crime and justice.
— Mary Helen Becker in *Mystery News*

The story rockets along . . . a fast-moving, well-told story with a surprising conclusion that blurs the line between crime and justice.
— Joseph Scarpato, Jr. in *Mystery Scene*

Jack Grant, the Vietnam vet and Pasadena-based PI who debuted in Frozen Stare (1989), returns in this engrossing sequel by Schwartz, author of several scholarly studies of Samuel Johnson. Schwartz knows his London, but surprisingly he evokes California with equal ease, mainly with vividly etched strokes. An apparently maniacal killer is on the loose in London, someone strong and very practiced at impalement. So far, so nasty. But when a victim is dispatched in similar fashion in Disneyland, of all places, Jack Grant is called in. He discovers the killer's identity, but there's a problem: there's a method to the killer's madness. Moreover, Grant has an ethical problem of his own: he's plagued by his conscience, since he understands and even sympathizes with the murderer's cause. The cinematic climax takes place high above the floor of the California desert, and Schwartz squeezes every last drop of suspense from his setting. . . . The result is a high-tension thriller awash in sanguinary detail. Paper towels, anyone?
— *Publishers Weekly*

Frozen Stare

I welcome Richard Schwartz to the club. It's been a long time since I've seen two more engaging characters entering the series scene.
— Sandra Scoppettone

Grant and White play nicely off each other and the switch-on-a-switch works well.
— *Kirkus Reviews*

This tale, in the California private eye tradition, has a rousing finish and is an enjoyable read.
— *Publishers Weekly*

A new author devoted to the hard-boiled tradition. . . . Schwartz has the hard-boiled formula down pat. . . . Schwartz does not break any rules in Frozen Stare. . . . He writes crisply. The narrative moves at a slam-bang pace as bodies pile up. . . . As a dedicated student of the hard-boiled school of detective fiction [Schwartz] has learned his lessons well.
— *The Washington Post Book World*

Gives a whole new meaning to the phrase 'cold-blooded murder'. . . . This is a quick read with plenty of action. Schwartz's first novel is a winner!
— *Sarasota, FL Herald Tribune*

This is a delightful tale, full of amusing touches, and the relationship between Grant and his good cop friend, black Frank White, is a joy. I hope that Schwartz can keep this standard up for a long time to come.
— *The Armchair Detective*

Nice and Noir: Contemporary American Crime Fiction

Opinionated but always fascinating, shrewd and smart, but always readable. . . .
— *The Thrilling Detective*

BOOKS BY RICHARD B. SCHWARTZ
FICTION

The Jack Grant Novels
Frozen Stare
The Last Voice You Hear
Proof of Purchase

The Gwen Harrison Novels
No Exit
Red City
The Gray Twilight

The Tom Deaton Novels
Into the Dark
The Survivor's Song
Nightmare Man
Death Whispers
Poison Touch

Short Stories
Townhouse and Other Stories

CRITICISM

Samuel Johnson and the New Science
Samuel Johnson and the Problem of Evil
Boswell's Johnson: A Preface to the Life
Daily Life in Johnson's London
After the Death of Literature
Nice and Noir: Contemporary American Crime Fiction
The Wounds that Heal: Heroism and Human Development
(with Judith A. Schwartz)
ed. *The Plays of Arthur Murphy, 4 vols.*
ed. *Theory and Tradition in Eighteenth-Century Studies*

MEMOIRS
The Biggest City in America: A Fifties Boyhood in Ohio
Accidental Soldier: A Reserve Officer at West Point in the Vietnam Era
Postwar Higher Education in America: Just Yesterday

EBOOK
Is a College Education Still Worth the Price? A Dean's Sobering Perspective

A GWEN HARRISON NOVEL

THE GRAY TWILIGHT

RICHARD B. SCHWARTZ

THE GRAY TWILIGHT

Published by Dark Harbor Books
First Edition 2024

Cover design: Jana Rade

ISBN: 979-8-9899271-3-5 Paperback Edition
         979-8-9899271-4-2 Hardcover Edition
         979-8-9899271-5-9 Digital Edition

Library of Congress Control Number: 2024917548

Author services by Pedernales Publishing, LLC
www.pedernalespublishing.com

10 9 8 7 6 5 4 3 2 1

Printed in the United States of America

v7

For those who lit the way.

We sleep soundly in our beds because rough
men stand ready in the night to visit
violence on those who would
do us harm.

*(Inspired by Kipling, sometimes
attributed to Orwell and Churchill)*

I

___

GWEN

CHAPTER ONE

As she attempted to open her eyelids, working against the thin channels of sand and grit, she found herself enclosed within constraints: cables, wires, tubing…a clip covering the first joint of a fingertip…the expansion/contraction of a blood pressure cuff…cotton padding under tightening latex tape covering elbow puncture points. She felt the pressures, the pinch at the needle entry point on the back of her hand, the unfamiliar sensation caused by the catheter. Her eyes panned across a rolling landscape of white linen as the webs and tangles of lines, monitoring electrodes and drains began to come into clearer focus. In the background: hums and beeps; in her peripheral vision--green and red flashes, some of bars and one at least of waves.

To her right there was a clear line of light emerging between partially-drawn curtains. The top of the surrounding walls appeared to be gray cement which complimented the rich courses of red bricks. As she turned to her left she saw the floor—some form of linoleum or vinyl with tiny splashes of muted colors. Simple to mop. There was some tiling at the base of the walls and a call button just beyond her left hand. Everything was spotless. No whisps of dust in the room's corners. No dark points among the grout lines, no dust motes floating in the line of sunlight; a host of smells—Lysol perhaps, but also something with a touch of citrus, predominantly lemon but with a drop or two of orange, all overlayed with something harsher, something designed to sweep all invisible invaders from its path. Something lethal, purifying, definitive, the kind of smell you had hoped for in cheap hotel rooms or nocturnal observation posts in otherwise-abandoned spaces, something that would protect you from invisible threats, some source of reassurance amid the shabby surroundings, a layer of insulation and protection.

Above and to the left of her head: breakfast, lunch and dinner in a single, clear plastic pouch. She craned her neck to the side, watching the drips and assessing the fluid level. How often does the attending nurse check it? What if it runs dry? Is there a signal of some sort? Her lifeline, after all.

She tried to feel the pain through the induced numbness, tracing the feed and drain lines to their sources and containers. What, after all, had happened? She had heard noises and felt pressures before she fell into the darkness. She remembered standing by a doorway, or was it a gate? An arch of some sort? She had been on duty but not in assault or combat mode. Some sort of liaison role. The memory was faint and it was now clouded by sedation.

The door opened slowly. A woman in blue, v-necked nurse's scrubs entered the room. She was middle-aged and expressionless. Had she received some signal when Gwen had begun to stir in her bed?

"How do you feel?" she asked.

"Groggy. Numb," Gwen answered.

"That's normal," the woman responded. Gwen noticed that she wasn't wearing a nametag or carrying a stethoscope.

"What happened to me?" Gwen asked.

"You were hurt. We're taking good care of you."

"Where am I?" Gwen asked.

"Someplace safe," the nurse answered.

"Could you open the drapes a little?" Gwen asked.

"Of course," the woman answered. "Is this enough?" she asked, parting the drapes another foot on either side.

"Yes, thank you," Gwen answered. "I think I'll rest now."

"Go right ahead," the woman said. She then turned and left the room.

Gwen had closed her eyes as the woman left; when the door closed she reopened them, scooting into position to see what she could see through the window.

There were white pines in the middle distance and what looked like dogwoods, mostly white but one or two pink…no houses, though everything seemed neatly trimmed and well maintained. About ten yards from the window the red-brick wall…security or decoration? Both? At least six feet high, perhaps eight. Inside the wall a single magnolia tree in full bloom. Thick, with shiny leaves. Thick enough to block the light beyond. On either side, azaleas, mostly pink, but some purple. Someone had taken pains to decorate the space. All beyond the purely functional… nice. She was somewhere in the south, probably no farther north than Virginia. She looked for a clock in the room. None on the wall, none on the side table next to the bed. She reached for the drawer and felt a twinge in her shoulder. She slid it open. Empty, except for some tongue depressors and packaged bandages. Where were her things, her watch, her cellphone? Was she under care or in confinement?

She raised her arm and looked at the i.d. bracelet on her wrist— standard hospital-style, made of adhesive paper but durable and difficult to remove. There was no name on it, no date of admission, no information concerning condition or care, none concerning hospital division or room number. There was a single 8-digit number with interspersed letters, some capitalized. A password or a code. Was this for her protection—to keep any intruders from easily identifying potential targets—or was it part of an attempt to keep her ignorant or confused concerning her situation and condition?

She fell back against her pillow and thought about her situation. There was a noticeable pinch of pain in her left shoulder. She rearranged herself and the pain returned to numbness. Certain things were clear. They were going to be evasive concerning her questions. If she resisted them they would probably resist her with equal force. They had taken pains to construct a web of anonymity. She was behind walls, after all; lovely red-brick walls dotted with azaleas and (she now saw) some yellow roses, but walls nonetheless. Better to play along. Better to let them believe that she was groggy and numb. Play the wounded sleepyhead, but watch and listen. Learn what little she could, incrementally. Then bestir herself.

CHAPTER TWO

Two days passed. The same nurse continued to attend her. Gwen tested her, inquiring about her IV bag and feeding line. She joked that it didn't taste like steak or chicken noodle soup. She asked about the finger clip and what it measured, trying to determine whether the woman was an actual nurse or a handler. She appeared to be a little of both. Her answers were generally evasive but they were interspersed with minimal technical information. "It measures oxygen level and pulse. In your case, 97 and 72; good numbers."

Gwen thanked her for providing 'such good care' and the woman smiled. At first she leaned forward as if she were about to pat Gwen on the arm but then she stepped back, smiled politely and left the room.

Four hours later she returned and checked Gwen's dressings. Gwen kept her eyes closed. She had already checked them herself, but they were taped too securely to enable her to inspect the actual wounds. Had she tried she feared that the tape might curl or fail to adhere as it had originally. She wanted to project detachment and docility. Dependency. Let the nurse feel as if she was in complete charge and Gwen her willing and appreciative patient.

From the corner of her eye she could see that one of the dressings had a slight yellow stain. Was it something they swabbed on the wound before operating? ChloraPrep? Betadine? Or could it be indicative of an infection? Gwen assumed that the nurse would check. She practiced looking with one eye as she lay on her side. When the nurse returned that afternoon to check her Gwen moved her head slowly to the left as if she was unconsciously adjusting her position to increase her comfort level. She inhaled deeply and then returned to her regular breathing. The nurse took a brief look, touching the dressing with the fingertip of her right hand, and then left the room, returning a few seconds later with a small tray containing fresh dressings, tape and what appeared to be salves. When she had removed the tape and lifted the gauze Gwen stole a look with her left eye. The nurse wiped at the wound, applied some form of antiseptic from a tube and replaced the dressings. She said nothing and left the room. The wound was not pretty. The center was blackish red with a halo of pinkish red at the periphery. The hole was circular and neat along the edges--a bullet wound. A large caliber bullet wound. No wonder her shoulder hurt. The smaller wound in her arm was probably its mate. Two rounds, no killshot. Aiming for the heart? One shooter or two?

She tried to sit up and stretch her body. Perhaps there was a chart clipped to the base of her bed. A long shot, she knew, and she had not yet seen the nurse (she had become comfortable calling her that) reach for such an object, but her interest was piqued and she was ready to grasp at even the most improbable possibilities. As she angled her body her shoulder said no, emphatically. So did her arm and, curiously, her back, her ankles and her knees. Were they weaning her off of her painkillers?

Two days later Gwen was able to move her right hand to the wound on her left arm. She moistened her fingertip and dabbed at the dressing, trying to create a slight discoloration. Running her damp finger tip along the metal joints in the bed freed up enough dust to create some color. She knew she couldn't create a yellow stain, but the hint of gray might be enough to cause the nurse some concern. Dirt could lead to infection and dirt could have come from some wayward tubing. She wanted to prompt the nurse to change the dressing and give her an opportunity to see the second wound.

It worked. When the wound was exposed Gwen was able to see it briefly. More darkish red, more pinkish halo, another nearly-perfect circle, but this one smaller. Not perhaps to the untrained eye, but certainly to a trained special agent in the Federal Bureau of Investigation. There had been two guns and almost certainly two shooters. No skilled sniper brings along an arsenal and she must have been the victim of a sniper. All she could remember was standing in some sort of opening in a gate or wall and feeling pressure and some twinge of pain before the memories disappeared. No grand narrative; no charge of a team or squad or pair; no firefight. No warning.

A person who sends two snipers is a person of serious purpose. Perhaps she should be grateful to be sequestered in an anonymous room in an anonymous facility, a place without names or nameplates, a place with high walls and solid bricks.

There was one clear and nagging problem. Since she had been unable to see her assailants, much less to return fire, they were still out there, perhaps just beyond the walls. Whoever sent them would be unlikely to write off their failure and move on, assuming of course that he (or she) knew she was still alive. Trained snipers with professional scopes should have seen the impact of the bullets on her shoulder and arm. With satellites and drones you could evaluate the effects of bombs, rockets and missiles. With forward observers you could see the results of small and large artillery. Checking out the results of two rifle shots in a civilian setting without the smoke and dust of actual combat to obscure their vision would be part of the basic training of any true professionals. Had her attacker sent the second team? Was she simply lucky? Was she shot at a vast distance? It is only a matter of inches from the heart to the shoulder, particularly if her body was tilted slightly or jerked by the initial round. A strong wind would significantly alter the situation. She didn't remember such a wind. On the contrary, everything had been calm. She had been waiting and watching, not poised to attack or even to react. There was a speech of some kind to be given and she was there to escort the speaker. There was a pause. He had been introduced to someone just off the podium and they were talking. Gwen was standing in the background, waiting for them to proceed, not waiting to be shot.

CHAPTER THREE

A week and a half later the majority of the tubes and drains were removed and Gwen persuaded the nurse to allow her to use the restroom rather than the bed pan. She had to roll the IV stand with her, but she was building her legs along with her confidence, restoring a small bit of muscle tone. Two days later she asked if she could leave her room and draw some fresh air.

"Of course," the nurse responded, but she followed Gwen outside, positioning her on a small patio outside and to the left of her room. The hallway to the outside door turned out to be a few feet beyond the internal door to her room, so that she was still isolated. There were no other patients at that end of the facility and no other individuals outside except for the nurse who checked on her frequently. The sun was warm, the air thick, but the humidity was countered by the breeze that came along the inside of the external wall, moving the flowers and shrubs. It was early spring, the temperature in the upper 60's, the weather systems moving the clouds, blocking and unblocking the sun, bringing cooler temperatures with the shade.

Gwen was becoming more and more impatient. Still tethered to the IV there was talk of solid food. "I'll speak with your doctor," the nurse said, a presence she had not yet met and whose name, like the nurse's, remained a mystery. When Gwen told her that she felt awkward, not knowing her name, the nurse told her to relax, get well, and not worry about it. She would be there whenever Gwen pressed the button beside her bed, a reassuring fact but still disquieting in its way. She knows *my* name, Gwen thought. This gives her some odd advantage over me. But perhaps she does not. Perhaps she refers to me as the patient in room 9. Perhaps the anonymity was absolute and was safer for all of them.

Gwen tried pushing the button at odd times; surely the nurse wasn't there twenty-four hours, seven days a week. She didn't want to push it so often that her actions could be seen as a test or a breach of trust, but she could manufacture an occasional cough and ask for water or empty the tissue box and request a refill. Still, the same nurse appeared each time.

She would have to get into some common area where she might find another patient. The Bureau was a large organization but perhaps there was another person there whom she knew. Perhaps there was a practical nurse or a member of the cleaning staff who would be willing to talk, willing, perhaps, to convey a message or lend her a cellphone, someone who could connect her with the world beyond the brick wall.

Gwen wondered if her room was equipped with WiFi. If she only had a phone or laptop and two minutes to herself. . .just the thought of being isolated and cut off troubled her. She was completely dependent, completely defenseless. This was not her condition of choice.

She thought of other strategies. If she could feign some form of illness she might be taken to a different facility for treatment, a place with other patients, perhaps with a telephone or a set of computer stations, a place accessible at night when the staff numbers were diminished and lone individuals might take meal or bathroom breaks.

If she could transition to solid food she could retain certain elements—condiments, perhaps—and create an emetic that would provoke vomiting. If she could plausibly soil her bed (or the floor, en route to the bathroom) they would have to move her to a different station while they cleaned. Even if she was positioned in the hallway someone might pass by, someone who could be persuaded or even bribed. Though still young, Gwen was a senior agent, reporting directly to the Director. She worked on special projects, some of significant importance, some in the nature of favors, like her most recent assignment, the outlines of which were beginning to return. The Director had asked her to accompany a

VIP, a friend of a friend, not someone in significant danger, but a person who could provoke unpleasant responses. "Do this for me, Gwen," the Director had said. "You may well find the assignment interesting." While she couldn't yet remember the specific details she remembered the Director's tone. This was soft duty, a break in a challenging schedule, an opportunity to ratchet down, perhaps even to kick back, at least for a moment or two. So why was she then shot near the heart by two snipers?

CHAPTER FOUR

It was another week before she was put on so-called solid food: juice, odd-colored smoothies ("filled with vitamins," the nurse said), broth, cottage cheese, rice pudding, jello. As she tolerated it they added salads, soups with noodles and tiny pieces of meat, boiled rice with vegetables; for breakfast, eggs, oatmeal and an occasional piece of lightly-buttered toast. "Next stop, pork chops and sirloin steak," she said. "Not quite yet," the nurse responded, "but you're doing very well."

She was digesting things well, sleeping less. She was even given reading materials—books, no magazines or newspapers with telltale dates, but some novels and short stories. Someone had been trying to save money; there were remainder stripes on some, the remains of adhesive and library sleeves on others. Nothing electronic. No phones, no tablets, no laptops, no television. Still, she went outside whenever she could. They couldn't hide or suppress the ambient temperatures. It was getting warmer. The short spring had been succeeded by early summer, with temperatures spiking in the 80's.

Her ornithology skills were minimal, but all of the birds she saw (grackles, cardinals, wrens, nuthatches, jays, mourning doves) were common and, at least, native to Virginia. The air was thick with humidity, some of the rain showers intense. She watched the insects, flying through the paths of artificial light at night. She watched the ants, the isopods and the wood roaches working the top of the soil and mulch. While she could not yet identify her location with any confidence she was able to eliminate a growing list of possibilities.

She thought frequently of the notion of inducing illness but finally decided against it. Damaging a limb through an 'inadvertent' fall was also dismissed as an option. Her arm and shoulder were feeling better and her medication had been radically reduced. She took a few *Tylenol* and was developing some muscle tone through minimal, seated and prone exercises. Finally, she asked the nurse if she could have access to actual equipment. "I'll have to see," the nurse responded; two days later she was told that her doctor had approved it. "I'll accompany you to the exercise facility," the nurse said. "The staff have access to it and the patients use it for rehabilitation; it's very nice, but we want to make sure that you don't overdo."

You also don't want me to communicate with anyone else who might enter the room, Gwen thought, but that's alright. It's a start. It's a change, a break in the routine, an opportunity.

The exercise space was actually in a separate section of the rehab facility, a 5-10 minute walk: new things to see, new things to learn, potential contacts to be made. Gwen was first outfitted with some gym shorts and an elasticized athletic shirt, some short white socks and a pair of *New Balance* shoes. No sports bra, presumably because of her shoulder wound; she would begin very gradually and progress incrementally.

"Are you ready?" the nurse asked.

"I am," Gwen said. "The clothing all fits well. Thanks."

The nurse just nodded and said, "Good, let's go."

The room was small, perhaps 20'x20', but filled with equipment. A single wall of mirrors increased the sense of depth. There was a dual action elliptical, an upright bike, a recumbent bike, a programmable rower, two treadmills and a set of dual-handle wall weights. The nurse apologized for the small selection and positioned herself on a window seat near the towels and top-loaded water dispenser.

"This is just what I need," Gwen said, pointing to the wall weights. The nurse just smiled, folding her hands in her lap. Gwen set the weights, grasped the chest-high handles and pulled them gently toward her feet. She felt resistance in her arm and shoulder, but the pain was minimal. She did several repetitions and then pulled the handles above her head, pulled them parallel to the ground and did some curls, testing the sensitivity of her arm and shoulder. She felt soft and a little weak, but there was still far less pain than she had anticipated, perhaps because of her morning *Tylenol*. After fifteen minutes of exercise she moved to the treadmill, stealing a look at the nurse as she walked to the other side of the room. 'West,' she thought to herself, as she assessed the light beyond the rear window.

The shutoff cord was twisted. She disentangled it, attached the clip to her shorts and turned on the device. She set it at 1.5 mph, moving it up to 2.0 after she felt comfortable. "Not too fast," the nurse called to her. "You've only been ambulatory for a short time."

"Thanks," Gwen said, "it just feels good to get up and move around."

The nurse didn't respond; she just sat there, her hands still in her lap, her eyes on Gwen's side and back. She hadn't brought a book or magazine, a tablet or a smart phone. 'Watching me is her full-time job,' Gwen thought.

She walked for fifteen or sixteen minutes and began to tire. She was also both hungry and thirsty. She paused the treadmill, walked over to the water dispenser, pulled a cup from the plastic tube beside it, filled it and slowly sipped.

"That's probably enough for today," the nurse said.

"Just a few more minutes," Gwen said. "Not long."

"As you wish," the nurse responded. Gwen took one of the red hand towels from the stack on the adjoining bench, wiped her face and forehead and returned to the treadmill. As she watched the dot circle the track icon on the status screen she caught a flash of movement with her peripheral vision. The entry door had opened and the image of a young woman was caught in the mirror. Gwen looked at the mirror, trying to appear focused on her exercise routine. The woman was about Gwen's age—late twenties, perhaps early thirties. There were no apparent bruises or marks on her face, arms or legs. No bandages. She was too far away for Gwen to see whether or not she had any IV entry-point bruises. Her hair appeared to have been recently cut and styled. She carried a small gym bag. Staff.

Gwen tried to see if she and the nurse recognized one another but she couldn't look without appearing to gawk. More important, there was something else in the young woman's hand, a cell phone.

CHAPTER FIVE

The woman used the elliptical for a brisk ten minutes, wiped her forehead with one of the small red towels and caught her breath. She then walked over to the parallel treadmill, put the towel over the left handle and placed her keys and cell phone in the cup holder. When she turned on the machine she began to jog slowly. Within two or three minutes she was jogging faster and adjusted the angle of incline by what appeared to be at least 10 degrees. She was running uphill—a heavy-duty workout.

Gwen smiled at her initially, said 'Hi' and then went back to her own exercise routine. Every few minutes she gripped the handles and waited for her heart rate to appear on the status screen. 104. Good. Her rate was slightly higher than expected and she was elevating it comfortably. She was actually exercising, not just looking for an opportunity to poach a cell phone.

She was careful not to draw attention to herself. The facility was governed by rules—absolute rules—and she did not want to appear to be anxious to break them. She would first need to build trust and that could take weeks or even months, assuming she ever saw the person again.

She wanted to speak with her but she would have to wait until the person was finished with her routine. It took longer than Gwen would have liked. In the meantime she lowered the walk rate a tenth of a mile at a time, finally stopping at 1.5 mph. When she saw the woman level the angle of incline and slow her pace she could also see that the light bar on her screen had changed. She was in the 'cool down' phase. Gwen stopped first, reset the screen on her machine, wrapped the shutoff clip and cord around two of her fingers and put them in the cup holder.

As the woman got off her treadmill Gwen was wiping her face. "I've been recuperating," Gwen said. "I'm happy to be able to walk, much less run like you."

"All things in good time," the woman said. "They'll take proper care of you here."

"They already have," Gwen said. "It's a wonderful facility."

"I've been here two years now," the woman said. "It's a great place to work."

"And it's very nice that they have a workout room," Gwen said.

"Yes, they encourage us to use it."

Gwen caught a look at her nurse, sitting in the distance. She appeared to be trying to hear what she and the other woman were saying. She seemed nervous.

Gwen wiped her face and said, "Maybe I'll see you again; I'm going to get some water now."

"You probably will," the woman said. "I try to get here every other day. My doc says it's better to have three short sessions a week than one or two extended ones."

"Easier psychologically too," Gwen said. "Thirty minutes is not so daunting. You can make time for it more easily."

"Exactly," the woman said, "bye for now."

"Bye," Gwen said. She could feel the nurse's eyes on her as she smiled politely in the other woman's direction. She then turned and walked directly to the water cooler. Her body language was saying that she had had enough of the social chitchat and wanted something to drink. Suddenly she and the nurse were the only people in the room and the sense of quiet was heavy in the air. "This tastes good," Gwen said. "Can I get you a cup?"

"No thank you," the nurse answered. "I'm fine."

"I don't want you to overdue," the nurse said as she walked Gwen back to her room.

"I appreciate that," Gwen responded. "I feel good. A little tired, of course, but good. I'm ready to rest awhile."

"I thought so," the nurse said, smiling. She seemed pleased, as if the last thing she wanted to hear was a request to return to the exercise facility.

CHAPTER SIX

For the first time since she awoke Gwen was able to read the orderly's watch. She had switched from a small, more stylish one to a larger one, with a *Swiss Army* logo. The breakfast arrived at 7:02 a.m. As Gwen cut the pats of butter in two and positioned them between her pancakes something clicked in her memory banks. The *Swiss Army* logo had released some droplets of neurotransmitter and made a momentary connection. A cross and a shield. The cross was not like Jesus'; the beams were equal in length, but, somehow or other, they always evoked something more spiritual. Like the shield…she thought of crusaders' shields, not gladiators' shields or those of Roman legionaries. She poured some syrup over the pancakes and took a sip of coffee. So…something spiritual… something protective.

She cut the pancakes and ate several bites, then returned to the coffee. Black, the way she liked it, but too much like her memory. She remembered that she had been on a special detail, something requested by the Director, a favor of some sort. Not something tactical or at least nothing that was expected to become so. Shepherding. Hand-holding. Directing. Protecting…but from what? Not from snipers.

When you look at a person surrounded by people in suits with earpieces…you think, security. Armed probably, as she always was, but not in heavy gear. Assume it was in Washington…someone known to the Director…a VIP, but not someone already protected by an established security detail. And this was the Bureau, not the Capitol Police, not the Secret Service. She ate some more pancakes and put butter and preserves on her English muffin, cut the sausages and dragged a slice through the pool of syrup at the base of the pancakes. Better that way than with ketchup. Then back to the coffee, and the muffin…she was on some sort of security detail for a VIP. Light duty, or at least it was expected to be light duty. The attack was unexpected. No, it was a total surprise, because she was offstage at the time. They were in some kind of garden or park with a stone gated entrance or a stone, curved structure of some sort near the speaker's position. The person she was there to shepherd was on a stage or dais, gesturing. There was a large crowd, some carrying signs. Protesters or demonstrators of some sort. She was there as a spear carrier, a person at the edge of the stage whose role was to flesh out the scene, to project an image of authority. Not an active role, more an iconic role with a small i. She had ridden with the speaker there, in a black Bureau Suburban. There were some uniformed officers, District police probably. They looked bored, like bouncers at a concert whose principal job was to display their shoulders, pecs and biceps and look as if they were hoping for an excuse to cuff some ears or slap some faces.

The center plate was now empty, nothing remaining but some shallow puddles of syrup. The muffin was gone from the side plate. She held her coffee cup in both hands, hoping that the heat against her fingers might send some inspiration to her brain. She thought of a writer she had heard once…was it Lawrence Block? He was doing a TED talk or something, on her iPad. He used old Selectric typewriters and he typed and retyped his manuscripts. He liked the physical connection between his fingertips and his brain. He said he could feel the words moving down from his head to his shoulders, his elbows, wrists and fingertips, sliding onto the paper and feeling comfortable there. OK, she thought, if it works for you…then she took a long sip of coffee, reached for the scuffed carafe and refilled the cup, holding it tightly as she waited.

Nothing happened. She drank it down and still nothing happened. Then she noticed the sunshine coming between the drapes of her room. It had also been bright the day she was shot, even though it was then late afternoon and the sun was descending in the west.

The speaker wasn't talking about sunshine; he was talking about rain. A lot of rain. Then he said something about the fact that it wasn't really the rain, that that was a nice story, but that the real story was even nicer because we knew it to be true. We had proof, the kind of proof that would persuade skeptics…skeptics…and…*secularists*. That last word seemed to trouble the crowd carrying the placards. They became agitated and expressed their feelings with a carefully orchestrated chorus of boos.

CHAPTER SEVEN

Why 'secularists'? She remembered that specific word. This was a person of faith speaking to skeptics. He was being polite. 'Secularists' was more neutral than 'atheists' or 'unbelievers', perhaps a description that they might even welcome. He was going to persuade them of the error of their ways, but politely. He was going to give them evidence. Secular evidence. Scientific evidence. Empirical arguments. Put them all on common ground where they could agree and reason together.

Campbell. His name was Campbell. Where did that come from? George Campbell. With a middle name…one that she couldn't yet pull from her memory banks. Did it start with an S? It didn't matter. Get back to the rain, the rain that was a nice story but not as good as the real story.

Wait. George was his middle name but he was British; he went by initials: R. G. Campbell (call me 'George'). At first she thought the R was for Reginald or Ronald, maybe Roderick or Randolph, but no, it was just plain old Robert and he didn't want to be called Bob. R. George Campbell. R. G. Campbell. Professor R. G. Campbell. Biblical history. It wasn't called that though. Eastern History? Ancient Eastern History? Something like that.

And why were the demonstrators there? He was talking about the Bible and about historicity. The events that sounded like children's stories were really true or were at least anchored in historical fact. And why would people demonstrate against that? Militant secularists? People worried about Biblical authority as a challenge to state authority? They could be bothered by that, Gwen thought, as she reached for her cup of water, filled to the top with ice chips.

But the rain…of course. Rain that never seemed to end. *Forty days and forty nights, Lord?* But what actually brought the flood? George smiled and said *global warming*. Well, not to traditional scientists…he said…they would simply call it glacial melt. And with the melt the seas rose, in the case under consideration, the Mediterranean. And when the seas rose the waters broke through the Bosphorus strait, from the Aegean through the Sea of Marmara…and it turned the Black Lake into the Black Sea. Something like 7,600 years ago. Long before the Trojan War, assuming there was a Trojan War (probably a battle over trade routes, George thought). When the waters broke through, the sound was hellish and the process took months. The stuff of legend. But quite real. Oh yes, and on the west side of the Black Sea in eastern Turkey: Mt. Ararat.

Professor Campbell didn't go there…well, he had been there, but he didn't discuss the reports that the Ark's remains had actually been found there. He stopped with the Black Sea and the palpable evidence. There is a current from the Black Sea through the strait and into the Sea of Marmara. *And vice-versa.* And in the Black sea—at different levels—are mollusks that will only grow in salt water and mollusks that will only live in fresh. There are the remains of ancient civilizations beneath that sea. This is not disputed. The evidence was adduced by senior scientists in marine geology from Columbia University, a secular stronghold in a secular city. The story included an interesting sidebar— Russian ships followed the vessel of the American scientists who were studying the phenomena in a sometimes-forgotten episode from the Cold War.

So there *was* a flood and perhaps also some lessons in biblical demography, with thriving cities in Anatolia that were affected by it. And the doubters could take it up with the marine geologists, not the benighted people of faith. This didn't require faith; it only required scientific evidence and it existed in plentiful quantities.

But the demonstrators may not have been there in opposition to people of faith. They may have been there in defense of their own faith—their faith in man-caused warming. George reminded them that back in the day, thousands of years before Troy and thousands of years before the Gilgamesh epic, which recounts the story of a great flood, there were very few people and absolutely no Buicks, leaf blowers or gas stoves.

Gwen stared into her empty cup. Pity she didn't hear the conclusion of Professor Campbell's address. Her body was whipped back and forth by the entry of two snipers' bullets as her mind entered the place that begins with white and red flashes and ends in darkness.

CHAPTER EIGHT

So what should she assume? Secularists of any stripe might have some vague reason to dislike Professor Campbell's conclusions and some might even be willing to actively protest them and demonstrate against them. But why would any of the members of this group (or its splinter sects) wish to kill the spear carrier? Why would they go to the trouble of hiring not one but two snipers to accomplish the task? Professor Campbell's speech was learned and interesting and well-argued. It was witty and clever and informative. It dealt with a fascinating set of subjects and offered persuasive evidence for its conclusions. It was well-attended and well-delivered, but when all was said and all was done, it had nothing to do with the desire to kill her. She was not in the wrong place at the wrong time. She could have been anywhere, any place in which she presented a target, and the snipers would have taken aim and pulled triggers. In a way she was lucky. The shooters were forced to fire from a distance; they couldn't walk through the audience with *Glocks* or *Sigs* in their hands. The distance and the wind affected the bullets' trajectory. The smaller round probably traveled at greater velocity and jerked her enough to keep the larger round from hitting her heart or head. If you have to catch a bullet, pick the shoulder over the previous possibilities.

Gwen sketched some caliber numbers on her paper napkin, using her fingernail. When the young orderly came to refill her carafe of ice water she asked her if it would be possible to get a container of black coffee. "Of course, ma'am," the woman said.

"Ma'am." Better than nothing at all, but she would have preferred

"Special Agent Harrison." But then, this wasn't *Cheers*. This was a place where nobody knew your name and you didn't know theirs.

The woman returned in ten minutes with a full carafe. "I made you some fresh," she said. "But you don't take milk or cream or sugar?"

"No," Gwen said. "You've got it just the way I like it. Many thanks."

"Of course," the woman said, and left.

So let's talk bottom lines, Gwen thought to herself. Someone is protecting me. They may be maintaining strict anonymity to minimize the chance of anyone on site revealing my identity to someone on the outside with bad intentions. They don't want me to communicate because communications can be traced. They don't want me to interact with anyone in order to keep me from accidentally revealing my identity. They're on my side. If they weren't, they'd be feeding me something other than pancakes, sausage, English muffins and black coffee. Like something to stop my pulse or loosen my tongue.

So if they're on my side, they (or someone with whom they're connected) might just want to find out who shot me and improve the arc of their career paths. Sooner rather than later, and, hopefully, definitively.

But if my mini-tour of duty with Professor Campbell had nothing to do with my shooting (and if I personally am not aware of any recent or more distant events that might have precipitated the snipers' actions) the only way for anyone pursuing *my best interests* (finding the bastards and terminating their behavior) would be to work with me on the consideration of other possibilities. Where have I been? Who have I met? Who have I called? Who has called me? What have I seen? What cases have I been working? Obviously, the shooters had opportunity, but what was their motive? Or, more precisely, what was the motive of the individual who dug deep in his or her pockets and footed the not inconsiderable bill for an attempted hit of a relatively highly-placed (no time to invoke false modesty) special agent of the Federal Bureau of Investigation?

Three hours later, when the woman brought in her dinner tray,

Gwen asked her if her nurse was available to talk with her. "I'll let her know you want to see her," the woman replied.

The nurse was there in less than five minutes. "How may I help?" she asked.

"I have a request," Gwen said.

"Yes?" she answered.

"I would like to meet with the Director of this facility."

"I spoke with the Director this morning," she responded. "We have expected you to ask that. The best time would be tomorrow morning, after breakfast."

"That would be fine," Gwen said. "Thank you."

"Of course," the nurse said. "Breakfast at 7:00, meeting at 8:30?"

"8:30," Gwen answered.

CHAPTER NINE

"Did you enjoy your breakfast?" the nurse asked.

"Yes, thanks," Gwen answered. "I appreciate the fact that the menu is varied. Institutional French toast is hard to do. And Bacon goes with everything. I assume we're still on for 8:30."

"Yes, we can go there directly. The Director's in a building at the center of the complex; it's not too long of a walk. You can wear your gym clothes."

They walked quietly, Gwen smiling but not trying to make small talk. As they walked she was trying to remember each step, each feature and each building. The administrative building was about 150 yards from her ward. The buildings beyond it appeared to be infrastructural—a supply facility of some sort and what appeared to be a secure parking garage. Everywhere she looked there were cameras and coded entry points.

When they entered the administrative building the nurse took her to the end of the hall. Gwen saw a door that said 'Office of the Director' and paused. "Farther on," the nurse said.

They walked another ten yards and approached a double door. The nurse punched in a code and then held the first joint of her index finger against a small screen. When the door opened Gwen saw a second door. It was steel, with a more complex system of locks. Four ceiling cameras looked down on them, each with a red light at the base. The door opened from the inside and a man in a white shirt and tie with dark slacks and polished wingtips stood there, with his finger to his lips. Gwen entered and the door closed behind her.

"Sam," she said. "I didn't know you were the Director."

"Great to see you, Gwen, and great to see you ambulatory and returning to something approaching good health."

"Sam Barron…the last time I saw you you had returned from a stint as SAC in Cleveland. From the South Harbor and Lakeside Avenue to… the wilds of, what, Virginia?"

"Right outside Stafford, actually."

"And your office is actually a SCIF?"

"Well, I do spend a lot of time here. We take security very seriously; we have to."

"I've already figured out that this is all outside any usual norms."

"It's serious, Gwen. Your situation."

"I figured that I was the principal target and that Professor Campbell's talk was just a coincidence."

"He's back in Leeds. A little shaken, but functioning. MI6 has some handholders checking with him and providing reassurance, but no one believes that he's in danger. He couldn't have seen anything at Dumbarton Oaks."

"That's where I was, for the talk?"

"Yes, in their gardens. You were off to the side, actually standing under a rose arbor. Not in any normal line of fire."

"The only thing that I can't understand is why they missed. I figured the first round jerked me a bit and that affected the second round's trajectory. I don't remember any heavy winds…but I do remember there was a lot of foliage."

"Yes, they couldn't have been on the ground and gotten a clear shot. They wanted to take you out there because you were on the move before that, in and out of cars and buildings…Dulles…the Hoover Building… this was the first time you were in a stationary position, in the open. They were shooting from a helicopter; that's probably why they missed."

"A helicopter? In D.C.?"

"Yes. As you know, they established a 'Special Rules Flight Area' over the District—30 nautical miles around the city and up to 18,000 feet in the air. You can't tool around up there without having a unique transponder code and you have to be in constant contact with the air traffic controllers…"

"But military and intelligence aircraft are in and out of there all the time."

"That's right. They bop back and forth between the White House, Langley and Andrews. All they have to do is notify the air traffic controllers of their presence."

"Hard for some dark ops group to commandeer a government aircraft."

"Hard but not impossible," the Director said, "but there's a more likely possibility. The permitting process is also eased for news helicopters and emergency medical helicopters."

"So you put a hospital logo or a peacock logo on your chopper and all you need to do is follow some protocols…"

"It's still damned hard, but this kind of operation is not for the faint of heart and not for those without means."

"Both power and money."

"Yes, in significant quantities."

"That's what you meant when you said it was serious."

"Yes. That's why we've protected your identity here. The facility is used for multiple purposes. One is to house and rehabilitate agents in significant danger."

"I appreciate your work on my behalf, Sam."

"I report to the Director daily. He's been happy to hear of your progress. Needless to say he wants to protect you. He said you're one of his top assets."

"I'll take that as a compliment," Gwen said.

"He didn't mean it in the way it sounds," the Director said. "When I call him I say 'our recently-acquired asset' or something like that. We never use names."

"This is serious, then," Gwen said. "So how do we find out who's behind this and, more to the point, how do we…let me put this politely…respond?"

"We've got some ideas on that," he answered.

CHAPTER TEN

"I am at your disposal," Gwen said. "The only problem is that I'm not going anywhere on these feet and legs and my left arm and shoulder are a disaster area."

"That was a .223 to the arm, a .308 to the shoulder."

"No surprise there," Gwen said. "These were not amateurs."

"No, not this time," Sam Barron said. "However, there's now one very big thing on our side."

"I'm regaining my memory."

"Precisely," Barron responded. "So long as we have your mental capacity we can bring in another agent with an agile body."

"And some serious street smarts as well."

"We haven't forgotten that."

"Then you've already got somebody in mind, somebody who can work with me."

"As a matter of fact, we do."

"Could I have a piece of paper and a pen?" Gwen asked.

"Of course," Barron said, scooting his chair to an adjoining shelf and then handing her a sheet of 8x10 and a ball point. Gwen took them, thanked him, and quickly wrote something on one side and then turned the paper over, sliding it back to him. "That's my suggestion," Gwen said.

"Our preferred person is currently in Kansas City, working drug- and human-trafficking cases. Before that, in San Diego, working on Operation Trojan Shield…"

"The encrypted communications project, disrupting international criminal operations."

"Yes, the person is an engineer by trade, but I have to warn you that there's a checkered past…"

"A checkered past?"

"Let's say a person with exceptional qualifications and a record of using them."

"Walking the thin line separating our side from theirs," Gwen said.

"Unh-huh," Barron said.

Gwen thought for a moment, or appeared to. Then she spoke.

"Her mother was gang-raped and she found the perpetrators and dispatched them with extreme and, I might say, very creative prejudice. They could never convict her and she also had a record of doing a great deal of good in the world…not that taking out the three sleazebags didn't raise the general quality of our national life."

"The rest of her file was unblemished. She is end-of-the-spectrum intelligent and what the profilers at Quantico call 'fully mission-oriented'.

"She targets the jugular," Gwen said.

"Yes. When she applied for the Bureau the screening committee read between the lines and bucked it directly to the Director's desk. 'Do it,' he said. 'I want the best players on our team.'"

"We worked together on the Rosario kidnapping," Gwen said. "Classic MS-13 ugliness. She recovered the ransom and the little girl. Then she took out the gang leader and the people surrounding him. There were some issues with the L.A. press and the mayor's office. They thought a wall filled with C-4 was a little extreme, but there was nothing left of the gang members and their house and their garage and their cars and the sidewalks and the power lines and the fan palms in the adjoining yard to make any positive identifications. It was written off as a very severe gas explosion."

"The number of kidnappings significantly diminished thereafter," Barron said. "She was directed to report to the Director's office, presumably for some sort of discipline. He told me that he patted her on the shoulder and said, 'Next time, spare the sidewalk.'"

"I don't like being shot," Gwen said. "I don't want whoever did this to keep trying. Let them know we're serious also."

Barron turned over the sheet of paper and saw a name written across the center:

Karen Wilken

"Great minds…," he said.

"How soon can she get here?" Gwen asked.

"She'll be here tonight. She's flying into Reagan National this afternoon."

"Can we use your SCIF?"

"You'll be required to."

"Not a problem," Gwen answered.

CHAPTER ELEVEN

They set up their dinner in the SCIF. Gwen's still-unnamed nurse brought her to the room at 5:30. By then they had assembled some street clothes for her. Karen arrived ten minutes later. Gwen was surprised to see her dressed in a nurse's uniform. Anonymity was the facility's watchword. When Karen entered the room she paused for a second to assess Gwen's condition; then they embraced, separated, and embraced for a second time.

"You look good, all things considered," Karen said.

"I feel better knowing you're here," Gwen said. "How was the Shirley Dieway?"

"A parking lot. They used a Suburban and let me change clothes in the back. When we got to the edge of Stafford they gave me a Camry and let me drive in alone."

"Coming in for your evening shift," Gwen said.

"Right," Karen answered. "All very routine and contained."

She was taller than Gwen and a year or two older, but very fit, with a wiry leanness and dark eyes that seldom blinked.

"So…Ms. Inside and Ms. Outside, then?"

"For now at least," Karen said. "I don't know how long it will take to track the puppet master. That's what I'm calling him."

"I have every confidence in you," Gwen said.

"Just don't expect him (or her) to be able to stand trial," Karen said. "This was a serious move and it calls for a serious response. I don't mean rash or hotheaded, but this was an attempted assassination. They weren't trying to sideline you; they were trying to eliminate you. First we have to figure out why, then we have to insure that there are no repeat attempts."

"Understood," Gwen said. "Your point, that is. Why they tried to kill me…I have no idea. How about some dinner?"

"How about a drink first?" Karen said, slipping two 100 ml bottles of *Glenmorangie* from her purse. "Not easy to find the good stuff in small bottles. Had to get one of those tasting sets."

"You're on," Gwen said. "Very much appreciated. The ice chips and rust-colored jello have pretty much run their course of attractiveness."

Dinner was Salisbury Steak with mashed potatoes and gravy and green beans, with rolls and butter on the side and peach cobbler for dessert. "How American is this?" Gwen asked. "I don't know whether we should pray first or stand for the national anthem."

Karen smiled. "Looks tasty, though, and it will pair well with the scotch."

"Point," Gwen said. She smiled, paused, and then spoke again. "So how are we going to do this?"

"For starters I need to know what you've been up to," Karen said. "You must have poked a big hive to get the attention of someone with this level of resources."

"I was in Houston," Gwen said. "Sunnyside."

"The closest thing to hell in the Lone Star state."

"Right," Gwen said. "I was there in a liaison role. One of the local teams of distributors had hooked up with a counterfeiting ring. They were giving change in funny money and even tried to buy product with it. Jive Miguel and his friends in Bogotá were very displeased. The Treasury boys and girls were trying to bust the counterfeiters and the Bureau was watching the larger distribution channels. Meanwhile the Houston police were trying to prevent a full-blown range war. My job was to keep the Director posted and to handle the interagency communications and coordination."

"But you weren't on the streets, eyeball to eyeball."

"No, I was in a hotel room with a laptop and secure phone line. Not playing hero in any way."

"And they called you to Washington from there?"

"Yes. The counterfeiters were taken out by a combination of the Treasury team and, shall we say, some dissatisfied customers. The dealers decided to shop their wares elsewhere for awhile and things returned to normal, which is to say, the usual set of pitched battles. The Director brought me back to Washington and asked me to shepherd a history professor around. He was doing a lecture that drew a few protestors. I didn't expect it to result in my being shot."

"How about before that?"

"Salt Lake. They had a new SAC and he wasn't used to dealing with a three-state area. I know the open spaces there pretty well and the Director asked me to work with him for a couple of weeks…you know, get him off to a good start."

"And nothing nasty happened there?"

"No, I got reacquainted with the elk, the moose and the gray wolves and took a few days off to visit the pronghorns in Wyoming. It was one long drive in the country."

"And since then?"

"Nothing. That's why I wonder what drew the puppet master's attention."

"Nothing, nothing at all?"

"No, not really," Gwen said. "Before the professor came to town I visited Great Falls one morning, went to a college alumni dinner, binge-watched two 'Line of Duty' seasons and repainted my kitchen. I was a model citizen."

"What happened at Great Falls?"

"Nothing. A lot of water rushing over some big rocks. I was practically alone, sitting at a park bench and drinking a thermos of black coffee. I smiled at a family or two, had an early lunch in McLean and drove home to Alexandria."

"How about the alumni function?"

"Pretty much a non-event. We had a nice dinner, listened to a speech from a development officer, fiddled with name tags and vowed to do it all again, soon."

CHAPTER TWELVE

"Anything from the distant past?"

"Not that I can think of. I can't say that everyone's been happy to go to federal prison at my behest, but most of the heavier stuff happened months and years ago. Lately I keep getting TDY'd for special assignments. I've been pushing paper like a GS-15 and writing notes to myself to remember to keep my *Sig* cleaned, on the off chance that I might actually need it sometime."

"If you don't remember any specific encounter you may have heard something or seen something that didn't make an impression at the time. You saw something you weren't supposed to see or heard something you weren't supposed to hear."

"Possibly," Gwen said, "but I can't think of anything."

"That's the point," Karen said. "You're not aware of it but someone else is, someone willing to kill you to keep you from remembering it."

"Or they're trying to send a message to someone else."

"That's a possibility, but your parents are retired and have never been involved with anything political or governmental. They're…"

"In South Dakota," Gwen said. "My dad did family law—wills, real estate purchases, small business contracts; my mom taught school. They've lived in the same town for forty years and the same house for thirty."

"And no siblings."

"No. A couple of cousins who do IT work (and not for the Bureau or the Company with a capital C). We get together for the holidays, eat ham and turkey, green bean casseroles and mashed potatoes. A big time for us is a trip to a national park or some camping and fly fishing. Everyone connected with me is a pure civilian."

"And no romantic relationships…"

"I'm never around long enough," Gwen said.

"Talk to me about your college event."

"It was really just a meeting of the local club. The school sent out a speaker, in this case a development officer. She tried to persuade us to contribute to a scholarship fund, actually a sponsorship arrangement. The Washington area club would help reduce the tuition cost for a deserving local student. Most of the students already get a reduction in tuition based on need; this would make it easier for Kenyon to compete with other schools' offers. If we kicked in enough a top prospect student might have no tuition obligations at all. It was a pay-as-you-go deal; we would sponsor a student every year. Of course, they would love to have us endow such a scholarship but that would take megabucks and most of the grads in the area are fairly young."

"Kenyon was always big on literature and writing," Karen said, "but not you so much."

"No. I was something of a rarity. They're always trying to attract kids interested in science. The fact that I was a woman didn't hurt and the fact that I was from a small western state helped."

"They like to brag about their reach."

"Right," Gwen said.

"And you majored in chemistry?"

"Minored. I majored in Geography, but also took a lot of language courses. There was a time when I could get by in French and do a pretty good job of faking it in German."

"Did you contribute to the cause?"

"I sent a check for $500 the next day. They didn't actually pass the hat or shake the tambourine at the dinner."

"That's nice of you. Did you talk to anybody there?"

"Just small talk. Nothing significant. It was mostly people who were younger. It was also very D.C.—people came late, people left early; people handed out their business cards, blew air kisses, sipped a half a glass of wine and took off."

"Busy busy."

"Always. I don't think the development officer expected too much with a group of young people in starter positions with high rents and careers in perpetual transition. I met one woman who graduated the year after me and went to law school; she was one of the senior people at the Federal Trade Commission; she had been there for what they considered an eternity--eleven months--and was looking to move to Wisconsin for a job at *Blue Cross/Blue Shield*."

"Heavily-regulated industry," Karen said. "Get some Washington bona fides and then take your act on the road for real money."

"Exactly," Gwen said.

"Where was the dinner?"

"*Quaglino's*."

"Dupont Circle?"

"Just west of it," Gwen said.

"Haven't been there, but I've heard good things," Karen said.

"It was good. We had a long table on the far side of the main dining room. Maybe twenty people in all. Twenty-five? Choice of entrées: Salmon, Steak or some Shrimp concoction. I had the Salmon. Risotto on the side, some asparagus. Good stuff. Special entrée price, just for us. A mere $68.50."

"This was just before the history prof came to town."

"The Thursday before," Gwen said. "I didn't see any assassins there… aside from the guys who priced the entrées."

Karen smiled. "Let me check on some things and get back to you. Maybe I'll find out something. Maybe I'll have some questions. I'll see. We've got to start somewhere."

"First thing in the morning?"

"No, I'm going to sober up with some coffee and head out tonight.

I'll spend the night at the Key Bridge *Marriott*. Maybe by late tomorrow afternoon."

"If I can do anything, let me know."

"Rest," Karen said. "Remember. This wasn't an accident. If something nasty comes down I want you to be ready to join me for the fireworks."

"I'll need at least a week," Gwen said.

"Sam said you'd need a month," Karen said.

"He hasn't seen me when I'm really motivated," Gwen answered.

II

KAREN

CHAPTER THIRTEEN

Quaglino's was not a rip-off of the London eatery of the same name; it was more (the owner said in a *Washingtonian* interview) an *homage.* The St. James version was a brasserie, Karen noted; this was more of a trattoria with ristorante prices. She was having Italian wedding soup and a lunch portion of risotto. She had thought about multiple disguises but decided to hide in plain sight—no makeup, hair in a taut bun, wire-rimmed clear glasses. She picked up a tome on Venetian history at *Second Story Books*, just by the restaurant, on P. Full scale academic. She acted as if she had trouble putting it down when the waiter was there to take her order.

If something *had* happened at *Quaglino's* the night of the alumni event, whoever was responsible for the attempt on Gwen's life could still have some eyes in the area. At the very least one or more palms would have been greased to report any official voices asking prying questions. Edgar's Bureau had always prided itself on its gray suits and the ability of its special agents to fade into the wallpaper. Karen considered it a kind of costume and chose misdirection over uniformity and predictability.

When she pored over the pages of Professor Tinkley's history she made notes on a slip of paper she used as a putative bookmark. She switched from the soup spoon to the pencil with the moves of a library rat, but her notes concerned the layout of the restaurant and not the economic challenges of Fifteenth-century Venetian tradesmen.

The open kitchen was at the rear of the main dining room. There was no head chef in evidence, though the *Washingtonian* interview had touted the presence of a protegé of Rita Sodi who had also logged time in Lidia Bastianich's Kansas City restaurant. There were bright overhead lights in the kitchen area (nothing to hide here), an outsized pizza oven and a mural of the funicular on Capri, with the Tyrrhenian Sea to the west and Gulf of Naples in the background.

A bar that was all chrome and mirrors with dark blue tones adjoined the entry point and a walk-in wine refrigerator filled the area in between. The restrooms sat opposite, to the south. Next to the kitchen was an open door with a set of racks stacked with large cans—mostly Italian tomatoes. The good stuff, the San Marzanos. Karen could also see a large wheel of cheese. Again, probably the top-of-the-line, the Reggiano Parmigiano. *Costco* gets just under a grand for a 72-lb. wheel. This is for the discerning palate but not for the faint of heart. The second level was open, with steps along one side of the open kitchen. Behind a waist-high railing were three doors, all closed, probably space for an office, a storage room and a private dining area--an inner sanctum for those wishing not to be seen?

As she made notes and minimalist sketches, Karen tilted her head upward, as if she was seeking inspiration or *le mot juste*, while very delicately looking for CCTV cameras and security-system boxes.

The risotto was surprisingly good, better than the more generic soup. When she finished it the waiter approached and said, "*Dolci, Signora?*"

She wanted a high-test double espresso but decided instead to stay in character. "I know the Italians would never have it after a meal," she said, "but could I have a decaf cappuccino?"

"Certainly," the waiter said, tilting his head and adding a formal smile.

When it arrived she sat back, put her book aside, and nursed it for nearly fifteen minutes. Then, pretending that her phone had vibrated, she checked the screen and promptly signaled for the check, which was presented on a small black-and-white marble clipboard. Before leaving she went to the women's restroom, looked for a window (there was none) and left.

There has to be a back door, she thought to herself. They wouldn't permit deliveries through the main entry point. She walked outside, found the alleyway below P and saw the rear door. There were containers stacked outside, both classic plastic milk cartons and cardboard boxes. One of the line cooks was standing between them, smoking a cigarette and checking his watch.

She checked her own and returned to her hotel room, slipping into the complimentary robe, making herself a cup of coffee and logging on to one of the Bureau's most secure sites.

CHAPTER FOURTEEN

She had the blueprints for *Quaglino's* on her screen in four minutes. The modifications made by the new owner (a Clement Wilburn) were substantial. The previous occupants of the building had been a Chinese restaurant named *The Emperor's Palace* and, before then, a *Mail Boxes Etc.* operation. Wilburn was an area entrepreneur with restaurants in Springfield, VA, McLean, VA, Potomac, MD and a wine bar on the eastern shore at Dewey Beach, the latter, like Dupont Circle, enjoying a large gay population. That was the only commonality. The Springfield operation was a steak house, the McLean an Irish pub with a large CIA clientele and the Potomac a French bistro.

To set up *Quaglino's* Wilburn had stripped the place to the studs, put in new flooring, the open kitchen, walk-in wine refrigerator, bar, and a second bathroom on the landing, an en suite for the people in the small dining area there. With the Bureau software at her disposal she checked his business *Visa* account for the months prior to opening. He had sprung for top-of-the-line kitchen supplies but scrimped on the security system. Passing on the top shelf commercial sources, he went with *Rock Creek Security*, a small local company that installed a wireless system that any novice Bureau tech could hack in a matter of minutes. During her lunch she had spotted three cameras; *Rock Creek* had charged for four, the latter probably over the back door. With the line cook and his cigarette occupying that space she was unable to get close enough to check.

The restaurant didn't serve breakfast and it closed at 11:30 p.m. Their prime competition in the area, *Café Milano* on Wisconsin Avenue in Georgetown, closed at 10:30, so the late closing probably afforded a slight comparative advantage. Alcohol drives profits and the $16-$19/ glass house wines would do very nicely with the late night bar crowd. Assuming a generous two-hour cleanup and prep stations not active until 9:00 a.m. or so, she had a wide swath of time in which to enter the premises and examine things up close and personal.

The waning crescent moon was helpful and while the street lights were closely spaced on P, the alleyway was dark except for lights installed by private businesses. She took her black nylon pantsuit and black blouse from her suitcase and checked her valuables—a *SigSauer* P320compact with additional magazine, an *Emerson* CQC-7 knife, a set of lock picks and a pouch of IT devices. Her pride and joy was a narrow belt with holster, sheath and fanny pack--a Sam Browne for discerning women with a plain finish and single-prong buckle.

Normally the Bureau would liaise with the DC police and have an unmarked in the immediate area for backup, but in this case there was no way of knowing how far the reach of the puppet master's influence extended, so the mission was strictly solo. The fact that the local cops had other fish to fry helped. Make that great-white-shark-level fish to fry. Even on a quiet day the business community's security needs were a secondary or even tertiary concern for the local force.

She went in at 2:30 a.m. P Street was largely deserted and there was only a single light in the alleyway, above the rear door to *Second Story Books*. *Quaglino's* delivery door had a decent *Baldwin* lock. She disabled the WiFi system with her tablet, slipped on plastic gloves, got past the lock in less than a minute, and entered the building. A small passageway beside the kitchen took her to the steps to the landing and she quickly made her way to what she had started referring to as the mezzanine. The store room was unlocked. It contained fresh linen tablecloths and napkins and sixteen shelves of dishes, glassware and cooking staples. The extra-virgin olive oil came from Italy in 3-liter cans, a nice touch of authenticity. The private dining room was currently set up with an oblong table with four chairs. With additional leaves it would comfortably accommodate eight; two were positioned in the room's corners. She lifted prints from the table, table legs and chairs, from the bathroom's toilet seat and trip handle and from both sides of the doorframe on the off chance that they hadn't been wiped since Gwen's night there. Then she moved to the office.

The door had a simple knob lock. If there was any money kept inside, Mr. Wilburn was a fool, because a child could have made its way into the room. She was most interested in the CCTV system and she was pleased to see that it was little more than a glorified home device. The NVR system had a 2T built-in hard drive, expanded to 6T with a 4T external hard drive. That would provide about eight days of 24/7 video footage before overwriting, but Mr. Wilburn had been extremely thoughtful in downloading multi-day segments onto thumb drives, each labeled and stored in an unlocked, bottom desk drawer.

Like a batter who had just scored a walk-off home run, she looked to the heavens and raised a finger to the Lord. She found the day of Gwen's alumni dinner, downloaded its data, along with that of two days prior and two days following onto a pocket-sized *Samsung* external drive, and moved on to the file cabinet. Checking the hard-copy files of special events she found a sheet for the alumni function and its charges as well as a separate sheet for a private dinner upstairs. The client was probably a Beltway Bandit consulting firm—*FSG Associates*—since the address was on Dolley Madison Boulevard (aka Route 123, aka, at times, Chain Bridge Road), the endless broken strip of highway that ran through Fairfax County. Whatever they had been doing there that evening it had probably cost the taxpayers serious money. She took pictures of both documents with her cellphone and searched for a list of the restaurant's employees. Those were on separate cards but they also included addresses, phone numbers and (for some) social security numbers. She photographed each, checked the files for any other potentially-useful information, including the bills from service, food and utility providers, turned off the desk lamp and returned to the alleyway. She slipped her rubber gloves into her jacket pocket, reset the WiFi, congratulated herself on a good hour and a half's work, and left for her hotel.

CHAPTER FIFTEEN

It was 4:25 when she crossed Key Bridge and returned to the *Marriott*. Everything roiling in her head told her to break out her laptop and get to work, but her engineer's superego told her it would be inefficient and counterproductive. Better to get four or five hours of solid sleep, load up on coffee and carbs and settle in for the first leg of the marathon. She rested and then hit the breakfast bar at 8:45, passed the omelet station and went for the pancakes and sausages with a side of bacon, an English muffin with strawberry jelly, a large glass of juice and a 16 ounce carry-out cup of black coffee. She also passed on the barely-edible, miniature *Marriott* bagels (who makes those things?) and reserved the right to pick up a cinnamon roll, as needed.

She carried a coffee refill back to her room, caught the maid finishing up her next-door neighbor's mini-suite and talked her out of two additional *Keurig* cups of high test. Five minutes later she was at the desk, in her robe, hard at work. She began by scanning the fingerprint tapes and accessing the IAFIS next generation identification system (NGI), a modular setup which incorporated palm print, iris and facial identification. She didn't have high hopes for the friction ridge portion. Even with 100,000,000+ files there were a lot of ne'er-do-wells in the world's 8 billion+ souls who had never been printed.

She turned out to be right. No hits beyond the male restaurant employee who had been arrested (but not convicted) on an assault/battery rap and his female coworker who had been arrested (but, again, not convicted) for shoplifting. She had greater hopes for some facial recognition hits.

The three cameras inside the restaurant were strategically located. The first, behind the kitchen, was a wide-lens affair that included the entire downstairs dining room. The bottom of the image was the pass between the kitchen and the diners. You wouldn't see any cooks or dishwashers light-fingering the garlic bread but you would see anyone approaching the kitchen after hours, thinking about either vandalism or grand larceny. The second camera encompassed approximately 80 percent of the dining room but focused directly on the wine refrigerator. With *Gaja* big wines carrying mid six-figure price tags there was a lot at stake there. The third camera focused specifically on the bar area, with an angle that not only provided a look at the patrons but also at the cash register. The images were sharp on all of the daily tapes so that you could pan in or out without much loss of resolution. That was particularly important for the camera behind the kitchen because the central image was the front door and the guard-at-the-gate's station.

Unfortunately there were no cameras for the private dining areas. Karen scanned film for three hours and then rested, did a caffeine run to the tray above the minibar, and ran background checks on the restaurant's employees to give herself a break from the finely-tuned staring/stopping/panning. She was not surprised to learn that the server jobs turned over constantly, as establishments opened, closed, reopened and trolled for help. The prep stations were operated by individuals with questionable immigration status, but generally clean noses.

The executive chef was pulling down a cool 95K, above the DC median, but beneath the 90th percentile. She was probably looking around for a 'new challenge'. Restaurant profit margins in DC were always razor-thin, but they wouldn't be in business if there wasn't some profit. Wilburn had made a lot of notes on the invoices from his suppliers, breaking down the cost of each dish ingredient-by-ingredient. Karen was able to pull up some earlier iterations of the restaurant's menus and noted that there were clear correlations between the seasonal items and the unit costs. No big surprise there, of course, but her purpose was to determine how tight a ship Wilburn ran and she was generally impressed with what she saw. Italian restaurants compete with checked-tablecloth spaghetti houses and high-portion chains. The trick is to carve out a quality niche without gouging beyond all recognition and catching market share from the sometime diners looking for a special treat and not just a table-crushing pile of semolina. All in all the operation appeared to be tight. The bar was the savior, always, but the private dining arrangements were favorable for the house. In DC you were selling privacy as well as pasta and the positioning of the decimal points on the deals cut there could raise eyebrows to the hairline, especially for the citizens who ultimately paid for them.

In D.C., government agencies didn't even write their more important reports; they were contracted out to Beltway banditos. When it came to more serious activities, like the construction of aircraft and the missiles they carried, the wild blue yonder was well beyond the ozone layer and the budgets of most billionaires.

After two additional hours of scanning video images she realized that she had overlooked lunch. She power-napped for thirty minutes and went back to the desk, holding out any thoughts of dinner as a reward for finding something intriguing. Anything.

CHAPTER SIXTEEN

Unfortunately she found nothing. Nada. She thought about Gwen, waiting impatiently (no doubt) for information. She decided to stretch her legs and also break for dinner. She was in the right place. She walked across Key Bridge, looked at the Exorcist steps across the street on M, turned right and walked up to the local mainstay *Clyde's*. She went partial-paleo with a bowl of the signature chili and a plate of steak frites. She passed on dessert. When the waiter asked if she wanted any coffee she smiled and shook her head no. He didn't have to know that she already had had somewhere between ten and twelve cups.

She worked off her dinner by walking up to Prospect, turning left on 37th and descending the Exorcist steps back to M. She crossed the bridge, noting that the traffic had barely subsided, returned to the *Marriott*, showered and fired up her laptop for a long journey into night.

She began with a long shot, checking the rear door to *Quaglino's*. Finally an aha(!) moment. Earlier in the evening of the alumni dinner she saw three individuals, all well-dressed, entering by themselves. There were two women and one man, each separated by about five minutes. One of the women's head and face was largely covered by a *Hermès* scarf. The second woman was wearing large dark glasses with the collar of a very pricey wool (probably cashmere) coat covering her neck, throat and cheek bones. The man entered last. He was wearing dark glasses, a *Burberry's* dual-breast trench coat and a large hat, a shade or two darker than the coat. Karen googled…probably a Borsalino, brushed felt, five-six hundred bucks a throw.

When he stepped up into the rear of the restaurant he balanced himself by grasping the door frame with his left hand, exposing his watch. Karen froze the image and panned in. Then she googled…a *Patek Philippe* Nautilus…hard to tell if it was white gold or stainless…hard to see if there were any diamonds. Price? Anybody's guess…maybe a steal at 12K or 50K or the high-priced spread at 400K or 600K. Not a *Timex*.

"So, here's the question," she said aloud, "what do you three jolly musketeers have to hide? What's with all this sneaking around, coming in through the back door?" Once they were all inside she returned to the camera feed from behind the kitchen and advanced the time fifteen minutes. "Hey, disappearing act 101. If the three of you are not all in the rest room you must be in the private dining room, plotting and scheming, because you are nowhere else to be seen."

I guess I've earned a cup of coffee, she thought to herself. And thank you, JWM, Jr. for replenishing the *Keurig* cup supply. She passed on the sugar and 'whitener' and went straight for the high test. Three minutes later she was back at the desk. There was one significant problem. The caballeros were very good at concealing their faces. She couldn't get a clear enough image to utilize the Bureau's facial recognition software. She advanced the rear-door camera's timeframe by two hours, then three. Nothing. Was the food not to their satisfaction? Did they bolt early? She checked back to a half-hour after their arrival. Nothing. Then forty-five minutes. Fifty. Sixty. Seventy…three minutes…and there they were… two pretty maids in a row and the man with the big hat…all five minutes apart…one turning left at the door, two turning right. Unfortunately, they were entering a dark alleyway. Fortunately, she caught a lip or two, a nose here, a cheek there. Just maybe…enough.

The big question now, besides Who? was Why? and how did their shadowy lives intersect with Gwen Harrison's, if, indeed, they intersected at all. The answer could be simple and utterly irrelevant for Gwen's attempted murder. They were nothing more than the charter members of a *ménage à trois* popping in for a nightcap after some afternoon delight. They were skulkers in the shadows, glands calling out to glands and trying to stay off of their respective spouses' radars. If that was the case she could at least eliminate them from her enquiries and move on to other possibilities, but…yet…that seemed like a longshot. Why get all gussied up and meet downtown when you could simply call for room service at the No-Tell or, more likely, at the *Ritz Carlton* or *Willard*? If you could go for the *Patek Philippe* you could go for the *Dom* or the *Veuve Cliquot* and any of the top DC hoteliers would be happy to oblige. No reason to hit P Street unless you were there to deal.

CHAPTER SEVENTEEN

Time to plan next steps. Before turning in she sent every shot she had of the pieces of the triumvirs' faces to Special Agent Mike Liu, a tech-savvy friend in the Salt Lake City regional office. She didn't have the resources for an advanced facial rec search on her laptop and Mike would be ensconced behind at least two outsized screens at dawn the next day. He would also keep their work confidential. There were people with comparable skills at the Hoover Building, but the principal techs had the unfortunate tendency to yell the Bureauspeak equivalent of 'Eureka' whenever anything truly interesting hit their screens. While she doubted that they would disclose their discoveries to anyone beyond the Bureau walls it was always a good idea to take extra precautions, particularly when this much was at stake. Mike was a quiet, steady introvert whose word was as solid as Gwen's or the Director's. If he was told this matter was strictly confidential he would refuse to answer questions from his wife, his mother, his doctor, his priest, his lawyer, his accountant and, most important, his SAC. If that meant working at night or on weekends, so be it.

After a sizeable breakfast and a sea of coffee Karen drove up the GW Parkway and into the northern reaches of Arlington and the eastern edge of McLean. The part of Dolley Madison Boulevard on which *FSG Associates* sat was on the western edge of McLean, below Tysons Corner, near the interchange for the parallel Dulles Toll Road and Dulles Access Road. The real estate in this particular portion of America was so expensive that McMansions were often built in one another's backyards on so-called 'pipestems'. Commercial rates were similar, with tiny access roads metastasizing around thoroughfares, as three, four and eight-story buildings propagated, making room for more and more corporations dedicated to the proposition that there were enough government teats to fill the hungry mouths of opportunists from the metro Washington area to the late Senator Byrd's fiefdoms in West Virginia.

Finding *FSG Associates* among them proved to be a challenge. She knew their address from Clement Wilburn's files and she knew that they had been willing to spring for the $500 surcharge for the private dining room and the $750 minimum, but the size, reach and nature of the operation remained a mystery and nothing sprang to life during her late night *Google* search beyond their simple address and phone number.

As it turned out, their office was more like a library carrel than a corporate headquarters. Karen knew that many of the banditos spent their time chasing government contracts and farmed the actual work to suburban freelancers, working in their jammies as they wrote reports and polished other peoples' prose, but they still required meeting space, basic office machines and a room or two for the largest of the trough feeders. The major contractors had multistoried buildings with serious signage. *FSG* had a locked, steel door at the rear of a four-story building and one unoccupied, designated parking place. Your basic front. When Karen punched in their number on her cell there was no audible ring on the other side of the door and a perfunctory recorded message, inviting her to leave a message of her own and wait for a call-back.

She texted Mike Liu with their title and address and asked him to find out anything he could about the company. "Anything at all," she said. When she returned to the *Marriott* forty-five minutes later he called her.

"Still working on the facial rec," he said, but I can give you a quick rundown on your entity's corporate presence. It's nonexistent."

"Nonexistent?" Karen answered.

"All but," he said. "They incorporated and dotted their i's and crossed their required t's about ten years ago. Since then, nothing. And I do mean nothing. These characters don't even pay the $25 or $50 to take out a minimal ad on their local Sunday mass church bulletin."

"Like the real estate agents and insurance salesmen," Karen said.

"Right. At the least it lets the locals know that they're public-spirited and supportive."

"And available for business."

"Right. They haven't sponsored a Little League team or bought space in a high school yearbook, never mind something pricey or dramatic. I couldn't even find an internet or security contract."

"Bids on government contracts?"

"Nothing. Utter silence."

"But they pay their rent?"

"$1800 a month. Actually a ripoff for a space no larger than a medium-sized bedroom."

"They may like the fact that it's under the radar and off the beaten path."

"Well they don't have any other expenses," Mike said. "Not even a cleaning service."

"Maybe they do their dirty business elsewhere," Karen said.

"They don't do any there," Mike said. "Not so anyone would notice, at least."

"Did you see who paid the rent?"

"Automatically charged to a corporate credit card. The same with their utilities."

"Located where?"

"London."

"London, England."

"Yep."

"That's interesting," Karen said. "Street address?"

"Ropemaker Street. Quaint, I thought."

"I think that's in the City. International finance types. Those who move and those who shake."

"I checked *Google Earth* and got a red brick wall. I'm not speaking metaphorically. It was actually a red brick wall."

"Listen, I appreciate your help, Mike."

"Anytime, Karen. I'll get back to you on the faces. I may have to give you a handful of choices. You didn't give me much…not criticizing…"

"I know. If I had been there with my *Leica* it would have been much easier. These three were trying to dodge the camera."

"They can try…" Mike answered. Karen knew the modest smile he was probably displaying.

CHAPTER EIGHTEEN

Karen called Sam Barron's secure cell from the *Marriott*; he was in the SCIF. "Can I come down for dinner tonight?" she asked.

"I'll have your dining companion ready," he answered.

Dinner was some passable Chicken Marsala, with angel hair, some asparagus and pre-assembled, once-frozen profiteroles. "I appreciate the thought," Karen said, "even with the institutional execution. They're trying."

"It's designed to make you want to get well," Gwen said.

"And get back to home cooking," Karen answered.

"So what have you turned?" Gwen asked.

"Nothing specific yet, but there may be a lead."

"Tell me," Gwen said.

"I'm focusing on your alumni dinner, figuring that your trip to Great Falls was probably innocent; there was no one there to observe you (or vice-versa). The room was full at *Quaglino's* and some individuals there were behaving in what I would consider a suspicious manner."

"Specifically?"

"Guests entering from the alley way, through the service entrance, and systematically attempting to avoid any exposure to the CCTV camera."

"Pictures?"

"Just fragments," Karen said. "I've got a master computer jock working the facial rec software."

"They must have wanted some serious privacy," Gwen said. "Probably coming from different directions, so that the restaurant was most convenient for them. Or maybe there were people at home they were purposely keeping out of the loop. Secret meeting, you think?"

"Yes, and they didn't show up in the principal dining room; they weren't joining your group so I figure they were headed upstairs to the room above the kitchen, next to the office and the storage room."

"But no i.d."

"The room was reserved by a group called *FSG Associates*. They operate out of a linen closet on Dolley Madison."

"A front."

"Almost surely. Too small for anything else."

"CEO?"

"Nothing yet. The rent is paid by a corporate credit card in England."

"International muck-a-mucks."

"Looks like," Karen said.

"Plenty of unspeakable activity to choose from," Gwen said.

"No doubt."

"So they weren't in the main dining room."

"No, I panned that crowd over and over. Families with college-age kids. People on dates. Nothing really to hide."

"Very interesting."

"Why do you say that, Gwen?"

"Because Peggy O'Connor and I walked in on them in the private dining room."

"Really?" Karen said, putting down her fork and sipping some of the wine she had brought from the *Marriott* minibar.

"Peggy…well, Margaret. She asked me to call her Peggy. Poor thing has Crohn's. The downstairs women's room was full and she couldn't wait. I took her upstairs and we hunted for an employee's room."

"Why did she need you to take her?"

"She's legally blind. She can function with heavy-duty glasses and a desk magnifier, but she can't see anything at a distance."

"So did you get a good look at the three people in the private dining room?"

"Not really. I turned the knob and stood by the side so that Peggy could enter. She was desperate. I realized immediately that this was not a rest room and we left."

"But all you got was a peripheral vision shot."

"Right, and I was worried about Peggy. I had my right hand on her shoulder."

"But they didn't know how much you saw."

'No. I think it was two women and a man. He was sitting toward the back, between the two women. They were adults. He seemed elderly. That's about as specific as I can get."

"Did you know her before the dinner?"

"No, she's younger; just graduated a few years ago. Got a master's at Ohio State. Planning to do a Ph.D. The development officer introduced us. Rare to have several scientists from Kenyon. She thought we'd have something in common. Peggy's a physicist."

"But legally blind."

"It doesn't hold her back. You'd like her."

"Where does she work?"

"At ONR," Gwen said.

"The Office of Naval Research."

"Right, in Ballston, just by Glebe Road."

"Does she walk with a white cane or anything?"

"She had one, but I volunteered to help her find the rest room."

"Did she give you a card or a phone number?"

"No," Gwen said. "She told me she's in the White Pages and that I should call her the next time I'm in the area. I didn't tell her I was with the Bureau. I just said that I worked for the DOJ and that I travel around the country."

"True enough," Karen said. "Listen, you can have my dessert. I want to get back to town. She might be in danger."

"You can call from here. It doesn't get any more secure than this."

Karen got out her cell and hit the White Pages app. "Three Margaret O'Connors," she said. "One in Springfield, one in Vienna and one in Arlington."

"She mentioned that she can walk to work."

"North Quincy Street," Karen said.

"Expensive. Convenient. Right by the Metro line. Restaurants up the ying yang. Yuppie paradise."

"She's not answering," Karen said.

"Maybe she's still at work," Gwen said.

"I hope so," Karen said, as she slipped her phone into her jacket pocket and headed for the door.

CHAPTER NINETEEN

Karen was 35 miles from Ballston, weaving cautiously through the traffic on I-95. Traffic was still heavy coming out of Washington. The HOV lanes were open, which helped in both directions, but she was forced to drive more slowly than she would have liked. Better to play by the rules, she thought; there's no need to alert anyone in the area to my presence here.

Peggy's building was an eight-story red brick condo. When Karen buzzed her fourth-floor unit there was no response. The street was brightly lit and there was considerable pedestrian traffic, so she kept her tools in her purse and stood about 6-8 yards from the door, waiting for one of the occupants to depart so that she could enter. She had to wait nearly ten minutes, though it felt more like twenty. A nicely-dressed young man eventually left the elevator at the rear of the front entry as Karen timed her steps to permit her to slide beside him and enter the building. He actually held the door for her and she thanked him.

Karen knocked and pressed the doorbell, but there was no response. Peggy's perfunctory lock presented no problems and Karen was in in less than thirty seconds. The apartment was small: a living space with dining area and kitchen, a single bathroom and a bedroom that was not much larger than 9'x12'. Karen noted that everything was high-tech, with an internet-controlled thermostat, very high speed WiFi and a dedicated computer space in the hallway between the kitchen and bedroom. Peggy's 27" *iMac* was new, as was her *HP* printer. The deep drawer beneath the desktop contained a large magnifying glass, a ream of printer paper, and a large, sectioned tray of flash drives, pencils, pens, paper clips and post-it notes. On the floor next to the desk chair was a shredder. Everything was in its place and nothing appeared to have been disturbed. The only things on the desk proper besides the computer, keyboard, mouse and pad were a set of special reading glasses and a coffee cup. There were slight stains in the bottom of the cup. She was fastidious but not pathologically so.

The kitchen was fitted with decent appliances and the cabinets were stocked with the usual housewares and several weeks' supply of food. The food in the refrigerator had not passed its sell-by dates and there was a bottle of white wine and some artisanal cheese and beer. The apartment appeared to be lived-in but cared for carefully. Nothing was on the floor or left hanging over a chair back. Karen checked the bedroom; the bed had been made but the sheets and pillow slips were not crisp and fresh. The cupboard was half the size of the bedroom proper and all of her clothes were neatly stored. There was a white, extendable cane leaning in the corner—a spare, presumably—and one piece of luggage on the top shelf.

The bathroom was tidy as well. The medicine cabinet contained the usual analgesics, some *Benadryl, Allegra, Imodium*, as well as some anti-inflammatory and antibiotic drugs for the Crohn's. Karen assumed that Peggy required infusions for the disease, but there were no calendars anywhere in the apartment. Presumably all of the information concerning appointments and treatment schedules were on her computer and/or in her phone. There was a charging unit for the phone in the kitchen as well as on the nightstand in the bedroom, but the phone itself was not there. Any reasonable person would simply conclude that the apartment's occupant was out. There was no evidence of any disturbance and nothing untoward in any of the sink or tub drains. There was no check book or bank book, but the former was probably in her purse and the latter all now electronic.

Perhaps she was working late. Karen googled Peggy's name and found a *LinkedIn* page; she listed herself as a Research Analyst, which could mean almost anything. Then she thought, why not? It could be an actual emergency. She called the general number at ONR; an operator answered immediately. She identified herself as a personal friend and asked if Ms. O'Connor was available. "I understand that this is after hours," she said, "but I'm only in town for this evening. I called Peggy's apartment and got her answering machine. I don't have her current cell number and I'll be happy to give you mine if you would be so kind as to ask her to call me."

"Just one moment," the operator said. She returned in thirty seconds and said, "Ms. O'Connor is on vacation at the moment. I don't have access to any further details."

"Thank you very much," Karen said. "I'll catch her the next time I'm in town."

Karen clicked off and left Peggy's condo. She had eight to ten minutes to plan a call to Mike and thought through the details as she drove back to the *Marriott*. She took Spout Run to vary the scenery and as she entered it a light rain began to fall.

CHAPTER TWENTY

As soon as she entered her room she turned on her laptop and googled the White Pages. She typed in 'Margaret O'Connor' and 'Arlington, VA' and found the single listing. She used her premium subscription and, compulsively, verified the street address. Her cellphone number was unlisted. She also learned Peggy's middle name—Anne. Under 'other locations' there was a single address: Dublin, Ohio. Other occupants in Dublin included Lawrence O'Connor and Deborah O'Connor. Probably Mom and Dad. It made sense. Dublin was outside Columbus, an upscale place, probably 50-60 miles from Gambier. The O'Connors could afford Kenyon's tuition (or at least their share of it) and they were close enough to the college to drop off and pick up their daughter, whose health was no doubt a concern.

Salt Lake was on Mountain Time so it was still early in the evening. She used a secure phone to call Michael.

"Sorry, I still don't have anything for you," Mike said.

"I'm calling for something separate," Karen said.

"OK, it shouldn't be too long on the other request; I'm doing some serious narrowing."

"Great. Here's the deal. I'm trying to locate a woman named Margaret O'Connor. Current address: Arlington, Virginia. She works at ONR and I don't want to snoop around there. They say she's on vacation…"

"Unmarried, presumably…"

"Yes."

"So maybe a sibling or her parents would know…"

"That's what I'm thinking," Karen said. "The White Pages put them in Dublin, Ohio, but I don't want to make a cold call."

"Understandable," Mike said. "One of them could be dead; somebody else might answer the phone…you want to give them the sense that you and their daughter are pals or something…"

"Right."

"This is related to the situation with our mutual friend."

"Yes, both were at the alumni function in D.C."

"That makes it easy," Mike said. "Alumni associations and college fundraising operations know more about individuals than anyone but the immediate family and they can track them wherever they move. Remind me of the college."

"Kenyon."

"Right down the road, well…what…fifty miles or so from Dublin."

"Yes. Can you get me something by tomorrow morning?"

"Piece of cake. The development office there will probably use some standard software package for (what do they call it?) 'donor relations' or 'relationship management'? Probably *Advance* or *Raiser's Edge*. Even if they have their own system they're easy to crack. The thing is…they're always selling lists to credit card companies that give the school a kickback or trying to sell watches or other expensive gee-gaws with the school logo…they've got the good information but they're also particularly vulnerable. It's all about the webs they weave and the webs' weak points. I'll have something in a couple hours. You rest, take two aspirins and I'll call you in the morning."

"Thanks, Mike."

"I live to serve and I haven't forgotten your facial rec request."

"When you're on the case I sleep like a baby."

"Screaming and flailing all night?"

"You know what I mean."

"I know. Just kidding. Be back in touch soon. Peace, out."

Mike called at 7:00. "I didn't want to wake you," he said.

"What have you got?"

"Quite a bit. Her mom and dad—Lawrence and Deborah—still alive. Fifty six and fifty four, respectively. He's an engineer. Civil; works for the City of Columbus. She's a special ed teacher in Dublin. Both very active in their church: St. Brigid of Kildare. That's right, in Ohio, not Ireland. Catholic enough for you? Margaret/Peggy is active too—in Our Lady Queen of Peace in Arlington. She majored in physics. Magna grad. Couple of awards. She was also active in the church at Kenyon—St. Vincent de Paul."

"Possibly targeting her for some kind of gift involving faith and religion on campus."

"I think so," Mike said. "She contributes to the annual fund now. $500.00 or so usually. And she made a one-time gift to a scholarship fund in the sciences."

"Anything of a personal nature?"

"Significant other, that sort of thing? No."

"And no siblings?"

"No; she's an only child. With health challenges, as you know. By the way, I got into her health records via ONR. Her Crohn's is under control and her vision is more or less stabilized."

"Some good news, at least. How about phone numbers? I've got her parents' number."

"I've got her cell, no landline," Mike said. He dictated it to her and she put it in her phone directory.

"I'll start there," Karen said. "I pray that she answers."

"She's supposedly on vacation," Mike said. "Some of us turn off our phones then."

"You wouldn't turn yours off if you were getting married or being rolled in for major surgery."

"No, I probably wouldn't. Neither would you."

"Of course not," Karen said.

She thanked him profusely for his help, clicked off, and rang Peggy's cell. It went straight to voicemail as she felt her heart rate increase.

CHAPTER TWENTY-ONE

Karen began to call Peggy's parents but stopped, looked at her watch, considered the fact that a call this early would arouse suspicion as well as anxiety, and instead went downstairs for breakfast, her appetite diminishing with every thought of the girl's possible condition.

Her breakfast still in her throat, Karen waited until 9:00 Central Time to call the O'Connors in Ohio. The phone rang three times before it was answered by Peggy's mother.

"Mrs. O'Connor?" Karen said, "I apologize for calling this early but I wanted to catch you or your husband before you left for work."

"Yes?"

"My name is Carrie Wilkinson. I met your daughter Peggy at a Kenyon alumni function a few weeks ago. I was changing purses this morning and I realized that I had an address book that belonged to Peggy. She left it at the restaurant and I've neglected to call her. I figured she probably had most of the information in her phone, but…just in case…I thought she'd want it."

"That's very kind of you, Carrie. Did you try to call her?"

"Yes, I have her cellphone number but it's going straight to voicemail. I called the ONR and they said she's on vacation."

"Right, she's with a friend she travels with. Maryellen."

"Any idea where they are? I could call and just leave a message. I'm sure it's not urgent, but I'm Type A and I didn't want to put it off, especially since it's so long since she lost it."

"I understand," Mrs. O'Connor said. "She and Maryellen are in

Front Royal. There's a B&B there that they like. I think they're only going to be there for a few days. It's called the *Royal Oak*."

"Great. Thanks so much. And Maryellen's name? In case the room is in her name."

"Blanchard," Mrs. O'Connor said.

"I really appreciate it," Karen said. "Have a great Tuesday."

"I hope to," Mrs. O'Connor answered. There was warmth in her voice but a little apprehension as she faced her day.

The *Royal Oak* was on South Royal Ave. The website showed a three-story, slate-blue wooden house in good repair with a broad front porch and some brass lights on either side of a dark front door. Karen called the main desk.

"*Royal Oak*, this is Carol speaking."

"Hello, my name is Carrie Wilkinson and I'm trying to reach one of your guests. Her name is Margaret O'Connor. She may have registered as Peggy. She's with her friend Maryellen Blanchard."

"That's very interesting," the desk attendant said. "They were registered for last evening but they haven't arrived yet."

"Can I ask…did they call?"

"I'm sure they've been held up. They've booked for three days. This is not uncommon."

"Right. I'll check back later. Thanks for your help."

"No problem," the woman said.

They've probably paid in advance, Karen thought, so the B&B's not concerned. They figure they got sidetracked along the way…or couldn't get away on time…or had car trouble…or whatever. They owned the room for three days; they could use it any way they chose.

Long shot time, Karen thought. Perhaps they did get held up. Maybe they stopped for dinner, had a little too much to drink and just stayed where they were. The *Royal Oak's* rooms were reasonably priced; it wasn't as if they were abandoning a $600 reservation in New York.

Where would I go en route to Front Royal? Karen thought. First, I'd want to get out of the metropolitan D.C. traffic so I felt like I was on vacation. Front Royal's only an hour and change from the city. Where would I stop to have dinner? The Virginia hunt country…or maybe the *Inn at Little Washington*. Gastro paradise. She began with the hunt country and called the *Red Fox Inn* in Middleburg. Peanut soup, colonial decor, wallpaper with pictures of Sly Boots in red hunting garb…she told the concierge at the Inn that she was a friend of Peggy's and Maryellen's and that she needed to reach Peggy. "No big emergency…don't frighten her, I just have something that she needs to know for her trip."

"I can check our reservations at the restaurant and the credit card chits. Your friend isn't registered at the Inn."

"Thanks so much," Karen said. Five minutes later the concierge came back on the line. "Sorry," she said, "there's no record of their being here last evening."

Karen thanked her and called the *Inn at Little Washington*. Same rationale, same initial answer from the concierge. When she returned to the phone she said, "I can't really give details over the telephone," she said, "but I can tell you that Ms. O'Connor and Ms. Blanchard dined with us last evening."

"That's very helpful," Karen said, "but I take it they're not in residence at the Inn."

"No. We've been fully booked for weeks. They were probably lucky to get a table at the restaurant without a reservation."

"Probably a spur of the moment thing," Karen said. "I know your food is wonderful. If I was in the area I'd try to pop in whenever I could."

"Thank you; Chef O'Connell is a master."

Karen thanked her again and hung up. What happened between Washington and Front Royal? What happened on Route 522? Ten minutes later she was in her car, pulling out of the *Marriott* lot and heading toward Route 66.

CHAPTER TWENTY-TWO

The area traffic was still heavy until she was five miles beyond the Beltway. The drive from Arlington to Washington took nearly an hour and forty-five minutes. She turned off of 211, on to 522, toward Front Royal, slowing to 40 mph and looking on either side of the road for any sign of a traffic accident or anything else that might be considered suspicious. She passed through Huntly and Chester Gap; in the distance, to the northeast, she saw smoke and her heart sank.

The smoke was from smoldering trees on a rise just off the highway. A car had careened off of the road and into a culvert. It was a black and twisted SUV. A Front Royal police department car was parked behind the wreckage, along with a Warren County sheriff's office vehicle. A tow truck with the title and logo *Blue Ridge Towing* was parked along the side of the road. The driver was pacing back and forth, trying to figure the best way to remove the burned car from the culvert.

Karen parked behind the two law enforcement cruisers. She showed them her Bureau credentials. "Just passing through," she said, "checking out some issues up on 81, but I grew up in this area…outside of Markham. Hope this isn't anybody I know."

The sheriff smiled but first walked over to talk to the tow truck driver, who was now rigging the cables to extricate what was left of the SUV. The Front Royal officer then walked over to Karen and extended his hand. "Vince James," he said. "This one's a real mess."

"Any survivors?" Karen asked.

"Found the remains of two women," James said. "They've both

been taken to the funeral home that functions as our morgue. Medical examiner should be checking them out by now. Car's registered to a woman named Blanchard. North Arlington residence. Unless she's got a second place here, she's not one of our's."

"We had a neighbor named Blandings," Karen said, "but I don't know any Blanchards. I guess that's a relief. Looks like something serious happened…what with all that fire."

"Too early to say," Officer James responded. "You see this stuff in the movies all the time, but that there's a serious fire. If there was a gas leak or something, people would usually pull over to the side of the road and get out. They might see smoke coming from the engine or smell raw gas, but they'd know it was nothing to mess with and stop, get clear of the car and call triple-A or something."

"Exactly," Karen said. "Hope this wasn't caused by some third party. Somebody ugly and mean…road rage stuff." She paused and said, "I don't see any bullet holes or ram marks…"

"We'll have to tow it in and take it apart a piece at a time," the officer said. "Something like this…we'll work together with Sheriff Hemple. We've got a good relationship. We support one another and all. None of that agency jealousy stuff that you see in D.C."

"Well that's a blessing," Karen said. "My watchword is always the same—the more help the better. We all might see something that another might miss. The point is to figure out what happened and why."

"Amen," the officer said.

"Tell you what," Karen said. "I'm working a human trafficking case, just going off to do some interviews. More a forced-labor deal than a sex deal, but sometimes they can go hand-in-hand. I doubt very much that your case here has anything to do with mine but it never hurts to ask. What if I swing by later this afternoon, buy you a cup of coffee and see if you're looking at anything that could be of concern to the Bureau?"

"Works for me, but I'd say later rather than sooner. It's gonna take awhile to get that Highlander out of that drainage ditch. Then they'll start applying the fine-tooth combs. I'd say four hours before anything even preliminary…"

"Not a problem," Karen said. "I've got plenty to do. How late's your shift?"

"I'm off at 6:00, if the chief doesn't ask me to hang around longer."

"You'll want to get home to dinner," Karen said. "What if I swing around at 5:00 and we'll just do a quick coffee, just to cover any possible bases."

"Five it is, unless the creeks or rivers rise," Officer James said.

"Pleasure," Karen said, and gave him a firm handshake. "Is there a diner or something near the station? That late in the day…we may want a slice of pie, take the edge off."

"*Sunshine Diner*. Breakfast all day," he answered. "East 6th…or what the locals call Happy Creek Road."

"I'll find it," Karen said.

It took fifteen minutes to reach Gwen and talk on a secure line.

"What a filthy, despicable group of son-of-a-bitches," Karen said. "They took out a girl who was nearly blind and her friend as well. What in the world are they hiding?"

"Dogged, too," Gwen said. "My guess is they wouldn't go anywhere near ONR. Too many resources. Too many dangerous friends. They had to wait until she was out in the open. Terrible way to die too, especially if it wasn't instantaneous."

"What bothers me is that they had the resources and the chops to know when she was leaving, where she was going, who she was going with, what kind of car she drove…the whole scenario. Like we've been saying all along, this is serious."

"So are we," Gwen said, "but I keep telling myself, if we can find them they can find us. I've been mulling over how they could have identified Peggy and me when we were only in their private dining room for five or ten seconds. Finally I realized that it wouldn't be that hard.

All they had to do was find out who was there that evening. The easiest first stop was to i.d. the Kenyon event and then look at some yearbook photos. The only real challenge was to have someone in the room with a good enough eye to remember our faces."

"Someone who would have been edgy from the get-go," Karen said. "Someone with a lot to hide."

"And willing to kill to keep it hidden," Gwen said.

CHAPTER TWENTY-THREE

Karen pulled into the *Sunshine Diner* at 4:55. Officer James was in one of the four booths at the corners of the long silver car. He was sipping coffee from a thick beige mug. "I wanted to treat," Karen said.

"You can get the pie," he answered. "I've already got a mug here for you. Ginny will get you some fresh."

"Any favorites?"

"The peach is my favorite, if they have any." The waitress had approached her, her lips mouthing the word 'pie'?

"Two peach if there's any left," Karen said. The waitress just nodded her head. She didn't ask if they wanted ice cream or any other side with it. 'Purists around here,' Karen thought to herself.

After she settled in and had a sip of coffee and a forkful of pie, Officer James slid a piece of paper across the table. "Not too much yet," he said, "but we know a little. Both of the women's purses were there and survived well enough to enable us to salvage some credit cards and i.d.

"From the height and weight data on the driver's licenses the driver was Maryellen Blanchard, age 32. She lived in the Ballston area, near the other decedent, a Margaret O'Connor, age 28. My guess is that they were friends from church. Our Lady Queen of Peace. Maryellen had some literature about a program they run for immigrants and each of the women had a rosary in their purse. It's just a guess, but they probably didn't meet at work. Margaret worked for the Office of Naval Research and Maryellen commuted into the city. She was a nurse in a doctor's office down near 17th Street."

"Anything at all that might suggest foul play?"

"Nothing you could really sink your teeth into. The right front tire had blown out. We're figuring that the blowout caused the vehicle to swerve off the road. A gas line was severed and the tank was punctured, so the heat of the engine or possibly some grinding of the undercarriage caused enough heat or sparks for ignition. Hell of a way to die."

"Anything suspicious found at the scene?"

"A couple of wires and a little piece of plastic, but that could be anything from anywhere."

"Anybody take a picture?"

"I got the thing here," he said, reaching in his pocket and pulling out a plastic evidence bag. "It's all ground up. It could have been there for months."

"Of course," Karen said. "Boy, you're right about this pie, Officer James. This is the best peach I've tasted outside of Atlanta, though I did know that they grow peaches in Markham."

"Their apple's nothing to sneeze at either," he answered. "And I do love their pecan, but that's a waist killer. I allow myself a piece or two at Thanksgiving and, OK, a piece or two at Christmas, but I try to steer clear when my will power permits."

"I was always a sucker for the pecan, myself," Karen said. "Of course, the family tradition was pumpkin after the turkey, along with a bottle or two of that white wine from *Naked Mountain*."

"Harpers sold to the Morgans. Ten, fifteen years ago or so. You probably knew that. Still the best wine in the area. Certainly my wife's favorite. I'm more a beer and bourbon type, but I'll try a glass every now and again."

Karen picked up the evidence bag and looked at the remainder of a fuse. "You're right, this could be anything from anywhere," she said. "I should probably take a picture, just in case."

"You can have the whole thing," he said. "Your labs are bigger than ours. So long as you sign for it and let us know if it leads to anything of substance. We're almost certainly writing this off as a horrible accident."

"That wouldn't be a problem," Karen said, sounding as if she would rather be talking about pie and Chardonnay. "I put your name in my cell earlier—*Vincent* James, right?"

"Sounds funny to me," he said. "I'm Vin to my wife and Vinnie to my mom, but that's right. Here, I got a card with my number. I'll wait to hear from you."

He handed her the card and the chain-of-evidence document.

"May take a little while," Karen said, "because there's a long line of serious forensic material ahead of anything that appears to be a long shot, but I won't let it get lost in the shuffle. I'm indebted to you, Officer James."

"If you could just put your particulars down on the transfer sheet, we'll be in business," he said.

"Not a problem," she said. "How about one more cup for the road?"

"I wouldn't say no," he answered, as she scribbled her signature on the chain-of-evidence document.

An hour and forty minutes later she was at the FBI Lab at Quantico, meeting with a friend named Andy Hartman. She had worked with him on some incendiary devices associated with an attempted terrorist attack in 2019 and she trusted him to respect confidentiality. "I appreciate your staying late tonight, Andy," she said. "I wouldn't ask if it wasn't important."

"And you wouldn't be here if it wasn't something interesting," he said. "What've we got?"

"Looks like the remains of a fuse," she said. "Possibly used to blow a car tire. Possibly used to blow a gas tank."

"Let me just have a preliminary look," he said.

She asked if she could get them some coffee.

"Already had more than my share," he said. "You go ahead, though. I just need a couple minutes with a magnifying glass and a bright light."

"I'll just wait then," she answered, finding a chair and checking cellphone messages.

He came back in fifteen minutes. "You were right," he said. "I could see some of the black powder core in the inner, textile tube, with the waterproofing agent and the external plastic wrapper. There's not much here, though. To the untrained eye it just looks like roadside junk. I doubt that we'll find any prints or DNA evidence. Your average vehicular homicide type will just shoot or ram. In the movies they cut brake lines. This is something done by someone a lot more devious and professional, but I'll have a look and call you ASAP. I'll have to do it after hours. We work in pretty close quarters and I don't think you want anyone asking me leading questions."

"That would be a roger," she said.

"Two days, maybe?"

"That would be perfect," Karen said. "You're the best, Andy."

"I live to serve," he said, "and to help convict. And incarcerate. And execute, when possible."

CHAPTER TWENTY-FOUR

By the time she got back to the *Marriott* she was hungry for dinner. The pie was good for calories and taste but little else. She checked her watch. She wanted to call Mike; it was still early enough in Salt Lake, but she didn't want to appear to be nagging. He would contact her the minute he discovered anything with the facial rec software. 'I'll just eat,' she said to herself.

She thought about the fact that she wasn't getting in her daily exercise because of the unexpected tours of northern Virginia and the piedmont and decided to walk across the bridge again and eat in Georgetown. She went to *Martin's Tavern*, a local mainstay. She was hungry, so she ordered some French onion soup and meatloaf with beans and mashed potatoes ('our version of mom's favorite'). She thought about some followup cheesecake or bread pudding but decided that she'd already had her full complement with the peach pie and instead ordered some hot tea. The food was good but it seemed as if the prices had inflated considerably since her last visit.

That evening she slept reasonably well. Her cell rang at 8:15. It was Andy Hartman.

"I decided to work late last night," he said. "Your questions always pique my interest."

"And your answers pique mine," Karen said. "Where should I start?"

"Our hardware store probably," he said.

"Done. I owe you one, big time."

"Call with any questions."

"Will do."

She turned on her laptop and went to one of the Bureau's drop sites, an actual hardware store in Tampa. She went to the CONTACT US link, entered a code and pulled up Andy's report.

It was succinct: *Almost certainly designed to blow the tire, because there was a residuum of relevant materials—some natural rubber, bits of steel and textiles, synthetic polymers, some antioxidants, antiozonants, curing systems and filler material: your basic components of passenger/light truck tires. Rare to get a little of everything, but the blowback from the pop appears to have been significant. Some theory? You wouldn't want to make the fuse a timed device because it wouldn't help their cause if it detonated in a parking lot or a gas station. If I'm them and trying to do some serious damage I make the tire device operate on command, to remove the driver's ability to control the vehicle subsequent to an initial blast, doubtless to the gas tank. That would plunge the car into flames and the tire device would then be detonated to, in effect, run the car into a ditch, thus frustrating any chance of escape. The tank device could be timed, like some sort of mini-limpet device, but for greatest effectiveness it should be activated on demand. That way the bad guys follow the car at a distance, wait for difficult/dangerous terrain, blow the tank, then blow the tire. A little prior reconnaissance would aid the process. The opportunity would have come when the victims stopped for dinner. The killers rigged the car, waited in the shadows, followed them to the optimal site and killed them. No gasoline residue on the tire fuse, but if it were me I'd put the tank device as far aft as possible, so that the initial flame would be visible to the follow car. Just a guess, but it fits the facts. If you could find any remains from a tank device that would clinch the case.*

Karen copied the report onto a heavily-encrypted flash drive, erased the message on the drop site, and held her chin in her hands. 'That's the way I'd do it too,' she thought to herself, 'the bastards.' Before she had breakfast she called Gwen and brought her up to speed.

Gwen thanked her, shared her thoughts on the horrible deaths of Peggy and Maryellen and asked if there was any news from her facial rec specialist.

"Not yet," Karen said. "That'll be my next step."

She looked at the time in the corner of her laptop. It was too early to call Mike. She threw some cold water in her face, washed her hands and went down to the breakfast buffet, grabbing a yoghurt, an English muffin and some black coffee. When she returned to her room she checked her gun and three spare clips of ammunition. She didn't anticipate using it this early in the investigation but she found it comforting to hold it in her hand and extend her arm toward an imaginary set of targets. She wondered if the snipers who attacked Gwen were also involved in the killing of Peggy and Maryellen. Different techniques, but it was always better to reduce the total number of individuals involved. A large and powerful organization would have access to bomb makers. If it was the snipers doing the actual job, all that they would need was some elementary instruction on how to secure the devices to the intended areas. They didn't have to get involved in the design or fabrication processes. If you walked along a crowded street in certain sections of the middle east and threw a *Wham-o Super Ball* it would probably hit more certified bomb makers than doctors or lawyers. Was that stereotyping? Yes, but not by much.

CHAPTER TWENTY-FIVE

She returned her weapon to her purse, sat down again at the laptop and began to check on bombmaking techniques. As the search engine pulled up possibilities, her phone rang. The secure phone. She recognized the area code: 801--Salt Lake City, Utah.

"Hi, Mike," she said. "What news?"

"Well, nothing definitive yet, Karen, but progress. I've had to do one at a time because there's so little to go on. We can talk about one today; I'll then go to the next one in line and get back in touch, ASAP."

"Great, Mike, shoot."

"Well, it's not an exact science," he said. "We've got very good software and we can enhance lighting, sharpen edges, enhance the resolution and even correct for misleading changes in coloration, botox use, and, yes, plumpers. Ever heard of something like that? People puff up their sunken cheeks…anything to trick the camera or attract a date. There's little evidence of that here; your three simply tried to cover themselves up and deny us good camera angles."

"Right, but they can't change facial proportions."

"No, they can't, but they can just give us a small portion of the face to work with. I had hoped for a stupid mistake. Sometimes, for example, they hide their eyes behind dark glasses but they forget that they're exposing their hands, their rings, etc. That's usually a long shot, but with people like these three—all well-heeled and dressed to the nines—you might catch a glimpse of something unique. Unfortunately, that didn't happen here and remember, when they only give you half a face or less it's harder to do proportions."

"Because nobody's face is symmetrical," Karen said.

"Right. Anyway, that's just prologue. What I'm trying to tell you is that I don't have anything 99.9%; what I've got (and we're talking about the woman in the Hermès scarf, as candidate number one) is a handful of potential matches."

"I can work with that," Karen said.

"I think the news is better than that," Mike said. "One of them jumps off the screen, not because of the facial rec software, but because of the need for privacy."

"Now you've got my hopes up," Karen said.

"OK, here's what I'll do. I'll put the shot we've got on our normal drop site, along with matches for the left eye, left eyebrow, the bridge of the nose and part of the forehead. You take a look at the six partial matches and draw your own conclusions."

"Will do," Karen said. "And thanks. I'll wait to hear from you on installment two."

"Probably not by tomorrow," he said, "but soon."

Karen went to a different drop site, a custom tee shirt designer in Lincoln, Nebraska. She had to jump through several digital hoops to reach the page. There were six pictures, with descriptions below each of them.

Picture One: Rachel Kincaid, a vice-president for sales in a valve company in City of Industry, California. She lived in a small condo in Arcadia, California, had attended Whittier College and received a master's degree from Cal State, Northridge. There was no record of any recent trips to the east coast, nor to China, where the valves were produced.

Picture Two: Susan Benson, an associate professor of Art History at Arizona State University. She had done her graduate work at NYU and was an expert on Italian art of the Renaissance. In the previous six months she had traveled to Florence for a special exhibit and to academic conferences in Gainesville, Florida, Ann Arbor, Michigan, and San Diego, California.

Picture Three: Bernice Richardson, a fourth-grade teacher in Sandusky, Ohio. She had studied at Kent State University and had not traveled beyond her state in the last twelve months.

Picture Four: Rebecca Grosz, a pharmacist in Springfield, Missouri. She had received her education at UMKC and had traveled to conferences in Las Vegas, New Orleans and San Francisco, all in the last six months.

Picture Five: Ellen Anderson, a development officer for a hospital complex in Des Moines, Iowa. She was educated at Carlton College and had previously worked for the Norton Simon Gallery in Pasadena, California and the Archdiocese of Boston. She had moved to Des Moines after her second marriage, three years ago. She was widowed after her first husband's death to leukemia. She had frequent trips to Chicago, Minneapolis, St. Louis but none to the east coast except for a trip to Hartford, five months ago.

Picture Six: Eleanor Boerling. Educated at Mt. Holyoke and Yale law school. Currently engaged in a host of philanthropic enterprises, with a courtesy appointment at the Georgetown law school. Residence: Number One Observatory Circle. Wife of the Vice-President of the United States of America.

CHAPTER TWENTY-SIX

"Hello, Eleanor," Karen said. "Did you enjoy your dinner at *Quaglino's*? And just what in the hell were you doing there?" One thing you can probably be sure of, she said to herself: your presence there had something to do with money. Carlton Boerling, her husband of 32 years, had begun as a community organizer in Portland, Oregon, progressed to membership on the school board, the city council, legislative assembly, and—representing the third congressional district (Portland, east of the Willamette) in the House of Representatives. His father taught Sociology at Reed College and his mother was a counseling psychologist. He met Eleanor Turner in law school at Harvard. Her father had been an attorney at Skadden, Arps and her mother a predecessor at Mt. Holyoke before becoming an officer at the Mellon Foundation. Her parents, unlike his, were worth approximately $37,000,000, not including their east 68th street apartment and cottage in Seal Harbor, Maine. None of this, however, explained Carl and Ellie's net worth of $18,000,000, even with her inflated Georgetown salary of $125,000 and his longstanding rep's salary of $174,000, bumped to $235,100 when he donned the veep's mantle. His communications secretary had suggested "intelligent investments," whenever there were questions from a curious member of the press, but the smart money was on influence peddling and the ability to utilize campaign contributions in a host of creative ways.

Ellie herself had never practiced law or even taken the bar exam. She had sized up Carl as a class-A meal ticket who shared her profound concern for the weak, the downtrodden, and the ways in which they could propel the two of them to Easy Street. Once fused to his coattails, establishment Washington embraced her heartily and touted her activities with the same level of enthusiasm as they had devoted to her couture. If there was anyone in Georgetown, Kalorama, Adams Morgan or the Palisades who exuded greater D.C. chic they had not yet been formally identified. Karen summed her up in a single word: *gonef.*

Before she could notify Gwen of her discovery she saw an email hit her in-box. It was from Mike, using an alias, and indicating in very cryptic fashion that the second installment of his investigative results had been posted.

This time there were four possibles for the second woman, the one with the high wool collar and large dark glasses. The hits concerned the eyebrows, lined forehead and nose with a prominent bump. The forehead was particularly high, sufficiently disproportionate to draw statistical attention.

The first woman was a B-list actress from Britain named Sophie Walsh. With a place outside Edinburgh and a *pied `a terre* in south London, she had not traveled to the United States in years, at least not officially or noticeably. The interesting thing was that Karen actually recognized her. She usually played downscale character roles and did not carry herself with the hauteur of the woman on the *Quaglino's* security system.

The second woman was a lawyer from Albuquerque named JoEllen Robinson who handled personal injury cases and advertised on local television. Interesting, Karen thought; most of the chasers of ambulances are of the male persuasion. Her *LinkedIn* site listed four children, a husband, two dogs, a cat and active participation in local civic affairs. She was too busy to come to Washington and get into trouble with Ellie Boerling.

Number three was actually a nun. Lay name: Carolyn Tillson. No habit, no wimple, no yardstick tapping against her left palm. She was the principal of a parochial grammar school in Toledo, Ohio and she sported a genuine smile and personal warmth that Karen instantly embraced. The fact that her clothes were more *Penney's* than *Saks*, *Nieman's* or, God forbid, *Bergdorf's*, cinched the case. It was almost certainly number four, particularly considering Mike's propensity for saving the best until last.

Her name was Isabella Dominguez, the wife of Benjamin Dominguez, an Argentine cattle baron. While he owned vast grasslands he now developed his cattle via feedlots, particularly a humongous one in Saladillo. The feedlots were anathema to environmentalists, not just because of the emissions from the cattle into the atmosphere but also because of their waste materials polluting the ground water and local aquifers. Karen's initial guess was doubtless right—that wool coat that Isabella was sporting was most definitely cashmere, if not *vicuña.*

Any possible relationship between Dominguez and Boerling was a matter of guesswork and conjecture, but one thing was certain. The relationship involved money, power, global policy and, almost surely, a conspiracy against the public. So who was the squire in the *Burberry's* coat and Borsalino hat? He wasn't at *Quaglino's* for the cavatelli or the bomboloni.

Karen thanked Mike for his help and told him she anxiously awaited installment three. He sent her an emoji of a man tipping an oversized hat. She called Sam Barron and asked him to notify Gwen that she would be there as quickly as she could.

"Sounds like progress," he said. "I like progress."

"Not the beginning of the end but the end of the beginning," Karen said. "Isn't that what Winston called it?"

"Yes," Sam said. "Hopefully there's not as much blood, sweat and tears involved in this story."

CHAPTER TWENTY-SEVEN

"Lunch or early dinner?" Gwen asked.

"Let's get some coffee, talk, and work the internet for a little while," Karen said.

"Works for me," Gwen answered. They sat across the table from one another, with dueling laptops, the coffee carafe and two tall ceramic cups separating them.

"Reinforcements?" Gwen asked, an hour later.

Karen just nodded, made a second urn of coffee and refilled the brown plastic carafe. She noticed that Gwen was now largely free of bandages and was deeply focused on her tasks, but her eyes wavered slightly as fatigue set in. She was at 80% mentally, 60% physically, and heavily-powered by caffeine. Thirty minutes later she seemed to slump in her chair but promptly pushed herself up by her elbows and winced slightly.

"Want to take a break?" Karen asked. "You could get horizontal for a few minutes, stop fighting gravity."

"It's not that," Gwen said. "I've got all night to rest. I just can't help thinking that this is all very generic."

"Generic?"

"Yes, not some plot to rule the world, just to rule a part of it and make some serious coin in the process. The issue is the secrecy and the desire to secure it at all costs."

"You think they're plotting something obvious."

"I think they are."

"Cow farts," Karen said.

"Yes, cow farts. They wouldn't put it that crudely, of course. They would quote methane stats, the total human costs of beef production and the need to save the planet. The diehards would want us to eat bugs and grass. The moderates would allow us to eat grass that tastes like beef."

"And the people who got in on the ground floor of plant-based pseudo steaks would make a killing," Karen added.

"And those who still bred beef could sell it at Wagyu prices. It'd become like fois gras from the Dordogne. If you had both beef and land to grow plants, as Dominguez does, so much the better."

"And the government's pay-to-play gambit is obvious," Karen said. "Forbid private producers from letting their cattle graze on public lands. They're already making noises about doing that. So far they haven't succeeded, but with an environmentally-credentialed veep, they could make their move. Without access to public lands the cattle market would shrink precipitously."

"And producers in other countries with a running start (like Argentina, obviously), would benefit from our cutbacks."

"Carlton Boerling takes the backhander to end all backhanders and the circle is unbroken," Karen said. "We've already established what he is; now we're simply going out to dinner at *Quaglino's* and negotiating the price."

"Yep," Gwen said.

"Does that mean we're having fish for dinner?"

Gwen just smiled. "It means that we'll be having a lot of fish for dinner in the future, depending on how that plant-based meat tastes."

"At least Boerling will be able to afford some Kansas City strip," Karen said. "Not that that's any great source of consolation, particularly with two and a half cases of murder supporting his efforts so far."

"That's the issue," Gwen said. "Look at the lengths to which he'll go to line his pockets. If it isn't beef production it will be something else. Like old J.R. put it, 'Once you give up integrity the rest is easy.'"

"But who's the unindicted co-conspirator in the hat and raincoat?" Karen asked. "A facilitator? A consultant? Someone who's ultimately using all of them?"

"Boerling's as corrupt as they come, but there's nothing in his past to suggest that he's capable of murder. He's all about wheeling, dealing, bribes and payoffs. He keeps the right constituencies in his pocket and hides behind a compliant press. In their heart of hearts his supporters aren't troubled by his getting rich by stealing from the taxpayers. That's how they define politics. That's why you run and get elected—to have an opportunity to grift, big time. In return you give your supporters sinecures or blown kisses. *Thymos*. Recognition. At the core and at its most basic: attention. These are needy shlubs and down-and-dirty pols, not quoters of John Stuart Mill."

"I don't know about Dominguez," Karen said. "He plays hardball but he's not operating Murder Incorporated. His wife actually has a sister in a convent."

"Cloistered," Gwen added.

"You noticed that too."

"I did," Karen said. "He makes more money than God already. Not that he wouldn't always want more. I'm struck by the fact that so far he's been strictly 'Cattle 'R Us'; he hasn't branched out into a whole host of other operations."

"He's a major player in his industry," Gwen said, "but he doesn't appear to be an international criminal. He's producing a lot of food for European cattle while forcing his own to live in cramped quarters rather than grazing merrily across the Pampas, but that's common practice. The environmentalists all wring their hands but no one's singling him out for being some kind of evil lone ranger."

"No, that's right," Karen said. "It's your basic 'economy' of production in the darker corners of Latin America--standard operating procedure. He just does it on a large scale."

"I see him as a quintessential interested party," Gwen said, "but not the guy whose hand is at the top of Mario Puzo's jacket cover."

"No," Karen said, "but the guy in the hat and raincoat might be. He's the one I want to know more about."

As they spoke there was a tapping sound from the speaker next to the door. "Anyone hungry yet?" a disembodied voice said.

"Could we have another hour?" Gwen asked.

"You can have as long as you want," the voice said. "We've got two choices on the menu tonight—swordfish or tournedos of beef."

"Beef," they both said together.

CHAPTER TWENTY-EIGHT

While they were working Karen received a call from Vincent James. "Just thought you'd want to know," he said, "we swept the area around and under the burned car and there was nothing at the rear except scorch marks. No more road junk or anything remotely suspicious. It looks as if there was probably a fire beginning at the gas tank, but that probably followed after the tire blew. Car went into a heavy skid; the tank bounced off of the side of the road; the shield shredded; the tank cracked and the sparks from the drag ignited the gas. I checked everything twice…nothing on the road, so we're going with the 'accident' explanation. Closin' the books on it."

"Thanks for letting me know," Karen said. "I don't have anything to report from my end. If and when I do you'll be the first to know. Meanwhile, thanks again for touching base." She clicked off and thought to herself, 'Efficient device. Installed cleverly. Self-destructed, in effect. We *are* up against some pros.' She briefed Gwen and they settled down to dinner.

The beef was medium rare, with a Bordelaise sauce, crispy roast potatoes, green beans and homemade rolls. Dessert was pecan pie with a dollop of whipped cream. "To keep our strength up," Karen said. "Sorry I didn't bring any wine."

"Not a problem," Gwen said. "When I get out of here I'm going to spend the first month or two making up for lost time."

"As you should," Karen answered. "In the meantime it's important for you to stay sub rosa. As long as you're sequestered here no one but

Sam and I and the Director know that you survived the double attempt on your life. They can keep their IED's and long guns away from this part of the wilds of Virginia and leave you free to investigate with me."

"I'd rather be side by side with you in the field," Gwen said, "but I'm realistic enough to know that I'm not yet fully capable of doing that. I'm not that far away, but still not there yet."

"Your brain is your most dangerous weapon," Karen said. "Anybody can put a finger on a trigger or button."

"I'd like to believe that," Gwen said, "but I have a feeling we're going to need a very big boat and some deadly fishermen to protect us from the ruthless bastard or bastards behind this."

"I agree," Karen said. "In the meantime I'll wait for my facial rec expert to check in. It shouldn't be too long, considering what we now have and how little we had to begin with. My money's on the guy in the hat and raincoat. I simply don't see Boerling as a murderer."

"That may depend on how much he has to lose," Gwen said. "I do think he would have trouble killing an ONR analyst and her friend as well as attempting the life of a Bureau agent using government assets. There's no way he could convince government people assigned to do wet work to take on targets like us, particularly not with their access to information sources that would label us squeaky clean. You remember the movie about the Kennedy assassination, the one with the huge government plot underwriting the script?"

"Yes," Karen said. "Completely implausible. There's no way you can have that many tentacles reaching out from government ground zero and keep it all a complete secret. Think about the way in which so-called 'top officials' run to the press the moment one of their suggestions is turned down in what was reputed to be a high-level, private meeting. Too many bruised egos, too many personal agendas, too much ambition, too little loyalty."

"Exactly," Gwen said. "This operation was private. No, make that: the result of a private/public partnership in which the ruthless, private side not only did the dirty work but insulated the government gonefs from excessive exposure."

"It's the classic dirty circle," Karen said. "The outsiders with the unending greed fund the insiders to facilitate a process which redounds to both of their benefits. On the one hand, reelection and the chance to peddle the resulting influence for personal gain. On the other, the opportunity to defraud the public via a set of officials who are assumed, a priori, to be corrupt from the get-go. It's what they call the 'system' and there's so much money involved that we're never more than a step away from violence, whether it's publicly acknowledged in the form of war or intelligence operations or executed privately, in the shadows, away from the microphones, cameras and bright lights."

"The gray twilight," Gwen said.

"I've worked there," Karen said.

Gwen started to comment when they both heard the tapping sound at the box next to the door lock. As the door slowly opened on its heavy hinges Sam Barron entered the room with his finger across his lips. He closed the door and secured it. "We may have just gotten lucky," he said.

"In what way?" Gwen asked.

"I'll give you the short version," Sam said. "A former member of the Secret Service and his wife have an 81-foot *Hatteras* moored in Selby Bay, Maryland. Every now and then they cruise up the Potomac, settle in for the night at a D.C. marina and go up to Key Bridge at the next evening's rush hour. They commuted across it for years, putting up with its miseries. Now they sit and watch the traffic as they break out the martinis and toast the commuters and unlucky tourists. They were coming around this morning, approaching the Wilson Bridge and trying to dodge some driftwood. In the driftwood, along with some branches and junk was a human hand. The left hand, as it turns out."

"Severed neatly?" Karen asked.

"Well, not so neatly, but recently. Even with the time in the water it was still fresh enough to yield a clear print from the ring finger. The DNA was additional gravy."

"Somebody thought they could destroy some evidence and feed some fish at the same time," Gwen said.

"Right," Sam answered, "help out the shad, white perch and the game fish that are trying to make a comeback in the face of the nitrogen, phosphorus, sediment and other pollutants there. Actually, my guess is that their intentions were far less honorable than securing the marine ecology of the river and the bay. This was an attempt to eliminate evidence, pure and simple."

"Because the person's been identified," Karen said.

"Yes. One Ronald Grayson, not a name that you're probably familiar with."

Both women shook their heads no.

"Grayson was eased out of the Army and returned as a mercenary in a UK organization, from which he was promptly fired. Highly-skilled and willing to take extreme risks but too fond of dangerous missions. He was judged to be untrustworthy."

"Loose cannon," Karen said.

"He didn't know when to stop," Sam said.

"And his specialties?" Gwen asked.

"Explosives and long range marksmanship."

"Gwen's sniper," Karen said.

"We can't be sure," Sam said.

"If it is," Gwen said, "whoever hired him didn't take long to rid himself of him."

"If that scenario holds," Sam said, "the person ultimately behind the attempt on your life is covering his tracks quickly and decisively."

"He (and probably a partner) blow up Peggy and Maryellen, report in for their envelope of untraceable bills and instead get fed into a wood chipper or run over by a hay baler," Gwen said. "I take some small pleasure in that outcome but it just reinforces the fact that we're dealing with someone whose methods are…"

"Between grim and grimmer," Karen said. "We're not going to find any record of social security or 401K contributions, but if this is one of the people involved…"

"A statistical long shot," Sam added.

"Yes," Karen said, "a statistical long shot but if we're dealing in the world of timelines and circumstantial evidence, one that should move to the top of our list."

"No question about that," Sam said.

"I think we should get back to our computers," Gwen said. "Maybe with some additional coffee."

"I already asked the kitchen to grind some fresh and bring in some big mugs," Sam said.

CHAPTER TWENTY-NINE

"My guess," Gwen said, "is that there are two levels of insulation. The active wet work people (now sent, one hopes, to a deep corner of hell), and the longstanding single layer between the person pulling the strings and the guns for hire. Your basic evil servant or servants, the kind who populate a blood-drenched Elizabethan tragedy."

"The person or persons the string-puller can trust, or at least believes he can," Karen said. "He may have the means to hire an Army but he's not surrounded by one. Too obvious. The stench would attract flies. He works through a middleman, at least for the darker side of the operations, and may well restrict his most brazen work to simple mercenaries, mercenaries who can be eliminated if there's too much post-op heat."

"Flies with cameras, listening devices and software that sweeps the dark web," Gwen said, "to the extent that individuals like us still exist."

"Once upon a time we could count on the fourth estate to join us," Karen answered, "before the death of curiosity or the greed of their corporate overlords turned them into an echo chamber or Amen corner for the platform's political allegiances. Nevertheless, this guy still has to be *very* careful. When you hobnob with the powerful who refuse to live on their paltry government salaries it carries a significant risk because the government stiffs in gray suits can call on government resources, the resources that include real armies and the big guns. Plus, they have an exalted sense of self and a daily course of life that largely consists of mendacity and self-aggrandizement. On the other hand, a wannabe string puller can't reside in his basement and live as a recluse. He may not want to do his dirty work in public but he has to be willing to at least meet, because the government types aren't going to deal with flunkies. Their egos won't allow it. He can insulate himself from the wet work team but he can't send a faceless liaison to a meeting with someone who fancies himself a significant player."

"And when he thinks he's been seen he simply erases the onlookers," Gwen said, "or tries to."

"Right, but like I said, he still has to take the meeting."

"And in this case the veep's better half (or unindicted co-conspirator) was there to represent an immediately recognizable public official, one known for influence peddling. That probably means that the man in the hat possesses enough respectability to allay any risk aversion that a person like Ellie Boerling might reasonably be expected to have. You can't play Caesar's wife and dine out with the *capo di tutti capi* in a public restaurant."

"Maybe he's someone from the top of the food chain," Karen said. "Someone above the law or at least above the partisan fourth estate's curiosity. Dirty but sacrosanct."

"A significant donor?" Gwen asked.

"Why not? Money is the pols' mother's milk. If you've got it, they want it. If you give it to them you receive access. If you give it to them in serious quantities you receive unlimited access."

"And if you deliver it in serious quantities you'll want something in return besides veal marsala, stuffed squash blossoms and buratta/watermelon salad," Gwen said.

"The worst thing is that it's systematically unquestioned and accepted," Karen said. "You check the White House guest register and you often find that the people in the oval office and West Wing aren't meeting with well-meaning staff or with important foreign dignitaries; they're hosting the shadowy people who come to trick and trade."

"And on a proportion of occasions that might even shock the voters, if the voters were paying any attention," Gwen said.

"It is what it is," Karen said. "The way things are. Maybe even the way things are supposed to be, so long as the results are to their liking. The way business is conducted. To the press it's like the sun rising in the east and setting in the west. It's not news, particularly if that sun is shining on the members of their preferred team."

"Even if it's a conspiracy against the public," Gwen said. "Corruption and politics? We're talking scones and strawberry jam. PB&J. Yin and yang. Even if the process results in an occasional severed hand floating in driftwood down the Potomac."

"The broken eggs that make the omelet," Karen said. "Remember the D.C. college president who said that political corruption was one of the established ways for an ethnic group to develop its cultural and financial power? True, unfortunately, but it's like sex between your parents. You don't want to see it acknowledged and you most definitely don't want to hear it talked about."

"All true," Gwen said, "but it feels different when the abstractions turn into bullets that find their way to your own arm and shoulder. That's not something I'm ready to sit still for."

"Point taken," Karen responded. "Collateral damage is sometimes the most consequential damage of all."

CHAPTER THIRTY

Gwen suddenly realized that she had been gesturing with her fork, even though she hadn't touched her pie.

"I'm going to check on this Grayson character," Karen said, "see where he's been, what he's been doing, who he's been talking to. Maybe he's using London as a base, or somewhere else with cameras on every corner. I'll talk to my guy in Salt Lake. He's got contacts everywhere. He calls it the white web—the place for deep searches by the people on the side of the angels. I'm also hoping he'll give us some information on the man in the hat. We'll try to do this top to bottom as well as bottom to top. Meanwhile…I need some sustenance."

She cut her pie with the edge of her fork, tasted it approvingly, and looked at Gwen who was deep in thought.

"I want to be of more help," Gwen said. "I'm going to ask Sam to set me up with an office. You develop the secret stuff; I'll try to develop the public stuff. Sometimes the crucial tidbits are sitting in plain sight. The guy in the hat…he's not young. He's been at this for awhile. There has to be a trail. The Dominguez woman…? I see her on the margins. I'll see what I can see, but I don't expect much. She and her husband are specialized, a target of opportunity for the major bottom feeders. Ellie Boerling? She's gone from clubwoman to political arm candy to gonef…"

"None of those moves involved long distances," Karen said.

"No question," Gwen said, "but though the legacy media have protected her, the small-fry local media didn't anticipate her reaching her current position. She may have left some interesting bread crumbs along the way. What did the political scientist say—you understand people when you examine their hopes and dreams at the age of 18?"

"Who was she reading then," Karen asked, "Ayn Rand or Herbert Marcuse?"

"Whatever someone who could do something for her at the time was reading," Gwen responded.

The next morning Sam had created secure spaces for both Gwen and Karen. Gwen thanked him for his help. "Neither of you should return to the field until you know more about the players," he said. "The Director doesn't want to see any increase in the body count."

"Any more human limbs found in the Potomac?" Gwen asked.

"Not yet," he responded, "but Karen was in early. She's received some material on Grayson. Breakfast at 8:00?"

"Perfect," Gwen said.

"They're fueling us with plenty of sugar and grease," Karen said, "but I'm not complaining. You eat your sausage and syrup and I'll tell you what I've learned from my man in Salt Lake. First off, Grayson was not based in London. He's been sighted in Bucharest and Tehran, but that was several years ago. The people who check on these things have not been able to find a fixed point, but they think he moves between Los Angeles and Boston. They haven't been able to find a current bank account but they've worked backward from events to payments. (Thank God for the Israelis, by the way. They've been bird-dogging him for years.) The jobs that bear his mark were followed quickly by payoffs from several hostile governments to mail drops in Santa Monica and Lexington, Mass. The common link was that he was paid in commodities rather than in currency."

"Not wheat or oil, presumably," Gwen said.

"No. Gold, diamonds, black opals, platinum."

"Like ABBA, back in the day, when currency fluctuations were too dicey for their accountants."

"Right, but they didn't require something portable," Karen said, smiling. "Assuming he's taking $100K-250K for a job, he'd prefer something smallish, unmarked and easily converted to cash in any major country. At its current valuation a simple kilo of gold is worth nearly $80K."

"So he was taking international jobs but with payoffs that enabled him to stay on the move and hide in the shadows."

"Like I said, he hangs out in big cities with an ample supply of sleazy commodity traders and major international airports. Unfortunately, we don't have any intel that's recent, reliable and specific."

"I've got another idea," Gwen said. "When he was fired from his last mercenary group he had been operating in Afghanistan. Even the hard core found his methods too…undiscriminating. Instead of operating in the open in daylight he simply went to his targets' homes when they were unoccupied and lined their internal escape routes with odorless accelerant. Then, in the middle of the night, he used a simple device to ignite them while he positioned himself with a sightline to the front door. If the women and children came through first he let them escape and picked off the men when they hit the porches. If the men came through first he shot them and let the women and children fend for themselves. If he got the addresses wrong every now and then…well… we're back to eggs and omelettes. If at first you don't succeed…go out for a nice dinner and drinks and try again tomorrow."

"Scumbag," Karen said.

"Yes. Major league," Gwen answered. "Anyway, I did some work last night after dinner. When he was fired there was another pink slip issued, this time to a guy named Scherl. Robert Scherl. It seems that he and Grayson had served together in the past. Two happy little warriors, one a colour sergeant (that's a staff sergeant in an English infantry battalion) and the other a corporal."

"Grayson was the sergeant," Karen said.

"Yes, presumably leading the corporal astray," Gwen answered.

"And guess what? Scherl does not appear to be as elusive as Grayson. If we study his whereabouts we might be able to track Grayson's."

"Scherl is the hired help," Karen said. "Waiting for Grayson's call."

"That's my guess," Gwen responded.

CHAPTER THIRTY-ONE

"And you've located him?" Karen asked.

"Trying to," Gwen answered. "It seems too easy to be true."

"Best guess?"

"Like I said, it seems too easy. I found a car registration in Wisconsin and it seems legit. The address attached is sitting right there on *Google Earth*, a cottage in the woods with a long driveway."

"His idea of security, maybe," Karen said.

"Yes. Tiny town outside of Madison, Wisconsin called Black Earth."

"Not Scorched Earth?" Karen said.

"No, but maybe the name attracted his initial interest."

"Now tell me he has an account at the local bank."

"He does," Gwen said; "he actually pays his taxes and reported some interest income but I didn't want to hack the account and risk tipping our hand to someone local that we're investigating him. It's a small town, a small bank; everybody probably knows everybody else and there could be any number of personal relationships."

"He may feel invulnerable or at least invisible," Karen said, "playing the solid citizen with Uncle Sam. Maybe he only signs on for something dirty when he needs an infusion of serious cash. He could even have an honest job somewhere."

"Possibly," Gwen said. "If Michael can't access all of his bank files electronically you could pass for a green-eyeshade bureaucrat and check them out on the ground."

"Yes, and I want to see his house anyway," Karen said.

"I did see that there are direct flights from D.C. to Madison," Gwen said.

"I'll go through O'Hare. Whoever's behind this could have people, cameras, bribed agents…I'd rather be in larger spaces with masses of people."

"Good idea," Gwen said. "I don't think we should be running around in all directions, but Scherl looks like he could be a possible."

"I'll be discreet," Karen said.

The next morning Karen was in O'Hare, in the pedestrian tunnel beneath Terminal 1, walking between the B and C Concourses. She was dressed down, looking more like a slightly unkempt graduate student than a professional woman. Her tattered carry-on, with well-worn wheels, contained two changes of clothes, her *Sig* P320compact and two clips of ammunition, all encased in a composite metal box designed to foil the screeners. She could have easily flashed her Bureau credentials and bypassed the issue as well as the scans, but that might have drawn someone's attention.

She hadn't been in the Madison airport for years—the site of an engineering conference a decade earlier—and it appeared to have grown exponentially. She rented a nondescript car from *Enterprise* and drove west. She entered Cross Plains (the mothership for the branch bank in Black Earth), having changed her clothes at an inexpensive chain hotel in the industrial parks of Middleton. A dark green blouse and black pants would look professional enough at the bank and serve as camo when she checked out Scherl's house.

The teller at the bank in Black Earth was named Terry. Karen's red Badger baseball cap (an airport purchase) covered her eyes sufficiently to disrupt the corner camera's sightlines. She introduced herself as an FDIC tech and showed Terry an all-purpose badge with generic credentials. "This is not a surprise audit or anything like that," Karen said. "I'm simply making some rounds, checking the banks' IT systems for security purposes. If you can give me a cubby-hole with computer access I'll be out of your hair in ten minutes."

"Would you like to talk to the manager, Mr. Driscoll?" Terry asked.

"Not really necessary," Karen said. "The more spontaneous the better the check. I'm sure he's on the up and up, but the check needs to be as independent as possible, if you know what I mean."

"Of course," Terry said. "He's actually at lunch. Why don't you go in the meeting room by the restrooms? There's no one there now. If you've got a laptop I can give you the password to get into our network."

"Perfect," Karen said, silently congratulating herself on her timing.

She was actually done in eight minutes. Scherl had a money market account that also functioned as a checking account. The recent history was interesting. A balance of $17,000 had been augmented with a cash deposit of $75,000. Then the account was drained, leaving a residuum of enough change to keep the account open. "Real bastards," Karen said to herself. "He gets a cheap payoff for a middle-range job, then his masters take the money back, leaving enough there to limit attention. Maybe they at least left his body intact."

Scherl's home was a frame cottage, just off 14, on the Mazomanie side of Black Earth. The driveway was dotted with eastern white pines. 'They grow quickly,' Karen thought to herself, 'maybe he planted them for cover and concealment.'

The house was painted a dark brown. Adjoining, but not connected, was a metal garage with a window on either side. It afforded a protective entry point to the area by blocking any potential views of the main structure. Karen made her way through some northern white cedars and scattered wildflowers and looked into the garage. There was a year-old *Land Rover Defender* with visible dried mud spatter on the fenders. It had rained for the last several days. 'His indulgence,' she thought, 'probably $55K out the dealer's door, but it hasn't been outside for awhile. I wonder why they didn't take the car also. Probably wanted it to look as if he was still among the living. Transferring the money from his account and bouncing it electronically was lower-risk.'

For the next twenty minutes she walked around the house. She didn't want to surprise Scherl, if he was still alive, and—more to the point—she didn't want to walk in on one of their armed guards. She hadn't seen any cameras, tripwires or sensors, but pros would hide them carefully. One obvious entry point, the rear door (off the kitchen, presumably), had a small deck with two garbage bins. The earth beyond it was undisturbed. The only other ingress/egress point was the front door with a small porch covered in pine needles. A long downspout was free of pine needles at the drain site but at the house's corner was a thick, muddy puddle formed by a clogged gutter. She could also see the tips of some weeds that had taken root in the corner of the gutter. Since everything else appeared to be in good repair Karen assumed that Scherl was either a poor housekeeper, otherwise occupied or no longer present.

There were no lights on inside the house and no smoke rising from the chimney. The ring in the analog electric meter was turning so slowly that no significant usage beyond a refrigerator motor was likely. Security systems drew less electricity than a medium light bulb. Karen had some miniaturized listening devices but they gave no indication of human or animal presence. She disabled the simple security system, picked the *Schlage* lock and went in through the kitchen door.

CHAPTER THIRTY-TWO

The sinkboard was clear, the divided aluminum sink dry. Raising her *Sig* she did a quick inspection of the house. Either Scherl was a fastidious indoor housekeeper or he had been removed and a cleaning crew was brought in to create order, remove dust and put everything in its place. There were two bedrooms with a shared bath, the kitchen, living room, assorted closets and a storage room that functioned as an office. All very basic, even minimalist. The interesting but not surprising thing was that the principal structure contained no weapons. Real pros would acquire cold weapons for each job and discard them when the jobs were completed. No one wanted to establish a traceable record. Still, a civilian deer rifle or something comparable might have been expected in a rural cabin. The bathroom medicine chest contained the usual analgesics, tapes, pads, salves and creams but no prescription meds.

The beds were made with reasonably fresh linens and there were some guns and ammo and field and streamy mags on the nightstand and living room table. The flat screen was a 48" *Samsung*, with an aging all-region dvd player. A small collection of sports, military and English mystery discs were lined up in a cubby hole beneath the TV. Scherl was old school, not a streamer.

The kitchen cupboards contained standard cookware and bakeware and an interesting collection of foodstuffs. Scherl had a particular love of chili, but an eclectic taste—from *Armour, Steak 'n Shake, Wolf, Chilli Man*, and *Hormel* to the *Amy's* tofu vegan concoction. He could do with or without beans and even had a taste for white chicken chili, but his favorite appeared to be the Cincinnati brand, *Skyline*, a thinly-minced sauce with cinnamon, nutmeg, allspice and unsweetened chocolate--an acquired taste--usually served over spaghetti with shredded cheddar cheese.

Beyond that there were common canned vegetables and a large selection of soups. Except for the usual staples of flour, sugar and oil there was little evidence of any baking, beyond a box of cornbread whose sell-by date had recently passed.

The aged yellow refrigerator had a few blue cans of *Point Special* beer, a half-filled jug of *Diet Pepsi*, eggs with a tight sell-by date and a bag of red grapes that looked as if they were trying to turn into raisins. The freezer compartment was empty except for some ice cubes that were beginning to acquire a slight onion scent.

She checked the tub drain and spritzed the surfaces with luminol but there was no evidence of blood. She inspected the walls and door frames carefully but, again, everything appeared to be clean and free of any evidence of violence or physical altercations. There were no hidey-holes for contraband, not even the scent of *Hoppe's* oil or the tote bag of tools that one might expect in a cottage in the woods in a town like Black Earth.

Before checking the garage she used the oak kitchen table to access the attic. The entry point was in a bedroom closet. The only thing she found there were the remains of some poison cakes for mice and rats. Scherl hadn't bothered to buy the plastic traps; he had simply slid open the ceiling panel and tossed in a couple handfuls of poison. It must have worked, for there was no remaining smell of death and decay.

The garage was only slightly more interesting. One side contained two bookcases, made of a composite material and dotted in the corners with the remains of spider webs. At the base of one was an ancient wooden toolbox with a lockless hasp that had warped tight over time. It had once been painted a dark red that was now streaked with the remnants of dirt and grease. Inside was a brace and bit, an old-fashioned gear-driven hand drill and some dried paint brushes. They appeared to be at least fifty years old, inherited, perhaps from Scherl's father or grandfather. On the upper shelves of the bookcases were some paint cans of various sizes, with long side drips. A tray for a roller contained some stir sticks and a tool with a bottle opener at one end and a paint lid opener at the other. Along the shaft was an ad for a paint company in Mazomanie.

The *Defender* was a mid-shade of green, probably from their military color palette. There were no keys in the car (and none in the house), but when Karen opened the door the interior lights illuminated, so the battery still carried a charge. General rule of thumb for holding a charge on an undriven vehicle—two weeks.

There was nothing suspicious in any of the interior spaces of the car, but the dust on the garage floor had been rearranged. No biggie necessarily. Scherl could have unloaded some groceries several weeks earlier or one of the rodents who had escaped his attic traps had come into the garage to explore. There was no obvious blood or drag marks. The rakes and snow shovels leaning against a far corner of the garage were surrounded by orderly dust and interlaced with spider webs. There was no storage space above the garage, just open rafters with a few sheets of plywood and a long step ladder.

Bottom line: either Scherl had been away for a week or two or someone had set up his house and garage to appear that way. There was always the outside chance that he had nothing to do with the attempted murder of Gwen Harrison. Karen tried to remain agnostic on that possibility but she now tilted toward the possibility that whoever had hired him and his sergeant for their recent jobs had thanked them for their service, took back their fees and killed them on the spot.

CHAPTER THIRTY-THREE

Karen passed along what she had learned, checked out of her hotel, returned her rental car and waited for her flight to Chicago. She hadn't seen anyone suspicious when she arrived and felt comfortable closing her eyes for a brief spot of time. Tilting her cap over her forehead she sat in the shadows and power-napped for fifteen minutes. The flight to O'Hare was on time, as was the flight to Reagan National.

The next morning she met with Sam Barron, who informed her that Gwen was back in bed. "Trying to overdo," he said. "She felt like you were doing all of the real work and that she had to do something to pull her weight. I told her that the case was in good hands and that we wanted her to heal completely. She just looked at me, said she was fine, and turned back to her computer. By noon she was slumped in her chair, fighting off sleep. I had a cot set up next to her work station. When she woke up in mid-afternoon she drank some juice, thanked me for the cot and went back to sleep. When I told her she was going to take the night off, whether she wanted to or not, she didn't argue with me. She had a good breakfast this morning and said she wanted to rest a little before returning to work."

"I'll meet with her in her room," Karen said.

"Treat the room as if it's not a secure space," Sam said.

"Will do," Karen said.

She briefed Gwen on her trip to Wisconsin, speaking softly and using broad, general terms. Anything specific, such as the money in Scherl's money market account was written on post-it notes and returned to Karen's pocket.

"Any word from your friend in Utah?" Gwen whispered.

Karen gestured 'no' with her head. "He's very methodical," she whispered. "When he knows something he'll let me know immediately."

"See you this afternoon," Gwen said. "I think I'll have lunch here."

"Of course," Karen said. While they spoke she had been pleased to see that there was no I-V tube, blood pressure cuff, oxygen meter, catheter or any other line or tube attached to Gwen. She simply needed rest. There were no leaks or infections or other forms of regression. When she returned to the work station adjacent to Barron's office she accepted his offer of lunch and worked at her computer, fortified with a BLT, some cottage cheese and pineapple salad and a glass of tea/lemonade. By mid-afternoon Gwen joined her, worked for a few hours, had a light dinner and returned to her room. Karen's assessment: she's exhausted. Her body has put her on notice that it's time to rest.

CHAPTER THIRTY-FOUR

Michael's text interrupted Karen's sleep. "I think it's time for a wardrobe change," Michael said. Karen opened a fashion blog that functioned as a Bureau drop site. The message was very long; it began with a set of pictures. As usual, Michael saved the best for last. The first four were possible facial rec hits.

Face one: an elderly lawyer from Miami named Paul Martinez. Semi-retired, the scion of his firm, now the client acquisition rainmaker. He specialized in corporate trial work but though he resembled the man in the hat in striking ways he had lost a limb in Vietnam and walked with a noticeable limp.

Face two: a Los Angeles businessman named Ralph Anderson. Pushing 100, he still appeared to be vigorous. He had invented two generations of state-of-the-art breast pumps for nursing mothers. He had studied biomedical engineering, taught for awhile, developed his inventions and retired to Malibu. A stroke at 88 had resulted in a slight sag of his left eye, enough to disqualify him from key overlaps with the man in the hat. Close. No cigar.

Face three: a former athlete. A relief pitcher for the Cincinnati Reds from back in the day. Country boy; his name was Sonny Lynn. Still vigorous, even tan, rested and ready, but without the financial means to do serious criminal damage. He had once been a partner in a steak house in Montgomery, Ohio and a Chevrolet dealership on Vine Street in what the locals called 'Auto Valley'. He had basically allowed the principals to use his name and image and show up for ad campaigns and special events.

As his name recognition faded he was reduced to falling back on earlier investments, the principal one being a set of apartments and townhouses in a section of the city called Mt. Healthy, a now-fading neighborhood that was once called 'Mt. Pleasant' but changed its name in the mid-nineteenth century when its residents fared better than their surrounding neighbors during a cholera epidemic. His income was sufficient to keep body and soul together, but would not permit him to conduct criminal activity on a significant scale.

The fourth face had been initially promising but its possessor had gone to his eternal reward three months earlier: a land speculator from Scottsdale named Richard Seymour. "He was rich enough and had been involved in some shady transactions, but mostly small-scale. The eyes are very similar. Anyway, no harm no foul. Just giving you everything I've turned," Michael said.

Number five was the home run or more likely the brief look into hell. "All the smart money will be on him," Michael said. "Working up separate file; go back to sleep; I'll be ready to share in the morning." The only material content that Michael left was a series of facial images.

'I hate when he does that,' Karen thought to herself. Michael could write teases for a cable news network. In the 1940's he would have written the endings to Saturday afternoon serials, in the 1840's the ends to chapters of melodramatic novels that were being published in parts.

For the next hour Karen tried to surf the web, the white web and the dark web for comparable images but she lacked Michael's software packages and technical skills. "He *does* look familiar," she said aloud. The key identifier was not so much the similar facial rec hits as it was the fact that he appeared to love expensive hats. In one picture he was wearing a tweed Baker Boy cap paired with a *Barbour* jacket and an Italian shotgun that looked like something King Charles would give one of his male offspring on a significant birthday. In another he was wearing a Panama Montecristi fedora that would have set him back $7 grand and change. Paired with a white suit he was accompanying a dark-haired beauty at twilight on the Ponte Vecchio. She was young enough to be his great granddaughter. The interesting thing was that he appeared to be strong enough to support her as he shepherded her through Florence on the evening stroll. No date on the picture, but it hadn't been taken decades before. Damn, he looked familiar, but he kept himself in the shadows with his eyes turned away and his hats darkening and slightly distorting his features.

III

SOL

CHAPTER THIRTY-FIVE

Karen had stayed overnight at the rehab facility but had slept fitfully. She awoke twice, once at 2:58 and a second time at 4:57. Each time she checked for messages from Michael but there were none in her secure inbox. She got up at 7:00, checked for messages, then showered and dressed. She had breakfast at 7:45—a Denver omelette with a side of fresh fruit and a carafe of black coffee. She reminded herself that Michael was on Mountain Time, with a two-hour lag. 'Unreasonable to expect him to be up at 5:45,' she thought, 'but then when he's in high gear he doesn't seem to stop to eat, sleep, rest or even pause.'

Barron joined her. He was carrying a 16 ounce cup of coffee with a Bureau logo on one side and a snarky motto on the other. "Waiting for serious news?" he asked.

"Yes," Karen said. "My facial recognition tech has sent some possibles for the man in the expensive hat, but he's saving his actual report for later… later being this morning. Not sure when 'morning' will actually be."

"Probably building a full file for you," Barron said. "If this guy is a serious player he'll have a long rap sheet and life story. It's very hard to tell from the CCTV pictures, but this guy is late 80's at least, probably older."

"Well-preserved, though," Karen said. "Big money brings top medical care and top plastic surgery."

"True," Barron said, "but criminal activity brings stress, even if the perp is insulated by several layers of underlings. He has to spend a little time, at least, looking over his shoulder and listening for the hoofbeats."

"Point," Karen said. "I hope he doesn't hear us until the door closes on his cell…or his coffin. How's Gwen?"

"Confined to quarters," Barron said, "not literally, but she's come to the point that she realizes she needs to stay horizontal for awhile and let her body catch up to the desires of her brain. We tend to think of her as the Bureau's tracker, the raw intellect with heightened senses and pitch-perfect instincts. And she is all that, but there's another side to her. Did you ever hear about the Drogden case?"

"Rings a slight bell," Karen said. "Anthony Drogden?"

"Antony, actually. Rapist and general molester. Worked the upper Midwest, five, six years ago. His DNA was connected with a crime on the north shore of Chicago. The Director TDY'd Gwen to the local office; the SAC wasn't happy about it, thought it was a criticism of his leadership (which, to a degree, it was). The Director convinced him that Drogden was too smart and too elusive and that the usual means of finding him were proving unsuccessful. He didn't use credit cards; he never held on to a stolen car for more than 24 hours. He had no fixed abode and committed his crimes in the woods or in abandoned houses. The women he attacked were of all ages and races and our profilers were disagreeing among themselves whenever they tried to analyze his life and behavior."

"How did Gwen find him?"

"She noticed that he always struck on the weekends. That had been true when he attacked women in Indiana a decade earlier, before his time in federal prison in Terre Haute. The usual conclusion was that his crimes involved complex planning and that he was working a job during the week. That wasn't the reason. The fact was that he was going to churches and synagogues, looking for single women who would be both available and vulnerable. Actually, Gwen didn't find him; one of the other agents did. She had persuaded the SAC to position people—including some local police—in the churches and synagogues. They even had an agent at the Bahá'í in Wilmette. When they caught Drogden he was in Skokie at St. Peter's Church. The agent assigned there saw him panning the church earlier and then following a woman to the parking lot. Drogden followed her home, pulled into her driveway, abducted her and pulled out, heading toward Wisconsin on Interstate 94. By then, suddenly, there was a convoy of unmarkeds, with Gwen taking point. They surrounded him in a wooded area in Highland Park…"

"And Gwen took him down?"

"Literally. He had a knife and he was threatening to kill the woman. Gwen had a baton and approached him. The other agents and police were afraid that he might actually hurt the woman, even though he was surrounded, but they figured that Gwen would try to talk him into putting down the knife and surrendering. She figured that he was thinking the same thing and was waiting and watching to see what she would do. Instead she walked straight up to him and smashed the end of the baton into the bridge of his nose. He was totally surprised and suddenly spitting and slobbering with blood rivulets running over his cheeks, mouth and chin. He dropped the knife, grabbed at his face and mouth and then started to flail in her general direction. She dodged right and left and proceeded to work all of his tender areas—kneecaps, ears, elbows, knuckles, groin, ribs…while he screamed and fell and tried desperately to crab-crawl away. She 9-ironed his hands and ankles and when he finally stopped she put her foot on his throat. 'The fun's over,' she said. 'The next time I'll drive the tip of the baton into the center of your temple. You won't survive that.' He rolled over on his belly and extended his hands behind him so she could cuff him."

"And the woman was unharmed," Karen said.

"She was shaken up but every time Gwen struck him she said she began to feel better. She said he had made her feel helpless, but as he became more and more helpless himself she felt as if she was free of him. Gwen told her that that was the idea. And it wasn't just the fact that she kept swinging; it was the fact that she was connecting, and in all the right places."

"She reminds me of me," Karen said.

"We say 'mission-oriented'," Barron replied.

CHAPTER THIRTY-SIX

"What are you guys talking about?" Gwen asked, as she entered the room.

"Your contretemps with Antony Drogden," Barron said.

"Scumbag," Gwen replied. "Sometimes you have to let lowlifes like that know that you're serious."

"I don't think you left any doubt," Barron said. "He was hospitalized for two and a half months."

"How much damage do you think he had caused all of his victims?" Gwen asked.

"I don't think my calculator has enough decimal places to answer that," Barron said.

"He got off easy. Back on the great plains…back in the day…he would have been happy to have survived intact."

"Probably so," Karen said.

"I know *your* pomps and works; you would have impaled him," Gwen said, smiling.

"I'll plead the fifth on that," Karen answered, as Barron tried to hold his expression.

"Did you get a good breakfast?" he asked Gwen.

"Hunter/gatherer plate," she answered. "Sugar, grease…I passed on the plants."

"I thought that's what the hunter/gatherers ate," Karen said.

"When they had to," Gwen said. "That's why they really wanted sugar and grease, the stuff that was harder to find. It's still in our brains. It keeps the *Waffle House* in business, even if we now think we know better."

"I'm learning new things all the time," Barron said.

"Stick with us and you'll learn scary things," Karen said.

"Things that might come in handy," Gwen said.

Barron was about to respond when Karen's cell phone twitched on the table. She looked at the screen. The icon was a dark basement with a miniature dragon sitting in a *BarcaLounger*. "It's Michael," she said.

"Let me access the drop site…ok…a couple clicks…"

Barron's eyes widened. "That's…"

"Alex Sol," Gwen said. "He's…"

"The biggest contributor to the president's party; Carlton Boerling's party," Karen said. "He makes George Soros look like a penny-ante neophyte."

"Why didn't we see that immediately?" Barron asked.

"All faces are asymmetrical," Karen answered, "but his is especially so. The little wen above his left eye is too small to draw attention and everyone his age has the Howdy Doody chin lines, but the facial rec software caught the details and when the left side of his face was matched with the right, it became obvious. He's also notoriously well-preserved for his age. At first glance he looks like he's 70ish; when you check the records you see that his sons are nearly 60."

"He goes to Switzerland for some weird rejuvenation treatments," Gwen said. "There was a WaPo story about it, a couple years ago."

"Almost *National Enquirer*-level. Capybara placentas or something," Karen said. "He can afford the treatments; not that many people would want them…"

"Vanity is a dangerous trait," Gwen said. "It distracts and preoccupies."

"Anything that makes you fixate on yourself is dangerous," Barron said. "In this case—where it's combined with wealth beyond the dreams of avarice—it's particularly dangerous. It worms its way into your brain and electrifies the selfishness there."

"*Wealth beyond the dreams of avarice…*I like it," Gwen said. "Where'd you get it, Sam?"

"My favorite Sam," Barron responded, "Dr. Samuel Johnson."

"I don't think he'd approve of Alex Sol," Karen said.

"I'm sure he wouldn't," Barron answered. "Sol is a monster."

"No one approves of him," Gwen said, "except the politicians who grovel for his money. I'm not even sure *they* approve of him, but they hold their noses as they put out their hands."

"He may well be the one who tried to have you killed," Karen said.

Gwen paused and let that sink in. "Yes, there is that," she answered.

"Michael's attached a file," Karen said. "Alex Sol isn't even his real name."

"Let me print it out," Barron said, "and we can all take a look together."

CHAPTER THIRTY-SEVEN

"This is supposed to be eyes-only," Barron said, "but we'll read and shred. It's in multiple sections. The name change is only part one."

Alex Sol:

Not his actual name. He's Hungarian. His birth name was Sandor Szollos. His father (a major industrialist) was Csaba Szollos. Csaba was the name of the youngest son of Attila the Hun. (True; look it up.) Sandor is the Hungarian version of Alexander. During the war he fought for Germany. When he served in the Wehrmacht he used the German version of his surname—Sollos. He was in the SS, rising to the rank of Sturmbannführer. That's equivalent to a Major in the U.S. Army. (BTW, the Nazi records have all been expunged. I discovered his rank, etc. through a public record.) *He now calls himself Sol, probably because that's a common Jewish name in Spain. He's not Jewish. Alexander is not a Jewish name; it's Greek, of course, but the Jews use it because Alexander the Great did not destroy the Jewish Holy Temple. So the name Alex Sol is a fabrication. It suggests a sunny Jew who fought against the Persians. Alexander humiliated Darius III in the Battle of Gaugamela, sometimes called the Battle of Arbela. So now, with the Iranians attacking us on all fronts, he's associated with their nemesis. In actual fact, he has sold toxins to terrorist groups sponsored by Iran. The toxins are used in explosive devices to amplify their lethality.*

"I remember that," Karen said. "One of the cable sites brought it up and the story was immediately quashed. The claim was made that Sol had a legitimate chemical company and that some of his products had been stolen and given to terrorists. He expressed outrage, held hands with his political patrons, they made some calls to their preferred media and the story immediately disappeared."

"The chemical company was in Belarus," Barron said, "not in New Jersey."

"The story of his life," Gwen said. "He greases palms and the D.C. establishment lets him do whatever he wants to do, including betraying our country. They, of course, think that *they're* the country, so if he supports *them*, the rest of the elements in his life are purely incidental. 'Strange bedfellows' and all that bullshit. He tried to have me killed because he thinks I may have seen him working on a deal that he preferred to remain secret. It's all about the money and the bottom line. How many billion dollars does he already have? Somehow it's never enough. It's disgusting and unforgivable, but it might be somehow rationalized if he was thirty years old and this was a deal that would make or break him, his family, and a dozen important and worthwhile charities. But that's not the case. The son-of-a-bitch doesn't need any more money; he couldn't spend what he has in 100 years. He may only have 100 days. Why isn't he sitting with his great grandchildren and enjoying the little time he has left?"

"A hundred days?" Karen said. "Let's make sure he has a lot less than that."

"What are you saying?" Barron asked.

"Sorry, Sam," Karen said. "I didn't mean to frighten you."

Barron turned the page on the document from Michael, trying to conceal his smile.

"So, would you like to know how he got his financial start?" he asked.

"I've heard the rumors," Gwen said.

CHAPTER THIRTY-EIGHT

"Michael's attached a map of the Caribbean," Barron said. "He did some serious homework."

"He always does," Karen said.

"Anyway…northeast of Turks & Caicos and due north of Cockburn Town is an island called St. Peter's. It was previously unnamed because it was never developed for tourist traffic. Sol's father acquired it in the early twentieth century and grew some citrus there. Sol saw a different opportunity. He developed more crops—coffee, sugarcane, bananas and tobacco. He named the island after a Spanish Jesuit—Peter Claver. St. Peter, as he eventually became, ministered to the slaves in Cartagena, Colombia, the heart of the Spanish slave trade in the seventeenth century."

"Very empathetic of him," Gwen said, "but I'm sure that was calculated."

"Understatement of the year," Barron said. "Sol hired agricultural workers from throughout the Caribbean and paid the prevailing wage but included health insurance along with decent quarters."

"Generous of him," Karen said, "but there had to be an ulterior motive."

"Second understatement of the year," Barron said, reading ahead. "Each six months the workers received health exams, but the sad thing was that the exams often revealed failing organs—kidneys, corneas, and eventually hearts, lungs and livers. (It's not difficult to inject foreign substances that will give false positives for certain diseases.) Sol had figured out, early on, that these would be very valuable commodities, particularly if they weren't actually diseased. And there was a ready market, if only it could be exploited. Kidney transplants were easy; they were done as early as the 1950's, even if other organs would take awhile. This is a common practice today, with thousands of kidneys sold on the black market. In some ways it's the most vicious and evil form of colonialism, with rich nations literally taking the organs from poor nations, though some libertarians have argued that you should be permitted to sell your own organs."

"The only thing of immediate and significant value which the poor have," Karen said.

"Except for their children, which some wish to sell," Gwen said.

"It's all intertwined with issues concerning slavery and trafficking," Barron said, "but the bottom line here is that an evil man duped trusting people into believing that they were being treated well."

"And people do get sick and organs do fail," Karen said, "but if there's no tradition of widespread health care there's no way to determine or predict how often this might happen."

"And if you only take a kidney here and a kidney there…" Gwen said, "the workers keep on working for prevailing wages, thinking that they're being lovingly cared for, while unaware of the real money that their employer is making from them."

"*Evil* and *vicious* are not big words in Sol's lexicon," Barron said. "*Money* and *business plan* are. He could just as easily have imprisoned the workers and taken whatever organs he wanted whenever he wanted to, but that would have entailed risk without guaranteeing enhanced revenue."

"The key thing is the business acumen involved," Karen said, "soulless, evil and vicious though it might have been. Knowing the international demand; controlling the supply chain. Having the contacts in Europe, the U.S. and especially in the Middle East. Operating the sales, the extractions at one end and perhaps even the transplants at the other. Finding the technicians who won't botch the work but won't disclose it either. This was complicated."

"And St. Peter's is eight square miles," Barron said, "populated with hundreds and hundreds of workers. That complicates the secrecy and 'security' issues but it also creates what Sol probably would have called a significant harvesting pool."

"What did you call it," Gwen asked, "wealth beyond the dreams of avarice? What does a kidney bring today—150-160k? Most of that goes to middlemen, but if Sol controlled the majority of the operation and, of course, the 'donors' got nothing, the profits could be, as we say, maximized. Years later, when hearts and lungs and livers could be transplanted…"

"Like a license to print money," Barron said. "And this was only the start of his (what shall we call it) entrepreneurial career?"

"Why am I thinking that it gets worse?" Karen asked.

"It does," Gwen said, flipping through the pages of Michael's report. "He continued the island operation but then moved on to another form of exploitation. He trafficked young women and boys, set them up in brothels in large cities. The children came from distant countries and they had no knowledge of the local language--no social capital, no local contacts, no real options. And, of course, the local police had all been bribed and ordered to keep their distance. They were sex slaves, pure and simple. Even if they escaped from the brothels they would feel helpless and alone. In the brothels they received two or three simple meals a day and they had a place to sleep. Again, they were given health care, but that was simply to insure that they would not infect the paying customers. When they got older or worn out the management model changed. They were rented in increments of minutes rather than hours and marketed to the city's poor."

"Volume over quality," Karen said.

Gwen shook her head and Sam Barron walked away, doing his best to quell the urge to vomit.

"If it's any consolation," Gwen said, "he's mostly been involved in weapons sales for the last several decades. To our enemies, of course, and to terrorists of any stripe. Occasionally he'll do some currency manipulation and destroy third-world countries' economies…and then there's the fentanyl. He supplies materials to China from his chemical company in Belarus; China distances themselves a bit but then funnels them to the Mexican cartels for processing. They end up in the bodies of American teenagers."

"So-called precursor chemicals," Barron said. "Of course, fentanyl is used legally all the time. If you've had surgery you've probably had fentanyl."

"The son-of-a-bitch works both sides of the street, or maybe I should say border," Gwen said. "Every now and then he'll endow the wing of a children's hospital or create some philanthropic organization (all calculated very carefully, of course). He holds hands with a mayor or governor or senator at a photo-op and pretends he's a public benefactor. He's funded a few free surgeries while his products have left tens of thousands of bodies in alleys and abandoned cars."

"The big question is…" Karen said.

"How do we get to him?" Gwen answered.

"That's not going to be easy," Barron answered.

CHAPTER THIRTY-NINE

"Michael knew you would ask that," Barron said. "He's listed four known, current locations. The first is in Beverly Park."

"Gated. In Beverly Hills," Karen said. "High security; stratospheric prices."

"He tore down and built," Barron said, "so there are no interior pictures on *Realtor.com* or *Zillow*. There are some aerial pictures, but thick foliage reduces the visibility."

"The second is in England," Gwen said. "Berkshire. By the *Sunningdale Country Club*."

"Beaucoup expensive and a hop, skip and jump to central London," Barron said, "but check out Michael's sidebar note. The *Daily Mail* reported in 2017 that Sol had applied for membership at the country club and been turned down."

"Probably more like blackballed," Karen said. "The club is very exclusive and they don't want any riff-raff, no matter how wealthy or influential they might be."

"That's encouraging," Gwen said. "At least someone in the world is upholding standards."

"The third is in Lausanne," Barron said. "The Olympic Committee is there, but not much else. Gibbon lived there for awhile. Pretty, and all that. He may go there for privacy when he's not wheeling and dealing in the U.S. or U.K."

"Number four is interesting," Gwen said. "Quito."

"Just outside," Barron said. His property there is on the site of an inactive volcano; probably likes the solitude; the property is measured in square kilometers, not acres or hectares. It's the kind of place where the disparity between wealth and poverty is almost immeasurable. Beautiful though, in its way. When you wake up in the morning and see Cotapaxi looming above you you suddenly realize what the Andes are all about."

"Nazis in South America; I thought that was passe´," Karen said.

"I don't know what he would be up to there," Barron said. "What's more interesting is Michael's note that he is reputed to have residences in China and Belarus. Nothing in the public record, of course. Maybe that's where all of the real work is done these days."

"Probably," Karen said. "So where does he spend most of his time? And which of the residences would be most easily…visited?"

"Michael doesn't say, but the place on St. Peter's is not on the list," Gwen asked. "Doesn't he still own it?"

"Let's get some coffee," Barron said. "If you could ask Michael…"

"Will do," Karen said.

Michael was prompt in responding. "He still owns the island," Karen said, "but he never lived there per se. He lived on St. Barts, with the beautiful people, the ones who prefer French food to banana bread."

"Did he own a residence there?" Gwen asked.

"Stayed in hotels, or with 'friends'," Karen said.

"Can we get some shots of St. Peter's on the screen?" Gwen asked.

"Sure," Barron answered. "I can get some generic shots from Langley, no problem."

"That's a landing strip," Gwen said.

"Paved," Karen added. "And long enough to accommodate larger aircraft."

"The house is modest," Gwen said, "a simple plantation house but with a dormitory nearby, probably for medical staff, overseers, whatever."

"The hired help," Karen said, "but it appears to be well maintained.

No rust on the metal roof, no large weeds in the paving stones in the walkways."

"The main house has some plantings. Not Versailles or Blenheim Palace, but also not overgrown. Someone visits there."

"Maybe it's like Mayor Daley's house in Chicago, modest by design," Barron said.

"And in the basement—S.P. E.C.T.R.E. headquarters?" Gwen asked.

"Possibly," Barron said.

"This could be his default position, where he goes to ground," Karen said.

"No one would expect it," Barron said, "and as long as you're flying private and avoiding Class B airspace you don't have to file flight plans. He could come and go as he pleased."

"The canopy is thick at the end of the landing strip. There could be a hangar in there," Gwen said.

"And God knows what else," Karen said.

"That's a fairly large dock at the waterside on the south end of the island," Gwen said. "Large enough to accommodate a nice yacht or commercial vessels."

"So what you're saying is that the island could be fully functioning, even if the organ trafficking scam is no longer in operation," Barron said.

Gwen and Karen both nodded in unison.

"We've got to get some eyes on that space," Barron said, "but how do we do it without drawing attention to ourselves?"

"I have an idea," Karen said.

CHAPTER FORTY

"What if I contacted a friend at a foreign security agency?" Karen asked.

Gwen held her expression, but Barron's eyebrows rose noticeably.

"You would have to speak to the Director about that," he said.

"I will," Gwen said.

"Let's all take a deep breath and think about this," Barron said. "Do you believe that the Director will approve of what you're actually considering?"

"Taking this pig off of the board?" Karen asked.

"Exactly," Barron said. "This is not an anonymous cartel member. This is…"

"A major contributor to the administration in power's party," Gwen said. "That's the problem, but that's also the issue. The president (and certainly the vice-president) would never approve of it, so Sol remains free to betray the country as long as he lines the pockets of the members of the administration."

"An administration for which the Director works," Barron added. "I can't believe we're having this discussion. No, wait, I'm not saying I'm not sympathetic. I'm saying…what kind of a mess have we created here? I don't mean 'we' the three of us; I mean the country. The level of acceptable corruption is, well, let's just say…unprecedented."

"Back in the day…" Gwen said, "President Eisenhower's Chief of Staff was forced to resign because he accepted a coat and an Oriental rug from a guy who was under investigation by the FTC. A vicuña coat is pricey and so are some oriental rugs, but we're not talking about a thousand pound block of gold or platinum. We're not talking about trafficking 12 year-old girls or stealing the kidneys from helpless field workers. And we're not talking about killing teenagers with fentanyl or arming terrorists with anthrax, botulism or plague—to be used against American soldiers and civilians. We're talking about an escalation in the degrees of evil that the public and the press are now prepared to take for granted. And we're talking about politicians who are prepared to place the perpetrators of that evil above the law. No regrets, no second thoughts. They're taking millions in backhanders and they're prepared to tolerate treason in return for it. I don't know how we got to this point, but that's where we are. The country is split politically; the press is completely compromised. If it makes you feel better you can blame it on the French Nietzscheans and postmodernism. They're the ones who were instrumental in undermining so-called *truth claims*. They're the ones who talked about narratives and relativism and the notion that everything comes down to power relationships. They infected the universities and the universities infected society…"

Gwen caught her breath and then continued. "Sorry if I'm sounding like a cable news channel. We've always had some Aaron Burrs in our country (and he was a vice-president, remember), but I've never seen what we're seeing now. The institutions have broken down, in part by intellectual design, but the Bureau is still supposed to be guarding the people, standing at the bridge…even if those in charge are prepared to flush everything we stand for in the interest of personal gain and political power. What do we do in a case like this? Go rogue? But who's the rogue and who's the defender of the faith? What did that writer say—a sane person must appear insane to an insane society? Sam, there's a reason why we keep making vigilante movies and telling vigilante stories; they're the only guardians we sometimes feel that we have. And it's horrible, I know that, but what do we do—stand by and let this kind of thing continue? Go through 'normal protocols' when normal protocols have been secretly abrogated? I understand your reticence, Sam. What I'm saying is that our situation is worse than being in uncharted waters. We had charts and they've all been shredded and burned. The new charts are all lies and obfuscation. And we know they're lies and we know that the complicit press knows that they're lies. It's all about the power and the greed and the pretense that things are normal. It's the *new* normal, when up is down and left is right and we're asked, no, we're told, to believe things that we know are palpably untrue. What's at stake is not simply justice for Sol's life of murder and fraud and greed. It's not about revenge for his killing Peggy O'Connor and Maryellen Blanchard or his attempts on my life. What's at stake, Sam, what's at stake is…everything."

CHAPTER FORTY-ONE

"This works at my level also," Barron said. "I'm responsible for your well-being. You're in my shop and my job is to help you get well. Not just your body, but your mind and heart. I'm not going to betray that trust."

"That's why we have Karen," Gwen said. "She's here to help, to be where I can't be."

"With all due respect," Barron said, "Karen is ready to drop both Fat Man and Little Boy through the roof and into Sol's living room. Not that I wouldn't like to see that happen."

Karen smiled.

"Your reputation precedes you," Barron said.

"Yes, we talked about that whole 'mission-oriented' thing," Karen said.

"And we need that," Barron said.

"Let's call the Director," Gwen said. "We can't let this go; we have to trust someone; I trust him."

Walter Gradison had been brought into the FBI largely under public pressure. The *New York Post* had described his job as 'beyond draining the swamp; it was more like cleansing the Augean Stables'. His earlier appointment as chair of the joint chiefs had been in part a sop to the few remaining blue dogs in the President's party. 'Walt' Gradison enjoyed a reputation for calmness under fire, scrupulous fairness and personal courage. Now he brought his organizational skills to the Bureau as well as his personal independence. He answered to both 'Director' and 'General'; Sam Barron called him *Director*; Karen called him *General*; Gwen called him *Sir*. Since Gwen worked with him directly on special assignments Sam asked her to make the initial inquiry concerning a meeting. Gradison took the call and agreed to the meeting. He knew that Karen had been working on the case and decided to invite her to come to the Hoover Building the next day. She would brief him there as well as on the way to Barron's facility. The four would have dinner together and discuss the situation. As soon as he checked the times and schedule he called Gwen back on the same secure line.

"Special Agent Wilken and I will meet earlier in the day," he said. "I know this entire situation is complicated; Sam Barron has kept me posted on the general details and I want some time to think it through before we get together. On a personal note, Gwen, I'm glad that you're recuperating well, but let me reinforce one thing at the outset: this has to be kept very low key and very low profile. Your principal person of interest thinks you're dead, or at least he has no reason to believe otherwise. We have to keep it that way. He absolutely cannot know that he's under investigation. He has too many resources to use to frustrate our actions."

"Understood, sir. I'm not going to do anything to give him any indication of what we're doing. I trust Karen and Sam completely. I will help all of you in any way you see fit. We'll see you tomorrow night."

"Right, I look forward to it," he said, and clicked off.

CHAPTER FORTY-TWO

Sam arranged the menu: Kansas City strips, medium rare; baked potatoes; grilled asparagus. No drinks. "We'll want to keep clear heads."

Gradison and Karen arrived at 5:30. "I don't see any wine glasses on the table," he said.

"We thought you'd want us stone sober, sir," Gwen said, taking the heat for Sam.

Gradison smiled. "How long have we worked together, Gwen?"

"Seven years, sir," she said.

"It's going to be a long night," he said. "I want to be fortified with the sacraments." He reached into his weathered leather brief bag and pulled out two bottles of nice red Bordeaux, handed them to Barron and asked him if he had any Scotch.

Barron unlocked the case next to his desk and pulled out a full bottle of 12 year-old *Macallan*. "I don't come from the world of Chris Wray or L. Patrick Gray," Gradison said. "I come from the world of Creighton Abrams."

"You were his aide right before he passed," Karen said.

"Right. Georgie's favorite tanker. Relieved the 101st at Bastogne. Made light colonel in his late 20's. The spearhead of Third Army. Not a pusher of paper. So why don't we just put our feet up for a few, taste some of Sam's scotch, and kick this business around."

Barron pulled his armchair up to the office coffee table, moved his client chair to the opposite side and invited the Director to make himself comfortable. Karen and Gwen sat on the lawyer's couch, the Director watching Gwen's movements and the degrees of her agility. He noticed that she winced very slightly as she leaned her arm against the side of the couch, but didn't comment on it. He took a sip of the scotch and said, "I've always liked the sherry oak *Macallan*. The fruit taste, the spice…and I'm a sucker for the color. Thanks, Sam."

"My pleasure, Director," Barron responded.

"So let's get to it. Let's mull some things. It'll give us an hour or so for reflection over dinner and then we can return to it after dessert. First off…kudos to Sam and his team for taking care of my chief tracker. And thanks to Special Agent Wilken for all of the yeoperson work. You *will* send along my best to your friend in Salt Lake."

"Of course, General," she said.

"So, first and foremost, the facial rec work is outstanding. This is our boy. I would have used a saltier description, but there are ladies present who might take the endorsement and start reaching for impaling sticks."

Both Gwen and Karen held their expressions.

"Or worse," Gradison said, "but all in good time. Let's start with the view from 30,000. Our politicians have lost their way, if indeed they had ever found it in the past, and they'll whore after money in ways that stretch the imagination to hitherto unknown lengths. You find us some enemies, excuse me, some international *adversaries*, no, sorry, some international *competitors*, and they'll find a way to make secret friends with them for fun and profit. Reclining with dogs may result in flea infestations but appointing or, worse, electing traitors without hesitation is beyond our previous experience. The WWII Brit aristocrats sometimes cuddled up with the paper-hanging son-of-a-bitch but as a rule they weren't sitting on the seats of state with responsibility for protecting the citizenry. I've always known that fallen human types were capable of doing some very bad things, but I never thought that we'd have the worst examples offered the Welcome mat at 1600 Pennsylvania Avenue and that the press would go all Sergeant Schultz at the sight. I know the game is not beanbag, but suffice to say I've never seen it played in quite this way, in part because it puts people such as ourselves in a position that is very, very awkward. Obeying the duly-elected is part of the job description, but treason is not. Allowing the traitors to have their way with us goes against all that is good, holy, right and true. So where does that put us—should we salute and betray, resign (knowing who they'll replace us with) or stand up, knowing that we could end our lives in a stone building with doors made of vertical steel bars?

"And if we don't like those choices, what choice or choices can we offer in their stead? How can we do the right thing, avoid prosecution and still look into that bathroom mirror every a.m. without immersing ourselves in shame? The hell of it is that those are not rhetorical questions. A sleazoid (or group of same) is coming and going in our town, killing innocent people, buying protection from the higher-ups in our chain of command and offering them business opportunities which may well jeopardize the well-being of the people we have sworn to protect. How do we address this problem without committing political and/or personal seppuku? How? And (need I say?), any suggestions you might have will remain at this table and be given the highest degree of confidentiality."

He looked around, smiled, took a long sip of his scotch, and said, "Just trying to get the ball rolling. But seriously, Special Agent Wilken broke up the monotony of the rush hour drive on the Shirley Highway by offering a thought on the subject. Karen…?"

"Her name is Mira."

CHAPTER FORTY-THREE

"Not so much a code name as a nickname. Her given name is Mary. For years they called her Miriam, but the name is so common in her country that they shortened it to Mira. Her surname has been changed so many times that everyone has more or less stopped using it."

"The Mossad," Gwen said. "Originally on the Caesarea operational team, but then the Kidon group, the elite unit of Caesarea."

"Yes," Karen responded. "A group of around 50 with a not inconsiderable number of women. We served together on an operation. How much can I share, General?"

"I'll tell the story," Gradison said. "I enjoy it and I'm not usually permitted to tell it. About two and a half years ago, the Iranian Revolutionary Guard Corps had sent a small group from the Quds Force to London. A group of our cyber warriors from Langley were meeting with their Israeli counterparts there to hash out some issues on software weapons and counter weapons. This is one of the Israeli long suits, of course, and they often run interference for us. They bedevil the Iranians' bomb building and other activities and keep us apprised of some (but probably not all) of the newest goodies in their toolbox. The Iranians were tired of watching their screens go black or, worse still, everything looking normal as it systematically imploded. At the very least they wanted to make a point by using an assassination team to express their displeasure. Anticipating that (and actually picking up active intelligence on it), we sent our own team as bodyguards. This is not usually a Bureau area of operations, particularly so far offshore, but Special Agent Wilken has some special skills and we sent her along on the off chance that those skills might be required. She linked up with Mira and, well, the rest is… eyes only.

"The men with the sharp knives and five o'clock shadow were found sitting around a table in the basement of an Italian restaurant in Jermyn Street. It was a spillover dining room and it was never made clear how they were invited there or why they decided to accept the invitation. One of the regular waitresses went downstairs to take their order and discovered that they had suddenly grown very silent. Instead of *Turnbull & Asser* or *Hilditch & Key* bespoke shirts they had red necklaces of blood at their throats and, in the case of their leader, a sharpened iron spike running through his heart and lodging in the back of his chair. It seems that that particular individual had blown up a school bus full of children in Tel Aviv. It was never clear how Mira and her accomplice had accomplished this feat and, even more interesting, why it was never reported in the London afternoon papers. Suffice to say the collaboration had been a successful one.

"Now, as to our Mr. Sol, he has succeeded in displeasing our Israeli friends on a number of occasions. He has sold nasty implements of terrorism to Hezbollah, Hamas, Islamic Jihad, and the Popular Front for the Liberation of Palestine. As usual, he has insulated himself from the direct sales, but there is no question of his involvement. The real question is why our government has not intervened on behalf of our key middle east ally. Dislike of that ally is not uncommon in some sectors of our government, but the principal answer is that Sol has given great gobs of cash to campaigns and campaigners and he appears—regaled in his tux—at the *Kennedy Center*, the *Willard* and other venues where philanthropy is the putative purpose of the exercise. He is, ultimately, too prominent to be subject to the law."

"Our original and ultimate problem," Gwen said.

"Yes," the Director said.

"But if we could include or even feature an Israeli presence in an operation," Gwen said, "we could insulate ourselves without compromising any principles. They could easily muster a hatred for him that would more than match ours and as the realities of his actions and character were exposed (not fabricated, simply exposed) the individuals who took him off the board would be seen, justifiably, as patriots and heroes, not assassins or partisan political activists."

"It's a thought," the Director said.

"But one that would necessarily involve a very small group of individuals capable of maintaining absolute secrecy," Barron said.

The Director nodded in approval.

"I appreciate the level of trust," Barron said.

Again, the Director nodded.

"And Karen could make the contact with Mira," Gwen said.

"It's a thought," the Director said, turning to Karen. "She would, of course, be equipped with every device needed to insure her anonymity. I could provide information as to Mira's accessibility and availability. The Director of the Mossad and I speak on a regular basis. I also have some back channels that we don't need to discuss here. The two organizations could provide an umbrella for our people and let them work out the operational details. They would, in effect, be silently TDY'd for the task and we would keep complete electronic and paper silence within our respective bureaucracies."

"Would you have to brief the AG?" Gwen asked. "That would give me qualms."

"Let me worry about that," the Director said.

CHAPTER FORTY-FOUR

"How soon can we start?" Karen asked.

"First, we need to do some serious planning," the Director said. "We need to know where Sol will be and what sort of security he will employ there. We need to decide which of our possible methodologies would be most effective, most *certain* and farthest beneath the radar."

"He is not a man without enemies," Karen said. "He may have friends in the highest of places, but sixty or seventy years of evil in his wake could yield a significant number of plausible external suspects, suspects who would, themselves, be beneath the radar."

"Point," the Director said.

"And his age increases the plausibility of putatively natural causes," Gwen added.

"True," the Director said.

"He has offspring," Barron said. "It would be nice to convey to them that they could be dealt with in similar fashion if they continued his operations."

"Indeed," the Director responded, "particularly in the case of the daughter. She is already involved in some trafficking activities on the southern border. You do see my point…this is complex. I suggest we enjoy our dinner and let all of this percolate for an hour or two."

"Compliments to the chef," the Director said. "Lovely char on the asparagus and the potato was one of Idaho's finest. Do I sound like one of those priggish judges on *Chopped?*"

No one responded.

"It was a rhetorical question," the Director said, smiling. "The question is (lifting his wine glass) does an army run on its stomach or on its liver?"

"Both," Gwen and Karen said.

"Yes, exactly," the Director said, as Sam returned to the cabinet next to his desk and retrieved a dusty bottle of cognac.

"You see why I trust you, Sam," the Director said. "Let's go back to the old chairs, have a sip or two and return to the question at hand."

"It's the middle of the night in Tel Aviv and I don't want to set off alarm bells. I'll contact one of my friends there tomorrow morning. Before Karen sits down with Mira we should think about some possible settings—his own island? How often does he visit? What kind of intel do we have on the setup there? One of his homes? I'd prefer not to operate in Switzerland or Ecuador. We could do southern California or Berkshire, but I'm wondering where he stays in Washington or New York. Maybe your man in Utah missed something. He spends a lot of time in eastern Europe and the middle east, but, again, there are no fixed addresses…"

"I'll contact my guy," Karen said. "It could be a little tricky. Sol doesn't fly commercial and I don't want to get into easily-hacked CCTV systems and tip him off that we're tracking his behavior. We can assume that he's got a lot of people on his pad, especially people in government and law enforcement. He has friends in the press but the world is filled with newspapers, even today. It would be harder for him to control the public record where we have a lot of searchable databases. Anyway…"

"Sounds good, Karen," the Director said. "We have a lot of technology we can deploy when we narrow our plans, but I would want to control the number of agents in the loop. This could end up being very old school. Eyeballs to eyeballs. Sharp steel against soft flesh."

Karen cocked her head with a terrier tilt; 'works for me' the posture said.

"We are not without our own press contacts," the Director said. "A story could be leaked in the interest of spin control…something to soften the impact, for example. A revelation here or there, some rumors from the past. Something to pique the public's interest. There's always a fundamental distrust concerning influence peddling. Those who buy and sell politicians are not high in the voters' pantheon. I also want all of you to access the Bureau files on his offspring. They might have some behavioral patterns that would suggest some operational possibilities. Why don't we end on that note. You still have some time this evening to check them out, while I return to D.C. And remember, we can reconvene at any time."

"Who does that?" Gwen asked. "His sons are Ian and Jan. That's the same name."

"Besides George Foreman?" Karen responded. "I don't know. A newspaper in upstate New York once called them TweedleDee and TweedleDoom…then the reporter was fired. A year later he perished in a boating accident. Ian is apparently a sweet kid, but sickly. He's in Lausanne in a healthcare facility. No public activities. Jan, on the other hand, is expanding the fentanyl trade. He keeps a low profile but there were rumors that he was working with MS-13 groups in California and on Long Island. He was also photographed at the *Four Seasons Punta Mita* in proximity to members of the Jalisco New Generation cartel. The picture was taken down from the internet in a matter of minutes and the public was reminded that prominent cartel members are regularly seen at top resorts. The photographer apologized but has not been seen recently."

"The one that is most feared is the daughter, Sara, the real TweedleDoom," Sam said. "You can see where daddy was going with the name. Somehow I doubt that she ever had a bat mitzvah. She is generally considered to be the most ruthless of the offspring, even though she's also the youngest."

"Overcompensating," Gwen said. "Age, sex, the usual components.

No husband or even boyfriend in the picture. She's focused. And serious. Ian was homeschooled and tutored; Jan went to Brown, spent all of his undergraduate days majoring in advanced self-indulgence. Sara studied chemical engineering at MIT."

"What was the subject of her undergraduate thesis—chemicals and genocide?" Sam said.

"Since you asked…" Karen said, accessing their library site, 'The Goldschmidt Reduction Process'…do you know what that means?"

"I did Geography," Gwen said.

"Russian Area Studies," Sam said.

"It's also called the alumino-thermic process," Karen said. "It involves reactions of the oxides of certain metals with aluminum. One resulting powder is called thermit, aka thermite. As in thermite bombs."

"Why am I not surprised?" Gwen asked.

"She probably aspires to inherit the family business," Sam said. "If I was Jan I'd watch my back."

"If I was Alex I'd be careful as well," Gwen said. "Normally I'd think of her as a candidate for the Electra Complex, but the wife is barely with us. She's trotted out occasionally for public events but most of the time she's on a steady diet of Benzodiazepines. She's logged more spa visits than the collective membership of the Bel-Air book clubs and garden societies. Sara and her mother Louisa see very little of one another. Louisa stays behind the gates in Beverly Hills and Sara lives in…ok…Georgetown. Not the one in Guyana. Or the one in Texas."

"Alex's home away from home?" Karen asked.

"Quite possibly," Gwen said.

"Where does Jan live?" Karen asked.

"You'll never guess," Sam said. "No, you *would* guess…East 64th Street."

"Amongst the beautiful people," Karen said.

CHAPTER FORTY-FIVE

Sam, Gwen and Karen all rallied early for breakfast.

"No word yet from the Director," Sam said.

"I've been checking the kiddos' addresses," Gwen said. "Jan's townhouse weighs in at 8,000 square feet, with five beds, eight baths and a *Zillow* guesstimate of $18 mil. Expensive habit; the taxes alone are well above the average person's total income. The backyard is all ornamental walls and gates, but elevated above the ground level. No easy points of ingress and egress behind the house."

"So if Daddy came to visit he could be seen from the street," Karen said.

"Yes, but probably not for long. He'd get out of a car or limo on the curbside and slip into the house in a matter of seconds. In the rain he'd be surrounded by large men with black umbrellas. We could certainly rig something inconspicuous, but it's Manhattan and there's always intervening pedestrian traffic. The good news is that there's a heavy gate in front of the door and that would take him and any entourage a moment or two to negotiate. There is a tree or two that would conceal small cameras and even if they were noticed security devices would draw little concern in that area. The below-street-level entrances are all heavily gated, with black iron nooks and crannies everywhere. Bottom line: we could watch the front of Jan's house fairly easily."

"How about Sara's digs in Georgetown?" Sam asked.

"A bit more complicated," Gwen answered. "A nice section of 34th Street. Originally built in the late 18thc (not the late 19th, like Jan's).

About two-thirds the size and one-third the price, but with large patio space surrounded by red brick walls and covered above by some leafy oak limbs. Not jungle canopy, of course, so we could observe large portions from multiple angles. However, there's been a garage added that's accessed from an inner courtyard so that no looky-loos would find it easy to see the faces of the passengers as they arrive and depart, particularly not with the darkened glass with which the cars there would almost surely be equipped. The home shares a small alleyway with the adjoining property. Again, the possibility for anonymous ingress and egress. Plenty of places in which to hide surveillance equipment, but Daddy could slip in and out at will and if Sara is mixing and mingling with other D.C. gonefs there would be constant traffic in, on and about the premises."

"Damn," Karen said.

Sam's phone rang--the private line.

"The Director," he whispered.

"All three there?" he said.

"Yes, sir," Sam answered.

"Put me on speaker."

"Good morning, all," the Director said. "I've spoken with a friend in Tel Aviv. He's more than game to cooperate. His operative is in the field; I'll text him the location and time in which we would like to meet. No information as yet on the current location of our primary person of interest. Any questions?"

Sam checked the women's eyes; no response. "We're good, sir," he said.

"Stay in touch," he said. "Have a productive day."

A few minutes later Karen's phone twitched. She read the text, which directed her to a secure site. Mira was in the U.S., in Vallejo, California. Karen was to meet with her in two days.

CHAPTER FORTY-SIX

Karen arrived the next evening but took the Golden Gate to Novato on the west side of the bay. Seeking to remain inconspicuous, she checked into the *Days Inn*. Gwen and Sam utilized a secure chat room on a Bureau drop site to fill her in on recent developments. Still no word on the whereabouts (or existence) of Grayson's likely partner, Robert Scherl. Jan Sol was reported being in New York, playing golf that afternoon at a club in Westchester. Sister Sara was in northwest D.C. at the dedication of a new facility within Sibley Hospital. The Sol family had endowed the space, no doubt hoping to grab a friendly headline as well as some most-favored-nation status at the city's country club hospital. No sign of Daddy Alex in New York, the nation's capital or elsewhere.

Karen took her compact P320 from its lead case along with a 15-round magazine and heavily-sharpened utility knife, locking them in the back of the room safe. She hung up the three lightweight outfits she had brought, one more formal, one informal, one tactical. She slipped out for some pasta at a local place called the *Chianti Cucina*, checked her phone for messages and set the alarm for 5:00 a.m. in case there were any early morning messages from Gwen, Sam or the Director.

At 7:00 the next morning she received an encoded message from Mira. They were to meet that afternoon at a winery in Sebastopol. She grabbed a light breakfast of yoghurt and toast, washed it down with two cups of black coffee, rechecked for any messages from Gwen, Sam or the Director and drove north. The boutique winery was owned by the Hunter family. It was located near the *Dehlinger* property which was renowned for its pinot noir and chardonnay. The Hunters' selectivity reduced their 20-acre yield to approximately 3,500 cases of premier pinot. The Dehlinger daughters, Carmen and Eva, were good friends and shared expertise and some equipment with Tom and Jane Hunter.

The Hunters' facility was small and the 'tasting room' was little more than an oak bar, mini-fridge and a small table and chairs in the center of the fermentation room. It was open by appointment only. When Karen arrived she saw a single sedan parked next to a tractor, a ½ ton red pickup, and a new, motorized crushing machine. She walked into the metal facility, stepped over some large hoses, passed two fermentation tanks and approached the tasting area and bar. It was illuminated by two simple light fixtures. Mira was sitting alone with her back to the wall, holding a glass of red wine. She hadn't aged at all; her brown hair was styled and highlighted. Her warm, brown, Ashkenazi eyes had always masked the steel beneath. Wearing an expensive summery dress she looked like a Tiburon or Pacific Heights lady who lunched well. Her *Cartier* watch partially covered the fading scar resulting from a contretemps with a Hamas terrorist who was probably still looking for his seventy-two virgins. When she saw Karen she rose and embraced her.

"Hello, my dear friend," she said. "You look lovely, but very businesslike. Is there any possibility that you were followed?"

"No, I've been in the area for several hours, eluding any possible observers."

"As I expected," Mira said. "Come, sit down, I have some wine and some crackers and cheese. No one will disturb us. We can stay here as long as we need to."

"How did you find this place?" Karen asked.

"Tom Hunter is an old associate. He consulted with us when he was in the software industry."

"I hear he makes good wine," Karen said.

"I like it; I think you will as well."

When Mira poured a second glass Karen asked her what brought her to northern California. Mira paused for a second.

"Whatever you can tell me…" Karen said.

"I can do broad brush," Mira said. "One of the members of the local professoriate is working with our Shia neighbors to perfect certain aspects of drone technology. I'm keeping an eye on him."

"If he or they become too successful you will do your best to see that their work never becomes operational and that they themselves are not present for the arrival of the Hidden Imam."

"No happy homecoming, I'm afraid," Mira said. "Doubtful that it will ever come to that. Our preventive measures should preclude any possibility of their weapons' success. In the meantime we're supporting some friends who were dealing with the current iteration of their technology."

The Americans? Karen thought to herself. She took a sip of the pinot and said, "This is very nice wine."

"I thought you would like it," Mira said. "Not a great burgundy, but quite special for California."

"How fully have you been briefed on our issues with Alex Sol?"

"The world's most evil pantomime Jew."

"Yes."

"We hear that his daughter is potentially worse," Mira said.

"So do we. And that's quite a high bar," Karen said.

"He's supplied and supported the Iranians for years," Mira said. "It is highly unlikely that his departure from the world would occasion significant mourning, except perhaps from the PAC's and the corrupt politicians he underwrites. He may be the world's most prominent unindicted co-conspirator as well as the best protected."

"A tuxedo at the Kennedy Center, a blood-stained butcher's apron in his everyday life," Karen said.

"Yes, that's him. A butcher in jackboots with a display rack of *Gucci* loafers," Mira said. "He puts visitation stones on the graves of those he's slaughtered."

"So you'd like to help me take him off of the board?" Karen asked.

"I wouldn't even ask for a fee," Mira said. "If I could select the method I might even offer to pay General Gradison. So where do you think he is?"

"Unfortunately, we don't know," Karen said. We know where his children are, but we don't know where he is."

"He's gone to ground," Mira said, "assuming that he's aware that you're looking for him."

"Our operation, or should I say our 'operational planning' has been heavily circumscribed," Karen said. "I doubt very much that he could be aware of it."

Suddenly Mira raised her hand, slipped off of her chair and rolled into the shadows. Karen followed suit. When she looked toward Mira she was assembling a weapon from parts in her tote bag.

CHAPTER FORTY-SEVEN

Karen looked to her for an answer but Mira was already moving toward the front of the facility, looking toward the sky. Karen scanned the horizon and saw a drone in the distance. She now realized why Mira was carrying a canvas bag instead of a small purse. The weapon she was carrying appeared to be an *ArmaLite* AR-7, a lightweight .22 caliber semi-automatic. She positioned herself by the entrance to the facility as Karen moved forward on the other side.

Mira gestured toward her, signaling her to join her on her side. Karen high-crawled on her elbows and knees. The sky was now clear. Mira put her right index finger to her lips, indicating the need for silence.

"Targeting us?" Karen whispered.

"Some wineries utilize drones," Mira said. "They check for moisture levels, weed growth, and so on, but the wineries here are relatively small. We're not talking about the monster growers who sell their wine in jugs and boxes. Tom Dehlinger has to worry about 45 acres, the Gallo team has 23,000 just in California and Washington."

"So you think the drone was hostile."

"Not willing to take any chances," Mira said. "From a great distance it's hard to estimate size, but when it came closer it looked like a reconnaissance drone, possibly a *Boeing* Blackjack. The Navy uses them and so do the Marines, but the Company has access to all the military goodies. What you don't want to deal with is a Reaper. If it was one of those and if it had intended to do us harm we wouldn't be having this conversation. Best guess? Tom Hunter was cleared by his old friends at the Company to cooperate with me but their curiosity was piqued and they wondered what my agency was doing in their country. They would have known where we were going to be and they were probably just keeping an eye on us. I suspect they're still out there, probably hovering above various sections of the 116, the 12 and especially the 101, waiting to see where we go and what we do."

"What would you like to do?" Karen asked. "Go in to Petaluma for lunch? Go to ground? You still have your mission to complete."

"That's not a pressing priority," Mira said, "more like long-term surveillance. We don't really need an agent on the ground. It helps, of course, but we can surveil electronically for awhile."

"They can't follow both of our cars with a single drone," Karen said. "Let's take circuitous routes to lunch and see if either of us is followed."

Mira put her finger to her lips, reached into her tote bag and took out a pad and pencil, writing "doubtful that we're being recorded, but just in case, let's rally in Yountville. *Mustards Grill*. Reliable, usually crowded. Blend in with the crowd."

Karen gave her a thumbs up.

CHAPTER FORTY-EIGHT

A Napa Valley stalwart that billed itself as a truck stop but specialized in recipes featuring rabbit, *Mustards* was indeed crowded. Both Mira and Karen ordered soup and crab cakes.

"Were you followed?" Mira asked.

"Not that I could tell," Karen said.

"Neither was I," Mira said. "We're probably being overly cautious. Still, overly cautious tends to contribute to longevity."

"Yes," Karen said.

"Back to the subject at hand…so you and your people plan to take your target off the board but not take credit for it in a conspicuous way."

"It would not go uncelebrated among the general population," Karen said, "but it would not go unnoticed among the intelligence and security bureaucracies. The politicians would be very unhappy to see the gravy train sidetracked but there would probably be some relief as well. Anyone with those kinds of resources and absence of any scruples would hold many secrets."

"But with that kind of money there would be heirs and assigns and they might already have his markers in their pockets."

"They might," Karen said.

"Still, you can't be overly cautious. Sometimes it's good to let the other side know that their misdeeds will not go unpunished."

"Exactly," Karen said. "I'd vote for a method that would carry a clear message, not something that could be interpreted with ambiguity."

"Suspended by the neck from a freeway?"

"Live by the cartels die by the cartels. It's a nice thought," Karen said.

"You could make the point but still distance yourself."

"Plutonium in his knockwurst?"

"That's an idea," Mira said. "I've always said that we should find joy in our work, but we should be careful not to look for too much joy. It could distract us, not just from the importance of the task, but also its likely difficulty."

"He's survived this long," Karen said. "That means he knows how to be careful and how to protect himself. He's also left a lot of bodies in his wake."

"As in your present case," Mira said. "You said that one of the likely assassins is dead and another is missing."

"Yes."

"How do you like the crab cakes?"

"Not bad. I like the places on the eastern shore in Maryland. You eat on picnic tables, break open the blue crabs and search for anything edible. You need a whole set of implements—mallets, picks, crackers, knives…"

"Bibs," Mira added.

"Essential," Karen said, "particularly if you're dressed nicely."

"Did it once," Mira said. "Very memorable. Less filler in the crab cakes there."

"Yes, but these came close," Karen said, as her phone vibrated on the table. She picked it up, said "Give me a second," and went to a quiet site.

"I have to return to D.C.," she said.

"Something serious?"

"Something good, I think, but something very curious. Alex Sol is dead."

"That *is* curious," Mira said. "One hopes he didn't pass away comfortably in his sleep."

"It doesn't appear so," Karen said.

IV

THE GENERAL

CHAPTER FORTY-NINE

Karen was forced to take a connecting flight from Santa Rosa via Seattle, arriving the next morning. She was able to sleep for several hours and she was spared the additional drive to Stafford. The Director wanted to meet first thing in the morning in his office in the Hoover Building. When she arrived he had black coffee fresh and ready. "Sorry about the redeye and the crappy little planes," he said. "I wanted to get on this ASAP and the morning flights would have put you here in the late afternoon."

"Completely understand, General," Karen said.

"I want you to connect with Sam and Gwen as soon as we're finished here," he said. "At this point we need to keep the team small."

"Then we still have an operation, sir," she said.

"We're just getting started, Karen," he answered. "Before, we had a clandestine reprisal operation that might have had some significant public repercussions. Now we have something that is, potentially, very serious."

"Can you brief me on the circumstances of his death?"

"I can tell you what we know, Karen. He had dinner at a restaurant in San Diego. Seafood. Nice. Very upscale. Dined with an unidentified man. The man paid in cash. Left a $150 tip on top of the $895 tab. They had to have that first class *Puligny-Montrachet* and two rounds of Armagnac. They parted amicably. Sol was picked up by a limo service. Took him to San Diego International. When he landed at LAX he was picked up by another limo driver who dropped him off at his hotel.

When the valet opened the door to let Sol out he just sat there. Probably because he had four rounds nesting in his forehead."

"Caliber?"

".22."

"Execution. Quadruple tap?"

"What we call your basic overkill."

"And the limo driver?"

"Nowhere to be seen."

"Why was Sol in San Diego?"

"No idea. Possibly meeting with a cartel rep? They're all over San Diego now."

"And did he fly down and return in a private plane?"

"Too early to tell yet, but that seems most likely. Sol wouldn't be the sort to stand in a line."

"First thought: we've got to get to the body before they can cremate it."

"Agreed. First order of business."

"Sure puts his political friends in a corner," Karen said. "If they don't control the narrative at this point it looks as if they're co-conspirators. If they do…it also looks as if they're co-conspirators."

"That's the second bit of good news after the fact of his death," the Director said. "Now: inquiring minds want to know: who did this and why? And who benefits, besides western civilization?"

"At least we didn't have to do the job," Karen said.

"Point. But who will *we* be investigating?"

"It will be a long list, sir."

"Indeed, but the names at the top of the list will be, shall we say, *familiar* ones."

"At least for those who still watch the evening news," Karen said.

"Some would say that we should leave it alone. The house landed on the witch. Time to remove her shoes, sell them on *eBay*, celebrate and move on."

"But then there's the obvious question," Karen said.

"Which is?"

"What if this is a hostile takeover? One of the heirs apparent got tired of waiting. One of his partners wanted 100 percent instead of 50 or 25. Or worse still, what if some scumbag or bags in the government want to take over one or more of his operations?"

"I think the word we're looking for is *exactamente*, Special Agent Wilken. Some will seize upon the first two possibilities, but the third…?"

"Unlikely if we were still a first-world country," Karen said, "but these days…?"

CHAPTER FIFTY

"What do you need from me first, General?"

"Brief Sam and Gwen and give me an honest estimate of her strength. We need her to be with you at the center of this. I'll take her at 80%, but I don't want to put her at risk."

"She'll want to go at 60%, of course."

"Always."

"And the background work? Facial rec on his dinner host in San Diego. CCTV at the airports. CCTV at the limo lines. Facial rec on both the driver and the valet at his L.A. hotel? And, presumably, on the driver and valet at the restaurant in San Diego."

"Already have the SAC in San Diego and the AD in L.A. on the case. You'll have access to their reports. You'll get texts and drop site info. whenever it becomes available. That will be funneled through me. No one in California needs to know what we're doing at this end."

"Appreciate that, sir."

"Basically you'll be taking on Gwen's special projects role, coordinating with me always, but also utilizing your techmeister in Salt Lake."

"Right, sir."

"In this case, *special* should be spelled with a capital S."

"We have nothing less than the possibility of direct criminal involvement from the highest reaches of the United States government. Committing capital crimes."

"That's where we stand, Karen."

As Karen drove to the Stafford facility Gradison sipped a second mug of black coffee, sometimes tapping the keys of his computer as he mused to himself: 'Well, General, this should be an interesting one. We could be looking at a simple execution by a drug lord who wanted to clear the accounts, eliminate a former partner and get on with his criminal life. Nothing at stake at our end but the renewed discussion of whether or not we should ready the Hellfire missiles and Special Forces troops and invade the *Estados-Unidos Mexicanos*. Some politicians may well want to do that. The voters have always been up for it, but the voters were always thinking of fentanyl deaths among their sons and daughters, not the eradication of an international dirtbag, in which case the murderer of my enemy is suddenly my friend. Break out the bubbly and let God sort it out.

'But what if we have a corrupt Attorney General or Vice President or President? What if one or more of the heads of our security agencies are on the take, big time, and are using government resources to bury their enemies and cover their own backsides? It's easy to say that we should solve all of this internally and protect the public from the knowledge that their government is battening on money from criminal enterprises and executing anyone with the capacity to sidetrack their gravy train. What does the poet say—humankind cannot bear very much reality? But how much delusion should be permitted? How much business-as-usual corruption can be tolerated? Why should the lives and well-being of 333,000,000 people be left in the hands of home-bred dirtbags?

'But be careful, Walter. It's not your job to go all messianic, put on the cape of Crusader Rabbit and presume to know what's best for all. After all, it's not like something like this has never happened before. The difference is the order of magnitude. The good thing, if there is any good thing involved here, is that as a soldier you faced these kinds of decisions constantly, but on a smaller scale. When you searched for magic solutions you were reminded that there generally weren't any, just a shavetail with a butter bar on his first combat operation or a middle-aged man with two stars on each of his shoulders, alone with his conscience and the need to act. So you do what you have to do: return to first principles and do the best you can.

'But you've already made some decisions. You've put a top agent on the case who is also a skilled assassin. For justice's sake, of course. That's all fine and dandy, but an assassin nonetheless. You didn't call on a bureaucrat from H.R. or P.R. Teddy thought…wait…it's here somewhere. (And a few keystrokes later…) *Far better it is to dare mighty things, to win glorious triumphs, even though chequered by failure…than to rank with those poor spirits who neither enjoy nor suffer much, because they live in a gray twilight that knows not victory nor defeat.* And then what? *The credit is due to the man who is actually in the arena…and spends himself in a worthy cause; who at the best knows in the end the triumph of high achievement; and who at the worst, if he fails, at least fails daring greatly.*

'Unfortunately, that's not where you're at, Walter. You're slogging in the darkness. There's no grand arena. There's a huge purse, but it's all ill-gotten gain sought by criminals who are happy to spend the better part of their time in that same gray twilight, to kill the innocent, to profit from the sufferings of the weak: soulless people who know nothing but greed and a variety of lusts that reflect very badly on God's creation. You see your first inclination. It's not to don the cape of self-righteousness and plunge into the amphitheatre with the bloody sand, but rather to set a thief to catch a thief, to find the person within *our* gray twilight who will eliminate evil without giving it a second thought, a person who will be completely satisfied if justice is served and all of the material benefits of heroism and duty remain out of reach. Your decision is to play at their game because…that's where we are now. They kill in the darkness; we have people who will also kill in the darkness. That's your starting point, General. There's no time here for dithering. It's time to sharpen the bayonets…time to *hone.* Now you have to hope and pray that you're right. Hope and pray that you can complete any necessary and justifiable operations without falling into a quagmire of self-delusion and self-destruction.'

CHAPTER FIFTY-ONE

"I've got to get out of here and get back in the game," Gwen said.

"That's the Director's choice," Karen said, "but he wants to be sure that you're in good enough shape to do so. He doesn't want to put you at any physical risk."

"I appreciate that. While you were in California I began a stronger exercise regimen."

"We've monitored her," Sam said. "She's doing well. Maybe a few more days…"

"Three," Gwen said.

"Five," Sam answered.

"I'm shooting for four," Gwen said. "Meanwhile, keep me posted of any developments."

"She's serious," Sam said, after Gwen had left the room and headed to the exercise facility. "Any new intel?"

"Not yet," Karen said. "I hate waiting for the phone to ring. I'm going to join her and stop the thoughts from swirling in my head. I'll have my phone, just in case."

Gwen nodded to Karen as she got on a distant treadmill, adjusted the angle and began walking on the two-ply belt. Twenty minutes later she had transitioned from a light jog to a serious run. Her hair was now matted with sweat and her small red towel was now around her neck, a sweat scarf. She was alert, focused and clearly attempting to fight off her frustration at the lack of other options. Gwen knew that feeling, even as she was resisting the cramping in her own legs and the inevitable pain in her side. She knew that she was making progress, even if it was not happening as quickly as she would have preferred.

At lunch they went all paleo with lean meats, vegetables, fruits and a cup of seeds. "Training table," Karen said.

"Sam's trying to get us ready," Gwen said, "but maybe the principal efforts will be mental. We're 'evidence-challenged' at this point and need to sort out the facts before we reach for the *Sigs* and *Ka-Bars*."

"The General has agreed to include my pal Mike on the digital work," Karen said. "He's gotten us pretty far already. He's taken some personal leave so that he can be on our case full-time. The San Diego SAC and L.A. AD aren't aware of it; Mike's working independently with us and has access to all of the available data. 'Another set of eyes…' and all that, but he's a guy we can trust. I'm not saying the Cali field offices are dirty, but they're closer to the temptations and the bribers and, well, you can never be too sure."

"Agreed," Gwen said. "When nearly all of Mexico is compromised it only takes one of the members of our team to succumb and we all know that the cartels have big sticks and big carrots at their disposal."

"Unfortunately," Karen said. "What does your gut tell you?"

"Really?"

"Yes, of course."

"Well…I think it's all the result of a web. At its heart it's institutional. Big government. Big business. Big crime. Big piles of cash. When they overlap the rot sets in; sometimes it's there to stay."

"Venn diagram," Karen said.

"In a way. That certainly works as a metaphor, and the fixity of the diagram is part of the issue. You put the elements together, stir in the worst human elements—the inclinations as well as the people—and you get that result. I don't think it's inevitable, however. Not that the passions and lusts and temptations aren't everpresent; they are. I think it's broader, though. I think it's cultural. It's the belief, in the bones, that you're entitled, that you're special, that you're above the letter of the law, the spirit of the law and any transcendent notion of right and wrong. It's a whole host of things; it's the lack of respect for the office, the contempt for the notion of the public trust. It's the imperial self. It's the little kid looking at the moon and saying, 'Mommy, I want it' and Mommy now believes that the kid should have it, regardless of the effect on the world and the tides and the 'little people'. Destroy everything, if that's what you need to be happy, at least for the moment. Maybe that's it entirely, the notion that there are little people and it's your right, maybe even your destiny, to take anything and everything from them. I don't know…you shouldn't get me started. I always end up spouting psychobabble."

"I don't think so," Karen said. "I see it another way. I think there are people who think in abstractions rather than facts and the abstractions are so attractive to them that they come to believe in their reality, regardless of the effects on everyone else. They stop seeing their own ulterior motives and believe that the suffering of others is simply collateral damage on the way to a brighter future, one in which, of course, they will be in charge. Certainly it's true of the politicians but it's also true of the detached businessmen and the detached criminal organizations. They're looking at statistics, bottom lines, X&Y axes, bar graphs…ultimately they're looking at abstractions that have become their realities. They live thirty stories above the wounds, the bodies and the blood splatter and cease to care about them."

"Works for me," Gwen said, "but how do we stop them without plunging to their level by thinking we're above the law ourselves? By realizing that they're not abstractions themselves but rather immediate threats? By crushing them before they can infect us further?"

"Maybe that's what we have to do," Karen said. "Anyway, there's a simple test that I've always thought was reliable."

"Really? What's that?" Gwen asked.

"After you've done what needed to be done you look in your heart and your mirror and ask, 'Can I live with this, forever'?"

"And if the answer is Yes…"

"Then you're either mad or you're a bringer of justice."

"Big either/or."

"Nobody said the stakes were low," Karen said.

CHAPTER FIFTY-TWO

The next morning there was intel. Karen led the discussion at the breakfast table.

"The dinner host in San Diego has not been conclusively identified, but he looks like a man named Perez, an accountant for the Sinaloa Cartel. No idea what the subject of their conversation was, but Sinaloa has extensive tunnels in both California and Arizona. Sol could have provided them any number of services, the most obvious being information on government activity there. By the way, Perez actually lives in La Jolla, which is, unfortunately, not unusual. The cartels are here now. Perez lives right in Raymond Chandler's old neighborhood; how's that for irony?

"The valet parker at the restaurant was the usual guy; he's been there for several years. Nothing fishy. Ditto the guy at the hotel in L.A. Actually, the hotel in Pasadena. The *Langham Huntington*. Old, historic place. Been a *Sheraton*, a *Ritz-Carlton*, etc. Old money protestants got married there. The driver waved at the parker, said he was going to use the bathroom, and went into the main hotel building. After a couple minutes the *Langham* guy opened the door and found the body. The hotel staff called the Pasadena PD but the driver was never found. According to the parker, the driver had been wearing a dark suit when he entered the hotel, but no hat or livery logo. He was, however, wearing dark glasses and he was sporting a dark beard, both probably long gone now. He's in the wind.

"The car—not a limo but a Caddy XTS—was a *Carey* car; perfectly legit. The question is: who was the driver? And how did he get the car?"

"Do we know where he picked up Sol?" Gwen asked

"At LAX. As we thought, Sol had flown to San Diego and back to L.A. The CCTV at both airports show him arriving and departing. The flight plans were registered. Everything kosher. When he was at LAX the driver was wearing a broad-billed cap and his face was completely in shadow. The CCTV at the *Langham* caught a side shot of his face. It corresponds precisely with the parker's description. Tall, dark, and blurry. A mustache and that aforementioned beard. Could be Mediterranean, Middle-Eastern. Wearing sunglasses, unfortunately; he had lost the cap by the time he got to the *Langham*. *Carey* checked their records. They couldn't identify the driver and there was no record of a reservation. It could be that Sol was informed of a reservation, but he was betrayed by his own people. It's also possible that the car was simply stolen from their lot or that a legit driver was carjacked. They're still checking their records. It gets pretty complicated. They're in Culver City with quick access to LAX and they dispatch a lot of vehicles from there."

"So we work on the assumption that the driver killed Sol," Gwen said.

"Lots of opportunity," Karen said. "You're talking about a distance of around 25 miles from the airport to the hotel. Usual route would be La Cienega to the 10, the 10 to the 110 and up to Pasadena. Plenty of places to turn off, particularly when you get to Pasadena. The driver has a pistol with a silencer, turns around, puts four rounds in Sol's forehead, and drives to the hotel. It's a fair question why he didn't just abandon the car at the kill site, but sometimes it's better to hide in plain sight. There are a host of places around the *Langham* where he could have parked a getaway car; it's not like a single, freestanding building. It's much more of a compound. Twenty, twenty-five acres or so with multiple segments, pool lanais. All nestled in a suburban neighborhood. The valet parking area is a huge circle with a building adjoining. They park the *Bentleys* and the *Ferraris* around the circle, to catch the eye and reinforce their own brand. The real question is…"

"How they knew when and where he was landing, what kind of limo reservation he had been promised, and where he was staying," Gwen said.

"Yes. And why he would stay at a hotel rather than simply go to the family manse in Beverly Hills--the place where his wife logs most of her time. That is very curious, and not something that anyone who lacked insider information would expect."

"Sloppy," Gwen said. "Unless there was an urgency in killing him. You could pick a time and place and method that was much less suspicious."

"A road accident, some nasty shellfish, home invasion, pick one," Karen said.

"This is progress," Gwen said. "And perhaps a whiff of desperation on their side?"

"Perhaps," Karen said. "I wouldn't expect Sol to make his own reservations. He issues orders, expects lackeys to do his bidding."

"Who would do that, usually?"

"I've asked Michael to check," Karen said. "In general Sol has a small operation with a tiny inner circle. I doubt that Jan or Sara would do gofer work. There's probably a general factotum who's much more than a travel agent. Sol's personal schedule would be heavily guarded. Even if he has friends in high places he has enemies everywhere. I'm thinking a single evil servant-type who's been with him for decades."

"A weasel," Gwen said. "A secretary with an executive's salary and a cabinet with more secrets than Dr. Caligari's."

"It certainly wouldn't be some temp service," Karen said, "not at the levels in which he operated. Wait a sec…"

Karen picked up her twitching cell phone. "It's Michael…" She made some keystrokes. "Damn, he's good. And fast too. The trusted assistant is named David Beauchamp. He lives in McLean. Wait…more incoming info.

"OK. Beauchamp lives in a townhouse on the grounds of the old Evans Farm. Used to be an Inn there—old Virginny type with spoonbread and that sort of thing. The property was sold in 2,000; 24 acres of prime northern Virginia real estate. Gated now, with 125 townhouses. They go for just under 2 Mil. Close proximity to the District; upscale; secure."

"Married? Kids? Guard dogs?"

"Not married," Karen said. "Don't know about any guard dogs. He bought about ten years ago and there are still some pictures up on *Zillow.* Very classy. All marble and pricey appliances. A showhouse."

"Wish we had a drone that could record sound," Gwen said. "The external mics just pick up motor noise and prop wash."

"I've got a phone number," Karen said. "I can call and ask if he wants to buy an extended warranty for his…just a sec…*Lexus* RX."

"We could at least find out if he's still alive," Gwen said.

Karen picked up a secure phone and called the number. She sat quietly and then clicked off. "Fifteen rings and no pickup. Doesn't prove anything. He probably screens everything."

"Turn Michael loose," Gwen said. "Bank records, credit cards, cellphone records, anything he can find. No way to be sure at this point, but someone had to make arrangements that ultimately involved an assassination. I'll let the Director know what we're doing."

"Done," Karen said.

CHAPTER FIFTY-THREE

"Already on it, Gwen, but thanks," the Director said. "Piecing together what little we know certainly points to an inside job. We weren't sure where Sol was, so it's doubtful that others would, much less what his immediate plans would include. I did check with our friends in Tel Aviv and they assure me that they were not involved. Mira expressed disappointment that someone else had the opportunity to welcome him to the infernal regions. In the meantime, work with Michael and keep me posted. I have some elements observing the area. So far, no sightings. You have images, I take it…"

"Yes, sir. It's always amazing how much they look the part. Short stature, thin comb-over, narrow eyes, and suits that look more like the *Nordstrom Rack* than Savile Row. Your basic weasel."

"Very harsh, Gwen, and completely spot-on," the Director said. "We're also watching Jan and Sara. And listening. They're not stupid, so they're probably operating under complete radio silence. If they're involved they would have distanced themselves from the get-go."

"I wouldn't sell David Beauchamp any serious insurance policies," Gwen said.

"No, but weasels are also good survivors. He would have made arrangements for eventualities."

"True, sir. Anyway, we'll stay in touch."

"Track that sumbitch, Gwen."

"Will do, sir."

"Interesting," Karen said, "but not surprising. Let's get some coffee and give Michael an hour or two to do his thing."

It actually took an hour and a half. "No recent financial transactions of any note," Michael said. "We can assume that his serious assets are all offshore. He maintains some purely functional *B of A* accounts. The checking account has 17K in it; he has a couple 60-day cd's that total 50K in value. This is walking-around money. He paid cash for his car two years ago. No rap sheet of any kind beyond a couple speeding tickets spread over the last two decades..."

"Education?" Karen asked.

"Haverford undergrad, majored in Econ. MBA from Wharton. Minimal work experience. Served time in a Philly investment firm between college and grad school. Since then he's been working for Sol Enterprises. Billed as 'assistant to the chairman' on his Virginia tax forms (most recent reported income--$450K)."

"He's either much more than a gofer or he's significantly underemployed," Gwen said.

"Right," Michael said. "He keeps a very low profile. A few WaPo stories about Sol's philanthropy: pictures with David 'looking on.' Probably reminding Sol what to say or who to thank."

"Anything on the recent reservations?" Karen asked.

"Everything just says 'Sol Enterprises'; no names attached to anything. One kicker however: there's nothing in the record concerning a reservation for the *Carey* car at LAX. Of course, Sol could have received a message that stated that there was such a reservation."

"Anything else in the *Sol Enterprises* materials that includes a list of staff?" Gwen asked.

"No one is listed on the website," Michael said. "Not even Beauchamp. It's purely generic. A few glowing testimonials from D.C. bigwigs, a list of philanthropic projects, pictures of Sol with some recent presidents and veeps, and a smarmy quote from Sol in flowing typeface, celebrating the glories of freedom, democracy and the American dream. Sorry. I wish there was more. I'll check back ASAP if I turn anything interesting."

Gwen and Karen thanked him and refilled their coffee cups. They drank a third cup, had a light snack and returned to work. An hour and a half later they were sitting at their tandem laptops when Karen's phone twitched.

"Just what I thought…" she said.

CHAPTER FIFTY-FOUR

"Film from the Director. A collage of clips from CCTV cameras."

"Wisconsin Avenue," Gwen said, holding Karen's phone in her left hand. "A jumble of eclectic operations. The crème de la crème restaurants where the spies and influence peddlers congregate, positioned cheek-by-jowl with the fortune tellers and euro trash stores that look more like money laundries than bona fide clothiers. Wait…there's Beauchamp, carrying a large manila envelope, walking south toward the river; dressed for work, not for shopping. He walks past windows without inspecting any of the merchandise. Is he preoccupied? On some sort of mission? He's walking at an even pace; not a daily constitutional, just moving from Point A to Point B…wait…he's suddenly turning west, on N Street, almost like a soldier with someone giving him orders to do a right turn…now he's not there…where did he go?…he's not a ghost; he's not on the sidewalk; not on the street…must have walked behind *Martin's Tavern*…always did like that place…where is he?…all of a sudden a lot of pedestrian traffic around N and Wisconsin…heading west…the looky-loos mixing with guys in white aprons, smoking…restaurant staff taking their breaks… turning now…all looking behind the Tavern…wait…a white van, Metro police with the white and red bars and blue stripe, pulling up fast… four officers hit the street… two quickly directing pedestrian traffic… new film…must be from police body cams…different quality images… jumpy…wish they'd move so we could get a more direct view… wait, on the ground, behind a telephone pole…police checking a body…blood everywhere…pooling on the ground next to his neck…what is that, a

Colombian necktie? Is that even possible? I thought it was some kind of urban legend. Maybe just a normal throat-slit with a lot of arterial spray…jugular…carotid…things can get messy fast."

The phone twitched in Gwen's hand. Message from the Director: "So what is this supposed to be—committed in broad daylight? In the center of town? With the risk of blood covering the assassin's clothes? Why not also set off bells and whistles, in case someone missed the show. Crazy. Why? Best guess at this end: they wanted it to look like a plausible mugging. Whole organization somehow unlucky. First the boss; then the staff. Bad days all around. Note that the manila folder is missing. Who steals something like that? It wasn't filled with currency or negotiable bonds; it was flat. Maybe a single 8x10 sheet. One thing clear; Beauchamp was set up. He wasn't walking into an ambush by choice. On the other hand, the mugging narrative is shaky. The killer did take his wallet, but left a decent ring. If you can cut a throat you can lop off a finger. He also left the watch. A *Tudor*. Your basic *Rolex* second. Not a knockoff. A second label. They go for 4-5K easily. This was one of those nice Black Bay GMT's. We're supposed to believe that the mugger was ignorant? They paid for a killer but this was his first time playing in the bigs? And why take out Beauchamp so soon after Sol's demise? Did they worry he'd run to the authorities and tell his own story? Why not hire the first team and make it look like an accident? Anyway, no more flailing. All hands now on deck. We'll continue to dig. Anxious to hear your thoughts."

"Here are my initial thoughts," Karen said to Gwen. "I'm not surprised. In fact, I'd be surprised if they had waited. The principal substance in their bodies is gall. They've always gotten away with criminal behavior. If the government wasn't protecting them, the press was. Usually both. They're not fearless because they think they're righteous or because they have courage. They're fearless because they believe they're untouchable."

"That's certainly true," Gwen said. "You're convinced it's Jan or Sara? Or Jan *and* Sara?"

"Almost surely. It's not like they were business people with direct competitors taking their market share," Karen said. "They're gonefs who'll embrace any grift that comes their way. Imperial-self narcissistic bastards. Not to put too fine a point on it."

"No disputing that," Gwen said, "but if it's them they're skating very close to the edge."

"That's where they live," Karen said. "They've got two big things working in their favor."

"Yes…?"

"The American low-info voter attention span is approximately 10 seconds and the government and press will happily provide any diversions that the Sol family feels it needs."

"Yes, unfortunately," Gwen said. "Government corruption—even on this scale--is as clear and compelling to the electorate as an advanced course in differential equations. The narcissism is omnipresent. Even as we speak there are some Hollywood types scoring some new form of genital plastic surgery that will draw public eyeballs from the blood on the street in Georgetown to their bandaged crotches in Bel Air."

"Why, Special Agent Harrison, that's the most edgy thing I've ever heard you say."

"What does the guy say in the Restoration comedy? 'I know the town.'"

"Only now it's more like tragedy," Karen said.

"The tragedy is that we're supposedly Horatius at the bridge, defending Rome against the Etruscans, when, really, we're a couple of women in a government agency facing the most mundane forms of greed, evil and corruption in a country where a significant portion of the electorate are watching their country slide into the sea while they play games for 6 year-olds on their cell phones."

"I think you're too optimistic," Karen said. "They're not paying any attention at all to what's happening to the country."

"You might be right," Gwen said. "They don't notice until it's affected them for…what…four years?"

"More like ten, I think," Karen said.

"But we're still not going to head to the sidelines."

"No. Maybe the Armory," Karen said.

CHAPTER FIFTY-FIVE

"So where do we start?" Karen asked.

"Let's see what the stakeout teams in New York and Georgetown have reported," Gwen answered.

"I can pull up the camera feeds," Karen said.

"If you're a mansion on a pricey street, what's it called when you're giving the camera a blank stare?"

"All quiet," Gwen said. "Or 'all seething' but behind closed doors and brick walls. Here, I can get the streaming reports from the Bureau monitors. There was a food delivery to Jan's home…I love this…the Bureau hacked into *Katz's* deli's computer. They got lunch in bulk. A couple pounds of pastrami, an equal amount of corned beef, two loaves of rye bread, some pickles, split pea soup, coleslaw and macaroni salad."

"Probably the only thing in that place that's kosher," Karen said.

"The quantity is interesting. There's a team there."

"Holding onto their peepees and jumping up and down, worrying," Karen said.

"No doubt. Worried that they're next or worried that they'll be discovered?"

"That's the question, isn't it?" Karen responded. "Let me check on Miss Sara…no food deliveries. Here I thought she'd be paying serious homage to the porcelain god with a finger or two down her throat."

"To each his own when it comes to worrying," Gwen said.

"She's not alone," Karen said. "Our team has a drone with a heat sensor. There's a lot of activity. The guesstimate is six human bodies at least and probably a dog or two."

"They better be Mastiffs or Alsatians with some industrial-sized teeth if she's next on the list," Gwen said. "That's the problem with ne'er-do-wells; they accumulate a list of people who would happily do them harm just to settle old scores. And there's always that matter of power vacuums and circling vultures. Even if Sara and Jan are responsible for daddy's demise (or one or the other) they could fear reprisal. It'll be awhile before either of them are actually celebrating. By the way, I trust that someone is checking on their respective lawyers. There are a lot of papers to be signed and accounts to be changed. The white shoes' computer systems could be hacked more easily than those at Sol & Company. The interesting question is whether or not Bro and Sis are rallying with their own teams and working against one another, or calling in the usual members of the larger organization for the grand consult and staying in touch with one another."

"I'll get Michael on it," Karen said.

CHAPTER FIFTY-SIX

"With all of the goodies the Director's put at my disposal I may be of more use now," Michael said. "Firstly…there has not been any significant contact between the devil's spawn beyond a single phone call on a personal cellphone. It lasted barely a minute. No text messages. No emails. Unless they're using carrier pigeons they're playing this separately."

"Which one called the other?" Karen asked.

"Jan called Sara," Michael responded, "but as I said, there was not enough time for any serious discussion. Perhaps they've arranged to talk or meet later after they've fully assessed the situation."

"Right," Karen said.

"They may be grateful for their physical distance," Gwen said. "If they don't know who iced the old man and they suspect that the other did it they can hunker down in their respective fortresses and put some defense mechanisms in place. It's probably safe to assume that some of the people noshing on *Katz's* best or holding Sara's hands are armed and reasonably dangerous. It's not as if they're in the boutique soaps and cologne business. Even if they've been cooperative and circumspect with one another and actually do trust one another, they know that daddy's tentacles embraced a host of slimy creatures, any one of whom might have had a beef that would have resulted in his demise. In many parts of the criminal kingdom the next step would be to take out those who might seek reprisals. Bottom line: they're right to be scared."

"But if one of them was behind the hit?" Karen said.

"Then they'd act the same way and play out the same scenarios rather than draw attention to themselves," Gwen said. "There's no reason for the guilty party to go after the innocent today. And if they colluded on this, the answer's the same. Better for each to hunker down and not draw any serious attention. If I'm them I'm weeping and wailing and incenting the police to look elsewhere."

"If I may…," Michael said.

"Of course," they responded simultaneously.

"I haven't been studying this for months, but from what I can see the offspring seem to get along. They're into different rackets, close to their father and basically waiting their turns. They may start maneuvering now that he's out of the picture, but he was older than dirt and not immortal. They each had nice shares of the family take and weren't consigned to convents or monasteries (or, as in the case of their brother, wheelchairs). Life was good and, if anything, the old man drew attention away from them and provided their separate enterprises protection. That doesn't mean that they won't start elbowing their way to his throne now that it's vacant, but while I wouldn't consider them in the Cleaver league the family was reasonably tight. They did, for example, all stay in touch with the disabled brother in Lausanne and provide for his welfare."

"But they were monsters in their operations," Gwen said.

"True," Michael said, "but there seems to have been enough in the way of affection or even purely prudential concerns to result in their mutual cooperation."

"Then you think they're innocent of their father's murder," Karen said.

"I wouldn't go that far," Michael said. "I'm just making broad-brush inferences based on the evidence that's before me."

"Fair enough," Karen said.

"We'll keep digging at this end," Gwen said.

"I'll stay in touch," Michael answered.

CHAPTER FIFTY-SEVEN

As Gradison poured himself a third cup of black coffee his subsidiary phone rang--the one that bypassed his standard office line.

"Gradison," he said to the AG.

"Good morning, Director," the AG said. "The president would like me to brief her on the Sol case; I'm calling for an update."

"Certainly," Gradison answered. "The Los Angeles AD is investigating with all hands. The working assumption is that the *Carey* car driver was a ringer and the direct assassin, but not, of course, the initiating agent. We're still investigating how Sol's system and *Carey's* were breached so that Sol willingly entered the car with no fear or anticipation of foul play."

"At LAX."

"Yes, that's where he was picked up. He flew private into L.A. from San Diego."

"Why did he go to the hotel in Pasadena rather than to his home in Beverly Hills?"

"Yet to be determined. He may have had a meeting scheduled there and didn't want to bring the person or persons into his home."

"Odd, don't you think?"

"Not necessarily, if you consider the kinds of individuals with whom he had regular dealings."

"What about the children?"

"Both under tight surveillance," Gradison responded. "The son is at his home in Manhattan; they've ordered in enough food to serve a significant number of individuals. The daughter is in the District;

no catering, but enough heat signatures to suggest that she's being accompanied by a reasonably large group as well."

"Probably giving each their condolences," the AG said.

"Or planning next steps," Gradison said.

"In what sense?"

"Inferring or actually identifying the perpetrators of the hit; covering their own tracks, coordinating their collective response or distancing themselves from the action and, perhaps, from one another."

"I wouldn't press too hard on that, Director. First and foremost, they were his children and there is every indication that he was a loving parent. The wife is somewhat incapacitated and Mr. Sol has been their primary parental contact. There is also, I understand, a disabled son in Switzerland who receives the very best medical care. Remember that Mr. Sol was a generous supporter of a multitude of causes and a faithful contributor to the efforts of our administration. Any other connections which he might have developed can be pursued separately and in good time. For now the president would like to postpone that discussion until the facts of the assassination have all been sorted and the case is effectively closed."

(And you're willing to play his obedient servant in that process), Gradison thought to himself.

"Is there any more information that I can provide?" Gradison asked.

"I'll call you, as necessary," the AG said, and clicked off.

That's interesting, Gradison thought, as he replenished his coffee. The president would generally want a personal briefing from her FBI director. She's keeping me at a distance, filtering the information on the case through a separate channel with her political toady. And keeping any talk of Sol's criminal operations at an equal distance, seeing TweedleDee and TweedleDoom as teary-eyed children, mourning the loss of dear old dad. Treating them as civilians rather than as indictable co-conspirators. 'General,' he said aloud, 'the wagons have been circled.' And then—to himself—'You did the right thing in putting together your own honest team and since the AG was basically keeping you at arm's length there was no need to share the matter of the attempted assassination of Gwen

Harrison, her sequestration, the private TDYing of Special Agent Wilken, the utilization of Michael Liu (above and beyond the work of the San Diego and L.A. field offices) and the little matter of the contact with Karen Wilken's old compadre from the Mossad.'

He sipped his coffee and called Sam Barron.

"What can I do for you, Director?" Sam said.

"Just checking in," Gradison said. "I just received a call from the AG, asking for an update on the Sol case so that he could brief the president."

Sam paused before responding. "Not to overstep, sir, but I would have thought that you would be included in that sort of oval office meeting."

"You're not overstepping, Sam. That's part of the point of my call—to let you know that the wagons are being circled and the hatches are battened down."

"I'll withhold any out-of-line comments on the AG's political loyalties, sir."

"No need for that, son," Gradison said. "You've got a well-functioning central nervous system. His allegiances to party over the law and our system of justice is a matter of public record. I do, however, appreciate your understanding where we all stand in this matter."

"Our two associates and their western compatriot are working the screens morning and night, Director. I regret that I have no new information that could be of any use. Both of the offspring are circumscribed, circumspect and basically silent. No one has been seen coming and going from their homes. You would already know that the L.A. AD is pressing hard but without any result to date. While we would love to enjoy the benefit of your wisdom and the pleasure of your company, we have nothing to offer at this time. Would you like to contact your counterpart in Tel Aviv? We don't anticipate any connection between his agent's current assignment and our case, but their general monitoring activities proceed apace and if we work through his agent she'll have to loop through him anyway."

"I'll keep you posted, if he has anything noteworthy."

"Much appreciated," Sam said.

CHAPTER FIFTY-EIGHT

Gradison checked his wall clocks. 4:10 p.m. in Tel Aviv. Gradison's primary 'counterpart' in Israel was not exclusively a member of Shin Bet, the internal security force comparable to the Bureau, but a liaison between that group and the Mossad. The integration of Israeli intelligence agencies was essential for a number of reasons, many of them geographical and demographic. He was thought of as a 'counterpart' because each of them shared a military past, including cooperative work during two major engagements. While they were unable to share all that they knew and all of the implements that they had at their disposal, the two of them always attempted to share what they could. Both men knew each other's system's strengths and often engaged in friendly barter. While the Americans possessed superior weapons systems the Israelis were masters of information technology. In this particular case they had access to a peerless system of surveillance expertise and equipment.

Gradison called on a direct line.

"Walter, I was just about to call you."

"Thank you, Daniel. Happy to hear that. What have you turned?"

"Something on the Sol case, but unfortunately no new developments on other pending concerns, though we have some emerging intel on one of the Iranian proxies and their activities that affect your country. I'll brief you when we have fuller information."

"Good, I was particularly interested in the Sol case."

"Well, the information may be significant; we believe we've identified the assassin."

"That would certainly be helpful. You had the picture from the Pasadena hotel…"

"Yes. Even though it was in profile it was helpful. What was essential was the timing. And the identification was embarrassingly easy, assuming that we haven't stumbled upon what we would consider to be a very implausible coincidence."

"You have my full attention."

"Fine. The murder took place in mid-afternoon. We assume that the assassin had to leave the hotel, secure transportation to some locale in which he could alter his clothing and his appearance. Shaving (or detaching) the mustache, for example, removing some of the swarthy 5:00 shadow and changing into clothing which was less—shall we say—stereotypical. After the adrenalin rush of the assassination and the departure from the rather extensive hotel grounds and after relocating to somewhere private and secure in the basin where he could attend to the issues concerning his appearance it would, simply, be time for dinner. Fortified with some strong drink, of course. We tapped into the CCTV's of likely upscale establishments and found him (or what we believe to be him) on an early pass."

"Not at a fern bar."

"I think I know what you mean by that, Walter, and no, it wasn't a fern bar. He dined at *Lawry's* prime rib restaurant in Beverly Hills. Significant quantities of expensive beef, plentiful amounts of aged, red wine and several glasses of brandy. We were even able to secure a picture of the items on his table. The alcohol was unidentifiable, unfortunately, but the slab of beef was not. We think it was the standard cut of prime rib at a modest $64.00 (served very rare, by the way), plus some potatoes and what the restaurant claims to be a 'classic' Yorkshire pudding. He may have been putting them to the test in that regard, since one of the locations from which he traditionally operates is London."

"And can you share the picture?"

"We do and we'll send it to you under our usual protocol. Enough suspense. It was Alexsei Volkov."

"The wolf."

"Yes, though his actual surname is common and pedestrian. He uses the *nom de guerre* for commercial purposes, presumably. Our people consider it pretentious though he remains an effective operative."

"Motivated purely by money."

"Yes, and that makes it easier to assess his movements and motivations."

"Were you able to trace his movements after his dinner?"

"As a matter of fact, we were. He went directly to LAX and flew to Atlanta."

"Busiest airport in America, as you doubtless know."

"Yes, unfortunately we lost him there. He was definitely at Hartsfield, but we were unable to follow him through the crowd."

"Even though you had positioned some agents there?"

"I'm afraid I can't speak about that. We had not made any arrangements with official liaison officials and we would have hesitated to attempt any action against him on foreign soil."

"In part because you don't fully trust our current administration."

"No comment, old friend."

"Volkov is a pro," Gradison said. "He could have arranged a private flight, secured a rental vehicle, even returned to California in an act of misdirection. It's very likely that he would have flown to Atlanta simply because of the level of activity there. His ultimate destination is anyone's guess. Still, I'm very happy that you were able to identify him and I'm grateful for the information."

"As you know, even plastic surgery cannot change the proportional relationships between facial features. When he arrived at Hartsfield he had switched from aviator glasses to some fashionably blue frames. It even gave him a slight look of innocence. He was, however, easily identified."

"Particularly if you are blessed with the best facial rec software."

"We are very proud of ours," Daniel said. "I do need to run, unfortunately. My betters are holding an upper-level meeting which I am obligated to attend. I hope this has been of help to you."

"A great deal of help," Gradison said.

A few minutes later an assistant knocked on his door and asked him if he needed a fresh urn of coffee. Gradison thanked him and said, "I need to be away for awhile, but I can be reached at any time."

He then called Sam Barron. "Can you set us up for a late lunch, Sam?"

"Of course," Barron said, his thoughts running to multiple possibilities concerning the news that the Director might bring.

CHAPTER FIFTY-NINE

The traffic was, predictably, horrendous. Even though the putative rush hour had passed, the lunch break constituted a third rush hour, particularly in the areas closer to the city. By the time he had reached the outer range of the 40+ mile trip there was some diminution in its density.

Lunch consisted of a corn chowder, authentic Maryland crab cakes and an accompanying salad. "There is some white wine," Barron said.

"I'll play against type and pass today," Gradison said, "though I appreciate your thoughtfulness. I'm afraid we don't have the time for a leisurely chat, but I wanted to meet with you all personally because I have important information to share."

Gwen, Karen and Sam paused from eating and let the Director continue.

"We (I should say our friends in Tel Aviv) have a likely identification on Sol's assassin. His name, which you will recognize, is Alexsei Volkov. I say 'likely' because he was in Los Angeles at the time of the murder (dining, afterwards) and the proportions of the partial facial elements in the hotel shot corresponded with the full shot available from the restaurant."

"Pure gun for hire. Or *knife*. Or *poison*," Gwen said.

"Or *garrote*," Karen added.

"Generally up close and personal," Sam said.

"Yes, he likes to make sure," Gradison said.

"Value for money," Gwen said. "He charges top dollar and delivers.

He also excels at evading capture. When you think about this it's actually very interesting…"

"Go on," Gradison said.

"Most important of all he's an independent operator. While little is known about his personal history and current movements, his reputation for successful wet work is well-known. If you want someone taken off the board this is the person you contact."

"Yes…?" Gradison said.

"So it's highly unlikely that he comes from within Sara's or Jan's organization. He likes to keep his prices high and that entails independence. I suppose he could be on some sort of retainer, but I think that's unlikely."

"And thus…?"

"He could have been hired by anyone. One of Sol's children; one of his MS-13 distributors; a cartel leader; a middleman from China; a system of sex traffickers. Maybe even an Argentine cattle baron (or the cattle baron's wife)."

"I agree," Gradison said.

"This is helpful in a number of ways," Karen said, "I think it helps clarify things. It does, for example, reduce the possibility that this was an act of revenge, anger or passing emotion."

"It wasn't personal; it was purely business," Sam said.

"Yes," Gradison said. "We can't be sure, of course, but bringing in the wolf (and at a considerable cost) would suggest something like a corporate decision rather than a spur-of-the-moment, blunt object kind of thing."

"And the more 'corporate' the more considered," Gwen said. "This is not a decision that one takes lightly, because there are results, implications, complications. You move Sol out of the way but you also, presumably, lose access to the political and social ties which he had so carefully constructed. His compadres in low places would lose the possibility of utilizing his friends in high places."

"Yes. I'm seeing it as a tectonic shift kind of thing," Gradison said.

"The old arrangements have been changed, irrevocably. So we not only have to ask '*cui bono*' but also who can sustain the 'strengths' which he brought to the table in the face of his absence from that table."

"General, how difficult would it be to trace the payment or payments to Volkov?" Karen asked. "I know it would be very, very hard, but that would seem to be one of the first questions we would want to answer."

"Well, we do know that he is open to be paid in commodities as well as cash. If the commodities are unidentifiable they would not be discounted heavily. We know that he is generally based in London, a major financial center, but he has also surfaced in places such as Belarus that are not known for their, shall we say, financial 'integrity'. His ultimate ancestry is thought to be Russian, so he could have a relationship with any one of the dozens of Russian oligarchs who deal in both commodities and cash. The difficulty here (I don't need to remind you) is that it's easier to track the dealings of someone with a known identity. The other problem is that the amounts of money with which we're dealing are relatively miniscule in terms of world markets. Let's say, for example, that he receives $1,000,000 for a hit. That's a lot of money. On the other hand, a bond trader in New York could easily sell billions of dollars in paper before lunch time. Five days a week. Fifty-two weeks out of the year. In other words, attempting to track transactions (absent a clear, identifiable actor) is probably a fool's errand, particularly when the transactions can occur globally. That doesn't mean that we should deter our ally in Utah from trying. I just wouldn't hold out too much hope. Anyway, you now know what I know and you can keep plugging with that knowledge in mind. I'll keep my friend in Tel Aviv apprised of the fact that we would appreciate his continuing help in trying to keep tabs on Volkov. We have resources of our own, of course, but the fact that the AG has asked me to go slowly gives me some justification for doing just that. My concern, of course, is that I don't want to send any ripples through our system that would arouse interest in, shall we say, *compromised* circles. Clear enough?"

Yes, they all nodded.

CHAPTER SIXTY

There was little time for any pleasantries. Karen contacted Michael and brought him up to date on the identification of the assassin.

"I'll see what I can find," he said. "No promises, of course. His trademark is his elusiveness. Meanwhile let me know if you hear anything from the surveillance teams in D.C. or Manhattan. I'm tapped into their systems, as you know, but there may be eyes and ears on the ground at either location that notice something that their cameras or drones miss."

"We'll keep you in the loop," Karen said. "If there's anything of interest it will come to us via the Director. The agents on the ground don't know that we're on the case."

"Right," Michael said.

A few hours later Karen and Gwen made a fresh pot of coffee. "I've had a thought," Gwen said. "It probably doesn't lead anywhere but it doesn't hurt to raise it."

"What are you thinking?" Karen answered.

"Ian. The brother in Lausanne."

"You're thinking that he justifies a second look."

"It couldn't hurt," Gwen said. "Apart from his health issues he may still be engaged. Even actively engaged."

"Playing Bro and Sis against one another?"

"Possibly. Maybe he's the ultimate chess master, playing a long game as they flounder."

"Let me have a look," Karen said, returning to her computer.

"Don't forget your coffee," Gwen said, following her with her cup.

"Sorry, thanks," Karen said.

"So what he has is called *arthrogryposis* or sometimes *arthrogryposis multiplex congenita*. Very uncommon. If you survive it early on you can probably expect to enjoy a normal life span, not that the experience would be all that enjoyable. Basically it makes your joints contract. The term is often used to cover a number of conditions. All of your limbs can become distorted as well as your facial features. You would usually be confined to a wheelchair."

"But you could still function intellectually," Gwen said.

"Oh yes. You look frail and even freakish in many cases, but you could still function mentally and, to a degree, physically. It simply depends on the severity of the disease (or diseases)."

"We have some pictures of him, don't we?" Gwen asked.

"Yes. Taken from a distance but we can sharpen the images," Karen said. "Here…"

She pulled up the pictures in a matter of seconds. "They're helping him into the wheelchair…here."

"He's smiling," Gwen said.

"Yes. Not like some malevolent Bond villain."

"Should we observe him more closely?"

"Are you saying you think I should go to Lausanne?"

"It wouldn't hurt," Gwen said. "What do you think?"

"Let me check with Sam."

"So it's not that complicated," Karen said. "You can fly nonstop to Geneva from New York and then take a train, bus, ferry or taxi to Lausanne."

"It's right on Lake Geneva, right?" Gwen asked.

"Yes, quite scenic. The big tourist attraction is the Olympic Museum; the Olympic Committee Headquarters are there."

"Not sure that *they're* always up to the acts that we would consider virtuous."

"No," Karen said, smiling. "On a more intellectual note, Gibbon lived there for awhile."

"*The Decline and Fall of the Roman Empire* guy," Gwen said.

"Yes. It apparently had a positive impact on him."

"Declines and falls are what we're all about," Gwen said. "When are you leaving?"

"The day after tomorrow."

"Will that be enough time for you to brush up on your French?"

"*Je l'espère vraiment,*" Karen answered.

CHAPTER SIXTY-ONE

Gwen gave Karen a full 36 hours before inquiring concerning Ian Sol. "Give me a few more hours; I finally have a direct sighting," Karen said.

"Not a problem. We have some movement at this end."

"On whose part?" Karen asked.

"Sara's. She's flying into LaGuardia."

"She's going to him," Karen said. "That's a sign of obeisance."

"Or maybe she just wants to get out of Washington; limit the family exposure in what is basically a small town."

"The smallest town in America, culturally," Karen said. "Keep me posted by text."

"She's at his house. No meeting on neutral ground at a hotel or restaurant," Gwen said. "They appear to be dining alone, from the heat signatures. An occasional person enters the room; we figure he or she is serving them food and drink."

"They seem calm enough. No herky-jerky movements. The table is small, given the proximity of their bodies. There even appears to be some personal interaction—handholding, that kind of thing."

"Expressing condolences, perhaps," Karen texted. "Maybe they're closer than anyone thought."

"She's leaving. We caught a brief glimpse of her before she got in a shiny new black *Escalade*. Heading back to the airport. Total time elapsed in NYC and environs: 3 hours and twenty-seven minutes. Enough time for a meal, some conversation, some emotional exchanges. Not enough time for any extensive planning and plotting. No one else in the room with them except for the wait staff. No other stops to and from the airport, at least not yet. They're acting like normal people who have lost someone close and need to share a moment."

"Back in a couple hours. Will call," Karen said.

It was three hours before Karen reconnected.

"Sorry to keep you up this late," Gwen said.

"Not a problem. When we texted earlier I was watching Ian directly and needed to double-task. First off, the place where he stays is very, very posh. More like a resort than a medical facility. It overlooks the lake; the staff are young and pretty and appear to be very competent. No scrimping on salaries, perks or bennies. Ian is significantly impaired and can barely transfer himself from his wheelchair to a chaise longue. His carer brought him out to sit in the sun this afternoon. He looked comfortable under his blanket, which was probably cashmere."

"Was he able to feed himself?"

"There were no snacks, just a crystal glass with a long straw. It took some effort for him to position himself to take a sip. We're talking more ice chips than *Trader Vic* cocktails with umbrellas and orange slices."

"Was he reading?"

"No. More nodding off than anything else. He appeared to be asleep for about half the time and resting his eyes for the other half. I feel certain that he was unaware that I was observing him. I changed positions and was as inconspicuous as I could be. They brought him outside at about two hours after lunch, so he wasn't falling asleep from a massive intake of food and drink. There was bright sun that they doubtless wanted to take advantage of; several other patients were out at the same time. 'Patients'?

Is that the right word? Probably so. No one was playing volleyball or taking a dip in the lake. I think these people are all largely incapacitated and I have a hard time imagining that Ian Sol in his current condition could even be thinking about masterminding some plot to take over a tidy portion of the world's criminal activities."

"What you see is what you get: a young man in a wheelchair who needs constant professional care."

"Yes, I think so. It was the struggles with the straw when no one was around to help him. I could see a certain degree of anguish in his face. Of course, he's just lost his father and may be concerned about the degree to which his brother or sister would continue his care regimen…"

"But there were no people around him, taking notes, whispering in his ear, looking out toward a security perimeter…"

"Not a one," Karen said. "I would say that he is certainly sentient, but so physically compromised that it would be difficult for him to carry on a systematic conversation or even to perform routine tasks of self-care."

"Sad," Gwen said, "assuming that he's not playing a serious role in the family businesses."

"I'm trying to think that way," Karen said. "I wouldn't want to have to include him in any operations which we might have to initiate."

"You're a softy," Gwen said. "I knew it."

"I wouldn't go that far," Karen answered. "Anyway, I think I've done about as much here as I can do. If he was involved in any serious family operations this would be the time in which he would be surrounded by a small army of evil partners and servants. All I could see was a young brunette in a nurse's uniform, slightly overweight, solicitous, perhaps even a little sad."

CHAPTER SIXTY-TWO

A day and a half later Karen was back in Stafford. Jan and Sara had hunkered down, taking a few isolated meetings, probably trying to get their heads together and plan next steps. Karen reminded Gwen that neither was likely to be the target of immediate attack or exploitation. "After all," Karen said, "these are basically nasty people with their own significant operations who are facing a temporary setback, not babes in boarding schools who have just discovered that their daddy was doing untoward things."

"He may have seen them as children; parents always do," Gwen said, "but these are middle-aged criminals with years of experience, even if their political connections have kept their rap sheets short and their exposure minimal."

"And they each have their own little charities," Karen said, "just like daddy."

Sam entered the workroom and asked if Gwen and Karen were ready for lunch.

"Something light for me," Gwen said, "I want to be able to put in a full afternoon. We need a break in the case."

"Works for me," Karen said. "Sandwiches and coffee?"

"We'll put something together," Sam said. "Any news from the Director?"

"Unfortunately not," Gwen said.

"No, nothing," Karen added.

As Sam opened his palms in a signal of discouragement, Karen's and Gwen's secure lines rang.

"It's Michael," Gwen said. "He wants to zoom."

"Hello, Michael," Karen said. "What do you have for us?"

"Something interesting, I think," he responded.

"Volkov?" Gwen asked.

"Well, it starts with him. In the Atlanta airport."

"You were able to track him?"

"Yes, but it wasn't easy. Your friends in Tel Aviv either punted early or they wanted to keep some things to themselves. I'm betting on the former, primarily because the situation there is so complicated."

"Big place," Gwen said.

"If you look at their brag page you get a sense of the dimensions," Mike said. "Sixty-three thousand employees on site. The 'site' is nearly 5,000 acres, with five parallel runways. Three hundred commercial venues for dining, shopping and miscellaneous services. Medical, nursing, interfaith chapel, lounges, charging stations and service animal 'relief' stations. They have art exhibits, musical performances; it's more like a city than an airport. In one year: 100 million passengers. Two terminals, seven concourses, 192 gates."

"But you tracked him," Karen said.

"Yes, but it took days to work my way through the camera footage."

"Did it look as if he was evading exposure?" Gwen asked.

"No question about that," Mike said, "unless he has the weakest bladder in the world he was in and out of more restrooms than the cleaning staff. And he was not there for a connecting flight. He was biding his time. A coffee here, a coffee there, then back to the restroom, then a stroll through the concourses, particularly the more crowded ones."

"And eventually he made contact with someone?" Karen asked.

"Yes, but in an incredibly well-planned way."

"How so?" Gwen asked.

"The pivot point was the route of the SkyTrain, an electric-powered automated people mover. The SkyTrain connects to the rental car facility, the west parking deck, the Gateway Center Arena and several hotels. The rallying point was on the SkyTrain, with Volkov taking the long route and his contact popping in and then back out at a single, precisely-timed moment."

"Did they speak?" Karen asked.

"Not that I could tell," Mike said. "The people mover was crowded and they intersected for no more than a second or two."

"With a handoff of some sort?" Gwen asked.

"Yes, but not with some James Bond briefcase or matching piece of luggage. More like a simple duty-free plastic bag, which, by the way, Volkov had been carrying from the time he emerged at Hartsfield."

"And the bag that was exchanged matched it precisely," Karen said.

"Yes."

"That is planning with a capital P," Gwen said. "These guys are absolute pros."

"The handoff was very impressive," Mike said. "Volkov knew that there was a camera on the people mover and he turned his body to the side as his contact slipped by."

"But you still saw it," Gwen said.

"The bag had a product logo on one side and a product image on the other. After the contact moved past him the sides were reversed. A small slip up."

"But one that you noticed," Karen said. "We've got pros on our team too."

"Well, I don't like to brag…" Michael said.

"And the contact disappeared and Volkov continued…" Gwen said.

"Yes, eventually getting off at the Gateway Center/GICC Station."

"And you lost him there," Karen said

"Yes, unfortunately."

"And you couldn't follow his contact," Gwen said.

"No, unfortunately. But I did get a glimpse of his face as they executed the handoff."

"Are you going to keep us in suspense?" Karen asked.

"Of course not. I think you'll recognize him."

With a single keystroke the image appeared on their screens.

"Robert Scherl," Gwen said. "As he lives and breathes. Bagman to the assassin."

V

SCHERL

CHAPTER SIXTY-THREE

"So we were wrong," Karen said.

"The assistant is the boss or at least the chief go-between. We figured Grayson for the team leader, but he sleeps with the fishes."

"Simple mystification," Karen said. "Scherl hides by releasing Grayson in parts. We figure he's the bossman, so Scherl must be dead as well. Sol simply cleaned house."

"I wonder if that's why his Wisconsin home was empty and sanitized. No possibility for him to be there if he's been dismembered and planted somewhere."

"Pretty crude place if he's moving in Volkov's circles," Karen said.

"Part of the mystification, perhaps," Gwen said. "Let me check some things."

"I'll put on a fresh pot of coffee," Karen said. "Fuel for your search."

They rallied an hour later. Gwen had finished a third cup of coffee while Karen had completed a brief workout. "Tricky little bastard," Gwen said.

"Did you find something?"

"As a matter of fact, I did," Gwen said. "His name is Robert Scherl, right?"

"On his military records," Karen answered.

"And on the lease to his place in Wisconsin," Gwen said.

"Thought he owned that," Karen said.

"Might as well have," Gwen answered. "He's been leasing it for years, long enough to embed himself in all of the internet websites. When you make a cursory check for his name you get the Wisconsin address. You figure he's a sidekick figure and the quality of his digs there square with your expectations. However…"

"Yes?"

"When you begin with his military records and go back to his birth certificate, you find out that his actual name is Lawrence Robert Scherl."

"Which could make him Larry Scherl, Lawrence R. Scherl, Larry R. Scherl, Lawrence Scherl, or…whatever," Karen said.

"Exactly, and when you're only signing a lease or showing up at a recruitment station with a sergeant trying to make his quota…"

"*Robert Scherl* is close enough for government work. But you found something under a different name…"

"I did," Gwen said.

"A house?" Karen asked.

"With a nice zip code," Gwen said.

"Which is?"

"01742," Gwen answered.

"Which is?"

"Concord, Massachusetts."

"Patriotic territory; doesn't sound like our boy," Karen said. "On the other hand, mucho dinero to live in that neighborhood. Plus a boatload of subsidiary benefits. Major airport. Train service to D.C. and other dens of iniquity. Easy ingress and egress; surrounded by history but also a broad landscape of rocks and trees and water."

"He sits on two and a half acres," Gwen said.

"And the name 'Robert Scherl' is not on the deed."

"Lawrence R. Scherl," Gwen said. "Paid $1.2 mil a decade ago. *Zillow* pegs it between $2.4 and $2.7 now."

"Wonder who he killed ten years ago for the down payment," Karen said.

CHAPTER SIXTY-FOUR

"I was just about to check," Gwen said. "Oh, and by the way, when we were checking out his partner Grayson there were some indications that Grayson had been spending time in both London and Boston."

"They may have rallied in Boston," Karen said, "renewing old ties from back in the day when they were in that British mercenary group."

"Very possibly," Gwen said.

An hour later Gwen pushed her chair back from her work station. "No specific assassinations a decade ago, but a lot of wet work in Africa and Latin America for those so inclined."

"Maybe cashing in on quantity rather than quality," Karen said. "Instead of taking out the dictator he was taking out a couple dozen members of the opposition."

"An equal opportunity murderer," Gwen said.

"I want to visit his home in Boston," Karen said.

"I think that would be a good idea," Gwen answered.

Karen made the dinner flight on *United* and landed in Boston in early evening. She rented a car at Logan and drove to Concord as the sun was setting. The house was off of the Concord Turnpike, on the south side of the road, across from the town proper. The connector was Manor Lane, which led to an extended cul-de-sac with 1970/1990-built manses spreading off into the woods. Short at their base they widened at the rear, with large stands of eastern white pines looming over heavily landscaped back yards.

Scherl's home sat at the head of the cul-de-sac, a 4,000 square-foot colonial in a tasteful gray with a slate blue door and a light on in the room over the garage. Karen parked approximately 100 yards away, just outside of the cul-de-sac, near a gravel road that had several mailboxes at its entry point. She then walked back toward Scherl's house, pulling up her hoodie and removing her binoculars from their black leather case. The lenses were designed for distance rather than breadth of vision so she would need a steadying implement but she easily found a dry spot free of leaves and the log of a dead pitch pine behind which she set up her station.

Before she detected any movement she heard a train coming through the northeast side of the woods. 'Thoreau's train,' she thought; the one he was contemplating when he said that trains run on us rather than the other way around. She knew that she was close to Walden Pond because she had seen a sign for it before she veered off of the Turnpike.

She focused on the lights that were visible from her position and figured that the principal light from the room over the garage was some sort of family room. A dimmer light in the background was probably in the kitchen and the blue glow a television screen. Someone was there but they didn't move for at least thirty minutes. Finally there was motion—a head, shoulders and a female form. Youngish. The woman went into what Karen assumed was the kitchen and returned with something in her hand. It wasn't a glass but it could have been a cup of some sort. Chamomile tea? Vodka, neat?

An hour later the blue glow disappeared, along with the bright light in the family room and the dimmer light in the kitchen. A light appeared in the foyer and was replaced by a light in an upstairs bedroom. A second light went on in the back of the room, probably the bathroom, since it was turned off five minutes later. The bedroom light went off but there was a slight glow from what were probably night lights.

So who is staying in Scherl's house—a friend? A squeeze? A caretaker?

A pet sitter? If it was a pet sitter there was no dog because none was let out right before the woman went to bed. There was no record of Scherl having a sister or niece. Karen remembered the number of windows when the bedroom light was on and figured that the woman was staying in the master, not in a guest room. So the house was operational; someone was there, if not Scherl, perhaps someone close enough to him to use his bedroom. On the other hand, if she was a housekeeper she could change the linen and sleep in the big bed whenever she pleased.

Karen moved her car to a distant corner of the area, caught several hours of sleep and returned to her post at daybreak. At 8:05 the kitchen light came on and at 9:47 the garage door opened. Karen hurried back to her car and prepared to follow the woman, who drove to the nearest *Wegmans*, bought some groceries and returned to Scherl's house. At the store Karen got close enough to take several pictures. The woman was 20ish, slim and fit, with dark hair and green eyes. The groceries she purchased were eggs, milk, fresh vegetables, fresh fruit and a baguette.

She sent the pictures to Gwen and to Michael for the application of facial rec software. Michael answered promptly. The match came through in less than twenty minutes: Dana Woodson. Local girl. Northeastern University grad in Communications. Parents living in Lexington. Either hired help or a girlfriend, but probably not a partner in crime.

"I'm coming home," she told Gwen. "I've installed some cameras outside Scherl's home, but my best guess is that the girl is a house sitter, hired locally. A civilian."

"I'll see you tonight," Gwen said.

CHAPTER SIXTY-FIVE

Karen's flight from Logan was delayed and by the time she got to Stafford it was 8:15.

"I saved you some dinner," Gwen said. "Italian beef OK?"

"Sure, thanks," Karen said.

Gwen broke up pieces of roast beef and doused them with Italian dressing, sautéing them over a gentle heat. Karen put two pieces of rye bread on a plate and added a handful of potato chips.

"Michael certainly id.'d the woman quickly," Karen said.

"University yearbooks are all online. The fact that she was close to those photos in age made it easier to identify her. She was all over the yearbook—political clubs, debate, sports teams…"

"Big woman on campus and now she's working for a professional assassin," Karen said.

"Not sure she's aware of that. He may have told her that he does international consulting and that her salary would be better than any offered by *Starbucks*," Gwen answered.

"True," Karen said. "There's not much call for Communications majors these days".

"It sounds interesting and wide-ranging but it may translate into a job in phone sales," Gwen said. "More fun sitting in a mansion in the woods and doing some light housekeeping, with plenty of time to read and prepare yourself for something better. As a line on a resumé (personal assistant to an international mover/shaker) it would work out better than most entry-level jobs."

"I saw a line on a Dean of Students' c.v. once," Karen said. "It stated that he had been an associate at the Great Atlantic and Pacific Tea Company."

"A bagger at the A&P," Gwen said.

"Precisely."

"That reminds me…speaking of groceries, one of our regular scans picked up some images of Scherl at a local restaurant, an Indian place in McLean."

"When was this?" Karen asked.

"Two days ago."

"So D.C. was his next stop after Atlanta."

"It would appear so," Gwen said. "I didn't put too much stock in it because it could just be mystification. He flew to Dulles, had dinner, and popped out again. There haven't been any other local sightings."

"Was he alone?"

"Yes, and sitting at the bar in plain sight, with one of those large bottles of Indian beer and a plate of what looked like tandoori chicken."

"One of my favorites," Karen said.

"With a side of naan bread."

"Have to have that," Karen said, "especially when it has all the little charred bubbles."

"You're making me hungry," Gwen said.

"Want some of the Italian beef?" Karen asked.

"I gorged earlier," Gwen answered. "There's some butter pecan ice cream in the freezer, if you're interested."

"I'll pass on that and have some coffee."

"We've got some of the K-cups with that half-caff stuff," Gwen said. "Just a little jolt and it won't keep you up all night."

"Sounds good," Karen said.

Ten minutes later they had left the table for more comfortable chairs in the corner.

"Next steps?" Karen asked.

"Full-court press on Scherl, more info on Ms. Woodson," Gwen said. "We'll bring Sam and the Director up to speed on what little progress we've made."

"I think we're getting closer," Karen said.

"You do?"

"Not close close, but closer. We know who passed the cash (or the way to find it) to the assassin who took out Sol. And we know that he's a middleman, not an initiator. The next step is to find out who hired him to play bagman."

"Could be insulated by multiple layers," Gwen said. "Makes me kind of wistful."

"In what sense?"

"The son-of-a-bitch tried to kill me. I was up for some major payback. Now it appears he's a pay-to-play functionary. It wasn't personal. He could have easily been defending me if that's what the buyer wanted."

"I don't need personal," Karen said.

"I don't either," Gwen said, "but it adds a little spark."

"You still wouldn't hold back," Karen said.

"Not for a moment," Gwen said. "When the situation arises and the opportunity presents itself, he's going down. Big time. In some ways a pure mercenary is more evil than a committed crusader."

"You'd take him out before he had a chance to finish that naan bread."

"Before he had a chance to take a sip of his 22-ounce *Taj Mahal*. Although…"

"Yes?"

"I might like to see him choke on a bit of it."

"My girl," Karen said.

As they finished their coffee their phones announced the arrival of a text. It was from Michael, directing them to a secure site.

CHAPTER SIXTY-SIX

"Wishing us a good evening?" Karen asked.

"Michael usually dispenses with the niceties and gets right to the point," Gwen said.

"OK, here we go," Karen said.

Sorry, G and K. I shouldn't have overlooked this. When I got facial rec from the Northeastern yearbook site I didn't check any further. The attached is from the Boston Globe. *When DW graduated she received a citation from one of the university's institutes, in this case the so-called* Center for the Promotion of Democracy. *The woman who is handing her the paper may be of interest to you. She had contributed to the creation of the center and was one of its 'trustees'. I think you may recognize her.*

"Eleanor Boerling," Gwen said.

"The veep's wife," Karen said.

"It could just be a coincidence," Gwen said. "Ellie probably throws a few thousand here and a few thousand there, if only to maintain her philanthropic street cred."

"I don't like coincidences," Karen said. "I'm not sure I even believe in them."

"Let me think about this for a second," Gwen said. "Ellie comes from old money. Big money. Carlton is a superannuated Oregon hippie who got into politics. He met Ellie at Yale law and may have actually had feelings for her. He certainly had feelings for her trust fund. Since then they've added to their personal fortune, probably through his influence peddling, since Ellie has never practiced law. She saw something in him (I'm not sure what) and has been a willing partner in his operations."

"Just a sec," Karen said, as she googled the Northeastern democracy center. "That center is directed by an existing faculty member. It appears to have a single secretary/receptionist and offers some coursework, mostly through adjuncts."

"So they'd receive some money from the instructional budget, buy off a course or two from the director, replace him with some cheap adjuncts receiving miniscule stipends and host a lecture or two. This is not an academic empire."

"More like a shell corporation," Karen said.

"Right, so we're talking an endowment in the thousands, not in the millions," Gwen said, "with how many members of the Board of Trustees?"

"Ten, right now," Karen said. "This pseudo institute runs on chicken feed from a handful of clubpersons who want to be honored at an annual luncheon and put an additional line on their *Who's Who* entries."

"Sounds about right," Gwen said.

"So this could all be pure happenstance that came back to bite them. Maybe the Boerlings' hireling mentioned that he was looking for a house sitter for his place in the woods and Ellie said, "I know just the person."

"It's not beyond the realm of possibility," Gwen said, "especially if Ellie wanted to demonstrate the level of her expertise to a business partner. Get out from under Carlton's shadow for a moment…but her lips moved before her brain was engaged."

"Stupid beyond comprehension, of course," Karen said, "but you have to remember that the first principles in these peoples' bible are that: a) they are above the law; and b) arrogance is not a failing but a natural entitlement to their position above and beyond the station of the little people."

"Maybe we just got very lucky," Gwen said.

"If you think it's lucky to be placed in the position where you have to remove the Vice-President of the United States and escape unscathed," Karen said.

"It would have the virtue of clarifying the situation," Gwen said.

"And that would be?"

"Oh, I don't know…perhaps the possibility that this son-of-a-bitch is attempting to take over the operations of Alex Sol."

"Ballsy," Karen said, "but perhaps not if he has Lady Macbeth whispering in his ear and asking him if he's ready to step up and be a real man."

"Overreaching. It's what they were born to do."

Karen paused before speaking. "Taking Sol out would not be a difficult task for those with the right connections, but taking Boerling out would be considerably more difficult, especially for those with a great deal to lose and, simultaneously, a great deal to fear."

"No," Gwen said, "we can't think that way. Remember what Patton said: 'Courage is fear holding out a moment longer.'"

"I love when you go all Georgie on me," Karen said.

"Most would probably go all TR and talk about the man in the arena who goes for broke and achieves success by daring greatly…even if he loses."

"But TR also talks about those who don't dare greatly and instead live in the gray twilight—the mediocrities."

"Not *our* gray twilight," Gwen said. "That's why you and I are having this discussion. The *real* gray twilight: remember it; you work there. It's the place of deep shadows, where the blood runs in bright red rivulets. The place where the villains suddenly find themselves facing the barbed wire fence or the brick wall that they're unable to climb. The place where reality sets in, where their eyes begin to moisten, their lips quiver and their only recourse is to beg. The place where justice is served in multiple courses."

CHAPTER SIXTY-SEVEN

"We're going to need a lot more information," Gwen said, "possibly a bigger boat, and at the very least the full approval of the admiral."

The Director responded immediately to their call and arranged to meet that evening. In this case their dinner was short on food and long on drink. Some cold roast beef on rye with a smear of horseradish and a scoop of potato salad was followed by some deep pours of Armagnac and conversation with long pauses. The urgency was palpable as the odds and challenges became increasingly clear.

"Of course he has a day job, no matter how poorly he performs it," Gwen said. "Sol could have devoted his every waking hour to running his various criminal enterprises. Boerling would have to subcontract and then take large kickbacks, far more than the occasional backhanders."

"True," the Director said, "but he would enjoy the support of various arms of the federal enforcement agencies. That would make it easier to keep the subcontractors on the straight and narrow. It's one thing to guard yourself against the occasional ambitious usurper in the ranks, quite another to know that the boss of bosses could pick up the phone and enlist the services of rogue elements within the Bureau, the Company or Seal Team Six."

"Perhaps he could throw some bones to Sol's offspring," Karen said. "They would still be in search of work with daddy gone; at the same time they would be fully cognizant of the ease with which he was removed."

"Right," the Director said. "Doubly motivated. That would also make for a smooth transition in several areas, but the negotiation would need a good interlocutor. Boerling couldn't just pick up the phone and identify himself."

"Hi kids, this is your uncle Carlton. I'm the new sheriff in town and I'm prepared to whack you like I whacked daddy," Gwen said. "That couldn't happen. With the family history of pseudo-philanthropy they would have contacts of their own and might be able to counterattack successfully. They could reach the president, for example, and could even do it via various circuitous routes. A Muffy here, a Muffy there, some CEO's…enough to force the president's hand and make her cut her losses."

"Right," Karen said. "If I'm doing it I'm keeping the kids in the dark. All that they are told is that they're dealing with the person who took out their father. Then apply a little stick…perhaps remove some people in their organizations in a way that would turn their stomachs and gather their full attention."

"That's a lot to put on a glorified hit man," the Director said. "We're talking about an enlisted mercenary, not the head of S.P.E.C.T.R.E. Would he be up to the tasks at hand?"

"He could certainly do the wet work," Gwen said, "but that's a good point. On the other hand, if you're thinking of evil servants straight out of central casting with Ivy League degrees, Boerling is surrounded by them. A retired rogue general or commandant from the third world would also have both the administrative skill and the taste for the jugular."

"True," the Director said. "The bottom line is that we've got beaucoup work to do and it has to be done in house by our own team. You'll need to determine if Boerling is, in fact, taking over Sol's operations and who is doing the work on the ground. You'll start with Scherl and his activities because we don't have anyone else, at least not at this point. If the investigation reinforces our theory and speculation we then have to decide what, specifically, we do with Boerling. This is the kind of thing that would be more than the subject of a future TED talk. It would literally shake up the world. However, things that have the capability of shaking up the world have a way of ending up with the dust under the palace-size Persian carpets. That would prompt a more definitive response: the plutonium cocktail rather than the congressional investigation. Of course the plutonium cocktail would also have the capability of arousing the world's interest and counterreaction, so there's no way this is going to lead to a set of easy choices. Fortunately, we are blessed with a team that enjoys the strengths of a rich imagination and the willingness to put Vlad the impaler to shame."

"Scherl *did* try to kill me," Gwen said. "He was acting on orders."

"Already noted," the Director said, as he sipped his brandy.

"And it's much more than personal," Karen said. "This network of activities gives new meaning to the adjective *evil*."

"Indeed," the Director said. "I don't like to preen and virtue-signal, but we do find ourselves in the position of defending the well-being of a vast number of innocent people who deserve the best efforts of their government."

"I'll drink to that," Gwen said.

"As will I," Karen said, emptying her glass and placing it on the table in a manner that nearly shattered it.

"So, Scherl first," the Director said. "We need to attach ourselves to his backside like a brigade of ticks in a woods full of amateur hikers. I'd also include your friend Michael. I like his instincts…and his tenacity."

"Michael's on the case already," Karen said. "Unless and until you tell him to stop, he keeps investigating."

CHAPTER SIXTY-EIGHT

The discussion ended with two double espressos for the Director and some half-caff for Karen and Gwen. He left for his home in the Virginia suburbs and they corresponded with Michael, briefing him on the outlines of their discussions.

"I'll keep an eye out for Scherl," he said. "Nothing new to report at this time. The Sol daughter will be tricky. She's into bomb making, a kind of consultant for terrorists, but that's a diffuse business. The precursor chemicals and components can be acquired just about anywhere and the devices are often assembled separately. You're not talking about major gangs or cartels; you're talking about basement and garage operations with a host of possible mischief makers. There's a government agency—the Cybersecurity and Infrastructure Security Agency—which has an Office for Bombing Prevention. It's part of Homeland Security and works with both public and private agencies to keep us from turning into red vapor. I don't have to explain to you that its reach would include fertilizer manufacturers as well as Farsi-speaking cells in the middle of the desert. I can try to nibble around her communication systems but this is huge, vastly complex, and in some cases so far underground that we'd need a bunker buster to get to their top floor.

"Jan, on the other hand, is an easier target. I can access some things on the fentanyl flow, particularly via MS-13 in Cali and on Long Island. I can also keep some tabs on the Jalisco New Generation Cartel and see if any of them are pen pals with Sonny boy. It'll be at some distance, because we don't want to tip our hand, but both the gangs and the cartels encourage a high profile, if only for intimidation purposes, while the bombers stay in the shadows, many, of course, simply hired guns for the actual users of the devices."

"What do you think of the general theory?" Gwen asked.

"That B and possibly Mrs. B are taking over the operations?"

"Yes."

"The potential connection between Mrs. B and Scherl's house sitter speaks volumes," Michael said. "In a country of 330 million+, that's too suspicious to overlook. At the same time we've got Scherl nailed as the bagman for the employer of Sol's killer. A two year-old could connect those dots. However, I think we've got some missing pieces. I see Scherl as an ideal person for field work and wet work, but it's hard to imagine him serving as the B and B's actual operations officer. That person would have to know D.C. like the back of both of his hands and know how to access the levers of government power without arousing suspicion from the media or opposition party. You're actually talking about a system of global criminal operations with an army of separate players, many of whom could be in competition with one another. At the same time the B's would have to keep their own apparatus tiny in order to avoid exposure. The fact that Mr. B is an intellectual nonentity (or appears to be so) is helpful, because few would expect him to carry something like this off. The wife is something of a different order, and we've all read *Macbeth*, but I'm thinking of someone longer in the tooth with deeper roots…"

"We thought maybe some retired military type," Karen said, "a person who knows where the weapons are stored, where the likely associates would be and, perhaps most important of all, how to enforce the notion of 'need to know' in a community that understands the concept and wouldn't question orders, no matter how suspicious or dubious, if they were coming from the top (or near the top)."

"Works for me," Michael said. "I'll compile a list and check to see who's been visiting the grounds of the Naval Observatory."

"Mrs. B likes Italian restaurants," Gwen said.

"Good point," Michael said. "Though they might attract more public attention there than if the muck-a-mucks were simply making formulaic calls on the veep. I'll keep an eye out for both public and private."

"Thanks, Michael," Karen said. "Any other thoughts?"

"Just some amateur psychologizing," he said.

"What are you thinking?" Gwen asked.

"The Mrs. is the source of the family income and the veep job has been compared with a bucket of warm spit. The family already has more money than they can ever spend, but when you get down to it an insecure man might still be driven to impress his wife, no matter how stupid or dangerous the actions."

"You look up the word *nonentity* in the dictionary and you see his face," Gwen said. "Maybe he's trying to change that image, at least at home."

"Right," Michael said, "because there are limits to what he can spend. Her wealth gives him a lot of cover, but they already have a place in Manhattan, a place in Hope Ranch and a large outpost on the Oregon coast. If they suddenly started flashing billions there would be questions asked, even by the otherwise compliant press. Even if they had stacks of bundled currency they would have to keep most of it stowed in a sealed basement."

"So it's not about the money," Karen said. "It's about the, what, *respect*? It's hard to think about violent criminal behavior as leading to love and affection. It's about the *recognition*."

"Yes," Gwen said. "It's like the actions of the tin pot dictators who like to sabre-rattle and intimidate their own citizens. They'll never be major players on the global stage but they want to be treated as such or considered as such. They want to leave the kids' table and be seated with the adults at theirs. They want to be fitted with golden helmets and carry the largest shields and spears, but when you remove the helmet all you find is a tiny head with a mouth full of threats and obscenities."

"And a willingness to do anything to avoid being considered a laughing stock," Karen said.

"Yes. What she said," Michael added.

CHAPTER SIXTY-NINE

The next morning they were up early and at their parallel work stations by 7:30. Sam tried to persuade them to eat a substantial breakfast but all he could manage was a serving of rye toast for each with a large carafe of black coffee.

"Nothing too exciting yet about MS-13," Karen said. "I knew about their initiation rituals (taking beatings, killing an innocent person), but their ugliness has never been in dispute. Jan Sol must really be hungry for money if he was willing to get into bed with the likes of them."

"The cartels aren't any better," Gwen said. "They have a special fondness for hanging the bodies of their victims in public places and threatening public officials and police who won't take their bribes with the prospect of the murder of their families, including small children and babies."

"The terrorists can at least plead that they're messianic and also virtue-driven."

"They may be lunatics," Gwen answered, "but they've persuaded themselves that they're operating with higher motives."

"So what do you think the Boerlings' plan would be?"

"In effect, extortion," Gwen said. "Convince the multiple criminal operations that they are now under the administrative control of a higher power, to whom they are to fork over 10% of their earnings. Or 15%. Or 20."

"Ten percent of six billion dollars a year would be 600 million. One cartel; one set of operations."

"And that would be off the top, without the incidental expenses of doling out the bribes and conducting the day-to-day activities, so it's a large bite."

"Some think the average take per cartel per year could be two-to-three times that much," Karen said. "What did Sam call that—wealth beyond the dreams of avarice?"

"A lot more than that," Gwen said. "Toss in terrorist gigs and MS-13 operations. And remember; this isn't a fly-by-night competitor; this is the U.S. government. They could make the threats stick. We've got stealth bombers that carry 40,000 pounds of munitions to use on their compounds and old-hand wet workers from the Company to take out the comfortable part of their membership living in La Jolla. And that's just for the first round."

"And that compliant press," Karen said. "A raid or two would redound to the administration's political benefit. It would be a case of cutting off noses to spite faces, but the criminal operations would continue after the messages had been sent."

"You could even see some queen sacrifices," Gwen said. "The Boerlings put in their own people to supervise the operations and if things are not sufficiently copacetic they could take them out in some extreme way."

"Convincing the bad guys that they're every bit as ruthless and vicious as they are," Karen added.

"You have to give them points for cleverness and cunning," Gwen said. "Assuming that they're never going to solve these problems, they can take their piece of the operations but hold out the threat that they can make some surgical strikes wherever and whenever they desire."

"And earn political points from the naïve general public," Karen said. "It's a license to print money, and in unimaginable quantities."

They had continued their conversations into lunch but were making no progress on actually developing evidence or identifying new players.

They worked through lunch with reuben sandwiches, pickles and chips and a resupply of coffee. At 2:15 they were contacted by Michael.

"Got something for you," he said. "I run airline passenger list programs constantly and I recently added the possible names for Scherl. A name popped: *Lawrence Roberts*."

"A lot of Lawrence Robertses across the globe," Gwen said.

"Yes," Michael said, "but not in Black Earth, Wisconsin."

"An Alias," Karen said.

"When and where to?" Gwen asked.

"Tomorrow afternoon," Michael said. "To Dulles from Philadelphia."

"Wonder what he's doing in Philly," Karen said.

"No idea," Michael answered. "Arrival time at Dulles: 1:55 p.m."

"Anyone suspicious arriving around that time?" Gwen asked.

"Not so far," Michael said, "but it's possible that he met with Jan in New York and took the train to Philly. I couldn't find any evidence of his flying to Philly, nor, for that matter, that he flew to New York. Maybe he's using other i.d. and breaking up his trips to keep us guessing. All I know is that he's flying to Dulles tomorrow."

"Perhaps to meet Sara," Karen said.

"That was my thought," Michael said. "There's something else I think we should remind ourselves of…"

"If he's working for the B's," Gwen said, "the Sols might never have seen him before. He can make the contact with them—doubtless using an assumed name—without relying on anyone else as an intermediary."

"Particularly if he *is* the intermediary and there's someone higher up on the food chain actually directing the traffic."

"The person Gwen and I are calling the *commandant*," Karen said.

"A person that the Sols would likely recognize," Gwen said.

"I'm going to Dulles," Karen said. "Text me the time, flight number and gate number if you have it. I'm going to put as many cameras in the area as I can and see if we can catch Scherl and his contacts in the act of being themselves."

CHAPTER SEVENTY

Michael and Karen were unable to ascertain the precise gate number, but they were able to identify the gate area. After installing all of her cameras Karen set up a mini-headquarters in an unmarked van. Michael had access to the other CCTV setups in the airport; Karen was fine-tuning to increase the likelihood that Scherl could be successfully tracked. Her feeds were on screens parallel with Michael's. The next day Scherl landed in the D gates but before he walked to the shuttle pickup point he entered the closest men's restroom.

"Pit stop," Michael said. "Maybe getting ready for an extended meeting."

"Possibly," Karen answered.

Five minutes later he was back on the Concourse, but he had changed his shirt, added a windbreaker from his carry-on, a Minnesota Twins baseball cap and a set of aviator sunglasses.

"Hiding from us," Michael asked, "or from the person he's contacting? Or both?"

"Hard to say," Karen responded, "but he's hiding from someone. Do we call that a data point?"

"You could," Michael said.

Scherl left the shuttle at the main terminal and walked directly to the *Starbucks* near Baggage Claim 14, pausing a few dozen yards away and scanning the customers at the shop.

"That was pretty straightforward," Michael said. "You didn't really have to go to all the trouble of locating your multiple cameras."

"Probably meeting someone on the open side of the security chutes. A local."

"Save them the trouble of buying a ticket or somehow finagling their way into the gate areas," Michael said. "I don't know why but I was thinking the meet might occur in one of the airline club lounges."

"Me too," Karen said. "Wait…he's moving."

Scherl was off camera for a minute or two, probably heading toward the counter to place an order. When he turned to face the camera, carrying a small cardboard cup in hand, he walked to an open seat on the other side of a table occupied by another customer. He looked around, as if to indicate that the shop was sufficiently crowded to justify his sharing a table with a stranger. He pulled out the chair and turned it to the side so that the other customer could only see him in profile.

"Close enough that he can talk to her," Karen said. "I wish she would turn her head and I wish that she wasn't wearing that scarf and those glasses."

"It's Sara," Michael said. "I've got enough of a view, even in profile, to run the facial rec software. He's talking to her."

"Smart bastard," Karen said. "He's talking into his coffee cup so that it's more difficult to read his lips."

"And he's holding his expression," Michael said. "He's not making small talk and exchanging pleasantries. This is transactional."

"Can you focus in on his eyes?" Karen asked.

"A little, but he's too smart to telegraph any emotion. He's passing information. All very pure and simple."

"Cold," Karen said.

"Yes, like a wolf talking to a small sheep about his possible dinner plans."

Gwen's voice came onto their net. "We should try to follow each of them after they finish."

"We'll try," Karen said. "I'll take Scherl; Michael can take Sara."

The conversation was finished in less than ten minutes, with Scherl doing nearly all of the talking. Scherl stood up and went back into the terminal, eventually entering a men's room, changing out of his glasses and hat, his shirt and his jacket. Eventually he entered a door marked Employees Only and somehow exited beyond the range of any of the CCTV cameras.

"That was planned," Karen said. "How would he know which doors were unlocked and which were not?"

"Points for cleverness," Michael said. "You have to hand it to him. This guy may be a four-star son-of-a-bitch but he's a professional one."

In the meantime Sara had proceeded to the edge of the Valet parking lot where she was picked up by a black Suburban with darkened windows and what appeared to be a very large driver.

"The meeting is over," Karen said. "She's been given her marching orders, probably laced with some threats to disrupt her sleep for the next month or two."

"I wonder if he had the same meeting with Jan," Michael said, "or if Scherl told Sara to send his message along to her brother."

"They say that she's the one to fear," Karen said. "She's the brains, the scientist from MIT who could blow up your home and the surrounding city block. She looked pretty sober to me when she got in the Suburban."

"Like she was doing all in her power to keep herself from shaking," Michael said.

CHAPTER SEVENTY-ONE

"First impressions?" Karen asked.

"I think our analysis makes sense. Fancy that," Gwen said.

"That was probably the easy part," Karen said. "Our next step... figuring out how we construct our intervention...that will be the hard part."

"You return to our base," Gwen said. "I'll update the Director and we can begin to plan our next steps."

Gwen contacted the Director and his message was brief: "Good work; good inclinations on your tentative analysis, but I don't need to tell you that before we can move forward with anything definitive we'll need proof that can stand up to decades of scrutiny. Full ahead, but with eyes open to all possibilities."

Meanwhile Karen completed the collection of her cameras, something she had to do as deftly as possible to avoid attracting attention. She was dressed like a technician, moving a cart that carried some light bulbs and cords on the top, open shelf. When she returned to the baggage claim area, preparing to return the cameras to the van, she decided to pick up a cup of strong coffee to caffeinate herself for the drive to Stafford. And there, big as life and twice as real, was Scherl.

"He likes his *Starbucks*," she said to Gwen. "This time he's gone full civilian, no disguises, just his simple self. Really kicking back too, even down to the blueberry muffin."

"And is he with anyone?" Gwen asked.

"He is indeed," Karen said. "Give me a sec to get into an inconspicuous position."

"Pictures on the way," Karen said. "Young, well-groomed, well-dressed. Overdressed for the airport. He looks like he should be kissing backsides on Capitol Hill. One of the Omegas from *Animal House.*"

"Thanks for the pics. May I have another?"

"Coming right up," Karen said.

"I don't recognize him," Gwen said. "Let me bounce the head shot to Michael and see what he can turn."

"No reason you should recognize him," Michael responded. "He stays in the background. One WaPo shot from five months ago, passing a document to Boerling when he had to break a tie in the Senate. Thomas Davis, age 28, unmarried…"

"Harvard or Yale?"

"Princeton. School of Public and International Affairs."

"Majored in the dismal science," Gwen added.

"Not exactly; they're organized in a more multidisciplinary way, but he would have had to take a lot of econ."

"He just looks dismal to me," Gwen said.

"Captain of the lacrosse team," Michael said. "Also played some chess."

"Not surprised," Gwen said. "Anything obviously shady in his bio?"

"Father's a hedge fund manager; divorced from mom. Daddy also happens to be a significant Boerling donor."

"How significant?"

"Seven figures, mostly through a PAC."

"You scratch my back, I'll hire little Tommy."

"Sounds about right," Michael said. "Now about the naughtiness in the past…"

"Yes…"

"Accused of sexual assault by a young Rutgers coed."

"And?"

"She withdrew her complaint."

"Daddy paid her off," Gwen said.

"More than likely."

"Or Tommy threatened her with something worse."

"What's worse than that?" Michael asked.

"An MS-13 initiation ritual?"

"Maybe Boerling is still holding that over his head in some way," Michael said.

"Could be. Maybe they just share a taste for arrogant, entitled violence."

"You haven't asked the big question," Michael said.

"What is an assistant to the vice president of the United States doing in a coffee shop with the hired assassin who tried to kill me?"

"Bingo. Give that lady the matched set of tea towels. I do know one thing for sure," Michael said. "He didn't drive twenty or so miles because he was in search of a cup of *Starbucks* coffee."

"Roger that," Gwen said. "I can tell you one thing about him…"

"What's that?" Michael asked.

"If Karen and I apprise him of the degree of our seriousness and assure him that he's out of the reach of anyone who could protect him he'll spill his guts faster than a drunken freshman on spring break."

"I suspect you're right," Michael said. "Two points for our side: a connection with Boerling and a snot nose who could play a leading role on *The Weakest Link*."

"Stay shtum; this is big, Michael."

CHAPTER SEVENTY-TWO

"Drive carefully, Karen," Gwen said.

"Always," Karen answered. "I'll be there as soon as I can and we can look at my film clips. We'll see if we can decipher some parts of their conversation."

When Karen arrived Gwen had some sandwiches ready, along with some double espressos. "I've found some more information on your little Neidermeyer. Do you want to hear it or do you want to try out our lip-reading skills?"

"You talk and I'll eat," Karen said.

"OK. There's not that much but it does confirm our initial impression. The rape allegation came during spring break in his senior year. It happened in Cabo. He and his pals met the girls from Rutgers and started talking about their shared experiences in the Garden State. One thing led to another (the 'another' almost surely being a handful of roofies) and suddenly we've got non-consensual sex on a grand scale. The girls might have had a better chance with the legal system in Miami or Ft. Lauderdale and the issue might have hit the front pages of the *Herald* or the *Sun Sentinel*, but 2,000 or so miles away in Mexico…not so much. There was also the simple fact that several of the parents of the boys were sufficiently *prominent* to make the problems disappear. The girls were either paid off or intimidated and decided not to press charges."

"Stereotypical. What pricks."

"Yes, quite, but there's another incident, equally nasty in its way. When Tommy Boy was a freshman he joined one of the eating societies (as they call them at Princeton). Apparently there was a running joke about some of the food selections and how they rhymed: lamb and ham, for example. Anyway, when Tommy and some upperclass men were on a road trip they stopped at a Mom and Pop place outside of Ocean City. The diner had antique pictures of the food on the walls and Tommy stole some of them in order to impress the older boys. Lamb and ham were mentioned in the local press. The diner owners were barely scraping by and didn't need to pay a photographer to try to mimic the style and color of the remaining pictures, but they had to either fill empty wall space or abandon their favorite form of downhome advertising. It was one of those small things that was bigger to struggling people than punks trying to prank their way into the good graces of their betters. The *Ocean City Sentinel* ran it as a human interest story, highlighting the arrogance of the rich boys and the gulf between their world and the world of the couple who owned the diner. In this case money changed hands, perfunctory apologies were offered and the story went away."

"I'm liking him less and less," Karen said. "Anything else?"

"Not on the kid per se, but I found a hard connection between his old man and Boerling."

"Criminal?"

"Some would say so," Gwen said. "It establishes a reason for the father's contributions to Boerling's political activities. It had to do with a set of subsidiary businesses. I'll give you the short version. Basically, Boerling's party is tight with the greens and they don't want to encourage fossil fuel use in the third world. The alternative, however, is often burning wood or waste products. The reality is that pollution would be reduced if, for example, natural gas was used as an energy source, but the greens don't want to encourage its use. Enter Boerling, who influenced the passage of legislation that would make an exception for Davis' business operations as part of a so-called 'demonstration project'—an exception to the usual rule that kept the greens in the fold. Since he was a prime rainmaker for the party the functionaries therein turned a blind eye on the hypocrisy, and since Davis had operations throughout Africa (or his 'people' did), the efficient fuels gave him a comparative advantage in the marketplace that yielded mucho dinero."

"You scratch my back; I'll line your pockets," Karen said.

"Exactly. The Washington that we've all come to know and hate," Gwen answered.

"Thanks for the food," Karen said. "And thanks for the coffee."

"Ready to lip-read?"

"Let's try," Karen said. "I had to work fast and I didn't want to draw any attention with the more serious cameras, so I just did some very brief clips with my *iPhone*. Let me transfer them to the desktop so we can get a better view…"

They both pulled their chairs as close as possible to the screen and Karen manipulated the mouse. "Number one," she said.

"It looks like he's saying something like, 'I explained it to her.' The hand gesture is as important as the speech," Gwen said. "It's as if he's saying 'I explained it to her and what choice did she have?'"

"I think the fact that they're so comfortable together is indicative of the nature of their relationship. They've done business before," Karen said.

"Yes, Tommy does a lot of nodding and he appears to be saying 'OK' which is more dominating than 'thank you, sir.' Actually, there's a lot of OK's, as if Tommy's going through a checklist as Scherl reports on an assignment."

"The kid is obviously not intimidated by Scherl," Karen said. "Of course, he's got all of Boerling's juice behind him. What does the poet say? This has always been about who's got the AR-15's and who's got the F-15's."

"Right," Gwen said. "If I'm looking at this for the first time and trying to figure out who's in charge the answer is clear: Scherl is the hired help; Davis is the one in control."

"Here's another clip," Karen said. "Watch carefully…I'll play it twice."

"He's saying, 'I'll tell…' Could be some code name for Boerling; it wasn't 'Carlton' or 'the vice president'."

"The principal?"

"Maybe," Gwen said.

"In general, the conversation seems innocuous, but the body language speaks volumes. This is a serious discussion and both Scherl and Davis are pleased with the result of Scherl's actions."

"And we can't overlook the fact that they're confident enough in their power and position to meet in a public place," Gwen said. "It's actually arrogant as hell. Dulles is a vast place with hotels and parking lots and a lot of dark corners. They're meeting in a frickin' *Starbucks*."

CHAPTER SEVENTY-THREE

"I'll brief the Director," Gwen said.

"I'll send my clips to Michael, see if he can decipher," Karen answered.

Michael called back in an hour and a quarter. "Essentially, you're right," he said. "Davis is the one in charge and he treats Scherl like a functionary five steps lower on the food chain. When you coordinate the body language with the clip answers it's almost as if Scherl was undergoing a performance review by a senior clerk at the DMV. The references to Sara were also interesting. Ample use of the "C" word; actually both of them. He kept talking about how Scherl made a Christian out of her, but his terminology was anything but religious. The 'small c' word was a constant in his speech. I felt as if I was looking at some high school kid trying to impress another man with his worldly-wise, dominant personality. 'You told the little c___ where she stood' and 'I could see the little c___ nearly wetting her pants' and on and on like that. This will come as no surprise, ladies, but I took an instant dislike to him and would be comfortable with any retribution which could be meted out to him."

"Sounds like you're trying to prompt us, Michael," Karen said.

"Seriously, I mean it," he said. "This is one very disagreeable little punk. Actually the worst kind of punk, one in a $5,000 suit and a general feeling of contempt for everyone unable to travel in his circle."

"You think he's Boerling's ultimate go-between?" Gwen asked.

"I wouldn't be surprised," Michael said. "His father's money is an inducement for Boerling, but Boerling's rich enough now to self-fund.

I would think that Sonny Boy is an attractive middleman for Boerling because he's probably vulnerable in a dozen ways we don't even know about. How many complaints about him has Boerling quashed? How many arrests has Boerling stopped, but then logged in a private file? The kid may be smart enough for Boerling's private workforce but he's also an easy target for blame, should the need arise. He's all strut and arrogance—exactly what you'd expect in a high-level staffer hiding behind his boss's juice, but he's also expendable."

"Big time," Karen said.

"Which doesn't mean that he isn't dangerous or that we let him skate," Gwen said. "If I'm naming him I'm calling him an 'accessory before, during and after the fact'. He's not going to plead that he was only following orders. In for a dime, in for a dollar, and this little shit has been in for it all."

"Agreed," Karen said. "Michael…"

"I'm still here…"

"Why don't you run searches on everything you can—his residence, phone traffic, financial transactions…all of it. I want to know who else he's articulating with. And how. And why."

"And I want to know the personal stuff," Gwen said. "What can we use on him and how could we use it?"

"On it," Michael said.

Michael checked back two hours later. "So what do they call it in D.C.—the first *tranche?* Anyway, I have it for you. Our boy lives in a newish development on Water Street, in Georgetown."

"Down by the canal, right by the river," Gwen said.

"Right you are. 3303 *Water Street Condos.* Just over 2,000 square feet; $3.5 mil. Plus a condo fee in the thousands, monthly. Daddy co-signed on a tiny mortgage and his name is also on the deed. Since Sonny's basic pay is just over $75K and there's no way he could even afford a janitor's closet in D.C. Daddy may be trying to teach him some personal responsibility by not funding the entire purchase price of the property."

"Good luck with that," Karen said. "Without taking significant money on the side he'd probably have trouble just paying the condo fees. This only feeds his sense of entitlement."

"Right," Michael answered. "There is no record of any sublet to a renter, so there's no roommate or mates. And from what I can determine there's no girlfriend, boyfriend, wife, husband, or significant other in any form. He is close to all of the action in D.C. as well as being close to the Naval Observatory. A little over two miles, depending on your migration route."

"And close to the restaurants and private clubs in that part of the District, if you're holding meetings," Gwen said.

"Ellie likes Italian," Michael said.

"*Café Milano* if you want to see and be seen," Gwen said. "*Filomena*, if you want to lowkey it."

"I ate there once--*Filomena*. Pretty good," Michael said.

"How about telephone traffic, money movement?" Karen asked.

"Haven't checked out the finances yet, but he's very guarded with regard to communications," Michael said. "I figure he works via burners. Calls, texts, et al. are kept to a minimum on his business cell phone. The office landline is filled with crap, but nearly always of a short duration. He's bouncing calls, doing quickie business transactions…nearly everything is within the government itself. Occasionally he'll call the Social *Safeway*, up on Wisconsin Avenue. I would have expected calls to that gourmet food store on M Street…"

"*Dean & Deluca*?" Gwen asked.

"Right. I was there a few years back."

"Closed a couple years ago," Gwen said. "Maybe 2018 or 2019?"

"That explains why he's not calling them," Michael said.

"We'll sit tight while you work on the financial stuff, Michael," Karen said.

"Sure," Michael said. "But I'm not quite finished yet…"

CHAPTER SEVENTY-FOUR

"What do you have?" Gwen asked.

"Medical records."

"Outstanding," Karen said.

"Ready when you are," Gwen added.

"OK. His primary care doc is actually just off 17th Street, cheek-by-jowl with the think tanks, lobbyists, and miscellaneous lampreys who make up the District culture and economy. His name is Lewis Tennent, M.D. William and Mary undergrad, Hopkins M.D. Subspecialties in endocrinology and urology. Surprised he didn't focus on one of those and draw the big bucks but…who knows…maybe he likes seeing and dealing with the whole picture."

"But these days that means he's constantly watching the clock and filling out forms for insurance companies and the federal government," Gwen said.

"True," Michael responded, "but he's got his own full-time assistant (one Lisa Ruffino, R.N.), so he may be able to hand off a lot of the paperwork to her. Anyway, Tommy Boy is on a statin to lower his cholesterol and Doc Tennent referred him to a podiatrist to make some orthotics to slip into his *Gucci* loafers. And here's something more interesting: he also prescribed some doxycycline…"

"That's an antibiotic for chlamydia," Karen said. "Not that I have any personal experience with it; I'm just well-informed."

"When did he have it?" Gwen asked.

"A year and a half ago," Michael said, "and yes, I checked his travel schedule just prior…no trips to Tijuana or Thailand."

"Keeping it local," Karen said. "A good doc would press his patient to notify his sexual partners about the diagnosis and the need for treatment."

"There is a brief note to that effect in the record," Michael said, "but no feedback from Tommy that he had fulfilled the obligation."

"Unfortunately, STD's are now as common as mumps, measles or chicken pox were back in the day," Gwen said. "And the shame factor is all but lost."

"There's something else," Michael said. "Not sure what category to list this under…maybe the 'strange'?"

"We're all ears," Karen said.

"He was circumcised as an adult."

"Before or after the chlamydia?" Gwen asked.

"Long before. Three and a half years or so. I understand the question. Some people think it reduces the transmission of STD's."

"And UTI's," Karen added. "Again, not that I have any personal experience in that regard. I would think his motivation might be more aesthetic. Like the girls in Hollywood searching for the perfect femmy parts."

"Always a possibility," Michael said. "He may consider himself God's gift to women and wants to present them with the perfect packaging. On the other hand, he may be experiencing rejection and is hoping to increase his odds. Anyway, I just thought it was strange."

"Not that I would know," Gwen said, "but I'm thinking pain factor. Given my druthers I'd rather have the Mohel do the bris at eight days or the Christian doc do it at 24-48 hours, at a time when I'm not aware of what's happening, when I'm sleeping most of the day and when I'm already being poked, prodded, cuddled and generally distracted."

"I do have experience in this regard," Michael said, "though I don't remember any of the details. Something for which I remain grateful. In other words, I'm agreeing with Gwen. It's not a form of surgery that one would wish to contemplate for days or weeks before and one that is probably done for hygienic or aesthetic reasons. However, I have trouble seeing this as related to some acute personality disorder or the motivation for committing major felonies on behalf of an evil master. That's just my opinion. I could be wrong."

"Anything else?" Karen asked.

"As a matter of fact there's one more thing," Michael said.

CHAPTER SEVENTY-FIVE

"Tommy had a bad case of acne. Not uncommon, of course, but this was something that required significant treatment. He started with a dermatologist who basically used lotions and potions but he was also referred to a full-blown clinic. An outfit out in Bethesda. Heavy duty industrial: lasers, peels, so-called acne extractions…the whole nine yards. I hadn't noticed any significant scarring when I saw his face on CCTV, so I went back, homed in and checked. Whoever did the work on him did a good job."

"So, your psych evaluation?" Karen asked.

"Nothing profound. Common problem among teens. May reduce his romantic life a tad, but it looks as if he had the best of the best treatments. Maybe made him more self-conscious. Made him over-compensate with aggressive behaviors? Made him over-compensate by wanting to draw attention rather than deflect it? Hard to say…"

"Every piece of the puzzle helps," Gwen said. "How soon will you be able to put together some financial information?"

"Top of my honey-do list," Michael said.

"We'll let you work," Karen said.

They looked at the clock, decided to catch some sleep and rally in the morning. This time they did the full measure—sausages, pancakes with maple syrup, toast with butter and preserves and a large carafe of black coffee. It was too early for a call from Michael so Karen went for a run and Gwen went to the exercise facility to work up a sweat and work off the breakfast. They showered and reassembled, made some fresh coffee and waited for Michael to call. It was just before noon Eastern Time when he contacted them.

"Ready to talk financials?" he asked.

"Absolutely," they answered simultaneously.

"All right. You were probably right about the condo costs. The HOA's, plus the heat, light, a/c (the water is included in the HOA, but not insurance on any of the 'improvements') take him over 3K a month. That's not counting the insurance on his furniture, artwork, etc. or his internet and streaming services. The mini-mortgage adds about another thousand. That amounts to more than two-thirds of his monthly income and we haven't begun to talk about his living expenses."

"He needs subsidiary income, big time," Karen said.

"An understatement," Michael said. "His VISA bill amounts to about 6K a month, on average, and he pays it off in full each time he receives it."

"What's he spending that kind of money on?" Gwen asked.

"Well, I'll tell you," Michael said. "First off, for general shopping he usually goes to *Saks* in Chevy Chase or one of the stores in *Tysons Galleria.*"

"The pricey one on the other side of the highway from the original *Tysons,*" Gwen said.

"Right. Let me put it this way, his favorite store is *Gucci.* You probably knew that their loafers set you back around a thousand dollars per pair. Did you know that they'll sell you a belt or a baseball cap for $500? And if you're into leather big time they'll sell you a jacket for ten times that much?"

"How about food?" Karen asked.

"Most of his favs will charge you $100 for dinner. Now if you also want wine…"

"And if he's staying in?" Gwen asked.

"Strictly custom grocers, with a yen for a place called *Odd Provisions.* When he's slumming he'll go to *Whole Foods.* He'll usually go to *Bassin's* for wine, but I noticed that a couple of times he was in a pinch and bought wine from hotels. Not the *Bide-a-Wee* or *Ken and Mitzie's in the Woods*; we're talking the *Ritz-Carlton*, Georgetown or the *Four Seasons* nearly in Georgetown. And he's paying their marked-up prices. Who does that? Not someone in his putative income bracket."

"Money is no object," Karen said.

"Did we talk about his car?" Gwen asked.

"Cars," Michael said. "He tools around town in a *Lexus* LC Hybrid; they run around $100K. When he's in the country he's in a *Range Rover*. A few dollars more."

"Conspicuous consumption," Gwen said, "but everyone would assume these are all gifts from daddy or the result of a continuing allowance, not that he's involved in criminal activities."

"His cover story," Karen said. "A glorified gofer who lives like a multi-millionaire."

"I'm liking him less and less," Gwen said, "not that I needed any further incentives."

"Unfortunately I can't give you any sense of what he's spending on hookers," Michael said, "because he's smart enough in that regard to pay cash."

"Not a heavy dater?" Karen asked.

"Not according to the paper trail," Michael said. "There's nothing in the record that I could find that suggests he has a real girlfriend or girlfriends."

"Too controlling," Karen said. "He wants something more… transactional."

"All rather predictable, don't you think?" Karen said. "Spoiled, decadent, soulless…dare I say *evil*?"

"Works for me," Michael said.

"He's going down," Gwen said. "It's part of our obligation to make the world a better place."

"I didn't hear that," Michael said.

"Hear what?" Gwen asked.

CHAPTER SEVENTY-SIX

"We're in your debt, Michael," Karen said, "as always."

"Forget it," Michael said. "This case has got me motivated." Gwen briefed the Director on the material concerning Davis; he responded that he would like to have a face-to-face with them. He came to Stafford the succeeding afternoon for a light lunch and meeting.

"As we've agreed," he said, "we have to have this hermetically sealed. No interventions at this order of magnitude unless and until we're certain beyond all imaginable forms of reasonable doubt. By your accounts Davis is the executive link, Scherl the operational link. Scherl is the more elusive of the two, so I think we should begin with Davis. He's Boerling's principal insulation and he's less cautious than he should be. If we can follow him he can lead us to Scherl and Scherl (once we've found him) can lead us to the criminal organizations that are kicking back to Boerling."

"Tricky with Scherl, because he protects himself with indirect flight plans and the consistent use of rental vehicles," Karen said.

"True," the Director said, "but he'll slip up sooner or later. Remember the words of Deep Throat. Ultimately these guys aren't very smart. Slick, perhaps, but not smart. If they were smart they'd realize that most of those who play at their game are either in prisons or cemeteries."

"Or floating down the Potomac in pieces," Gwen said.

"Exactly," the Director said. "So you'll need some help and the good news is that I can provide some. Have you ever heard of a device called the pinprick?"

"Just rumors," Gwen said. "Some kind of tracking device?"

"Yes," the Director said. "It's teeny tiny and it will adhere to nearly anything. The essential components are miniaturized to a previously-unimaginable degree and then encased in a pliable material that can be form-fitted to thousands of potential locations on a modern car. This isn't something that you put in a wheel well or behind a bumper. It can be slipped into a welding joint or wrapped around a fuel line. It can be placed inside a muffler clamp. It's nearly indestructible and its signal exceeds the abilities of any currently-available comparable device. You may or may not be able to get into Davis' parking garage, but when he goes shopping he'll be completely vulnerable and after a little practice you'll be able to install the device in a matter of seconds."

"I'd like to do it," Gwen said.

The Director paused before responding. "Can't risk it," he said. "They believe that you're dead. I don't want them to be disabused of that. The moment they know that it's possible that we're investigating them they'll shut down every action or operation that could link them with the gangs or the cartels. I know where you're coming from, Gwen. For godsakes, you probably want to just get out in the sunshine and get some legs and wheels under you, but you're too valuable for that."

Gwen didn't answer but she didn't express any anger or resentment. Karen said, "I can do it. It may also mean some long days sitting at departure points. I can't park outside his condo where I could be observed by one of their street soldiers or a curious member of the general public, but I can put some cameras on his points of ingress and egress and I can stay nearby, out of sight, waiting and watching."

Gwen nodded her approval.

"As a matter of fact I brought some pinpricks with me," the Director said, "just in case we decided to go in that direction. You'll want to practice manipulating the material. It feels a little like silly putty except that each device costs thousands to produce. I've actually got a couple dummy versions, so that you can crawl around and try them on your bathroom plumbing or on your actual vehicle."

"I'll get the cameras on his condo before daybreak," Karen said.

"I've got a full array for you in my car," the Director said.

"You pretty much had this figured out before you talked to us, General," Karen said.

"That's why I've got the big office," he said. "How about some coffee?"

"Espresso?" Gwen asked.

"A triple," the Director said.

"We can do that," Gwen answered.

CHAPTER SEVENTY-SEVEN

"So what do you think?" Karen asked.

"I think you should be very careful," Gwen said.

Davis stayed at home the next day, but he bestirred himself on Saturday, driving the LC to *Burberry* at City Center. Karen was on a secure line with Gwen. "He's going in to spend a couple thousand on a coat or a thousand on some shoes," Karen said. "Unfortunately, he was able to find a parking place on 9th Street. Too exposed for me. Let's hope he keeps shopping."

Forty minutes later she resumed her call. "Heading through Georgetown…on MacArthur Boulevard…oh good, he's going to *Bassin's* to buy some wine or single malt…and…and…yes; he's parking on V Street. Not too much pedestrian traffic…"

"Did you bring your uniform?" Gwen asked.

"Absolutely…slipping it on now," Karen said. "Kind of tricky but doable."

A few minutes later she got out of her car, wearing a charcoal baseball cap and an olive drab onesie with black lettering that read *Beltway Lock and Key*. She was carrying a small, well-worn bag in her left hand and a slim jim in her right. She had the driver's door open in less than eight seconds. She then popped the trunk and the driver's side rear door, looking for places to install the pinprick. She found a dark corner in the trunk which checked all the right boxes for cover and concealment, positioned the device, closed the trunk and the two driver's side doors, and returned to her car. She sat behind the wheel, jotting some notes on a clipboard sheet, and then drove to the *CVS* on MacArthur Boulevard, slipped out of her onesie, changed her ball cap for something more fashionable, put on a pair of large sunglasses, and walked over to *Bassin's*.

Usually now termed *MacArthur Beverages*, all of the District cave dwellers knew it as *Bassin's* (or *Addy Bassin's*), a 60+ year mainstay whose principal competition was *Calvert Woodley Fine Wines and Spirits* on Connecticut Avenue, a major migration route to the Maryland suburbs, as *Bassin's* fulfilled that function for the upscale sections of northern Virginia.

Karen entered the store just as Davis was completing a discussion with one of *Bassin's* highly-skilled advisors. The advisor was carrying two bottles for Davis, who was carrying two bottles of wine and a bottle of spirits. Karen chose not to risk photographing them, but she did manage to make her way past them without exposing her face for more than a few tenths of a second. She had to do a second pass to see what the advisor was carrying, but she was able to do that in a way that was completely inconspicuous.

The advisor was actually carrying two bottles of *Roederer Cristal*, while Davis was carrying a 2018 *Lynch Bages*, a 2019 *Palmer Alter Ego* and an 18 year-old *Macallan* from sherry casks. Karen did a rough calculation in her head. The *Lynch Bages* and second-label of *Chateau Palmer* would set you back about $250, give or take. For Davis: table wine to have with his pasta or pizza. The single malt probably around $475; semi-serious sipping whiskey. The *Cristal* was something around $800, but the interesting thing was that there were two bottles. When she got back in the car and called Gwen she said, "I think maybe he's got a heavy date and hopes to get lucky. If he can't make that happen with his overwhelming charm he'll try to get her drunk."

"She'll be impressed with the label," Gwen said. "What's D.C. about beyond surface glitter?"

"Right," Karen said. "I figure he'll invite her to his place. That will give him a sense of control. It may actually be happening tonight. He's driving home now even as we speak, or at least in that direction."

"And she'll drive there herself. Your basic independent woman. Gives her the opportunity to cut her losses fast. If he fails to impress, she's out of there. Power is as power does," Gwen said.

CHAPTER SEVENTY-EIGHT

And that, more or less, is what happened. Karen's cameras caught her plate as she drove into Davis' complex—District plates; a *Tesla* model S in a smashing silver metallic. The camera revealed some blonde hair and bare shoulders. The owner of same would have been surprised to learn that Karen (via Michael) had already hacked into the caterer's site and analyzed the meal that Davis had ordered.

The caterer was a woman named Marcia Li. Her resumé included a long tour of duty at *Le Bernadin* in New York. Famous for its chef, Eric Ripert, and his largely seafood menu, Marcia had presumably acquired the chops to justify prices that hovered in the stratosphere. In this case the happy couple would be starting with a shellfish tower, featuring Maine lobster, Maryland blue crab and Atlantic oysters and shrimp. This was followed by some lobster bisque, Dover sole, "seasonal vegetables" and rum baba. The cost was astronomical (approaching $1,000.00) because of Marcia's pedigree and the need to keep the cold food on ice and the hot food hot. This entailed the use of various devices and contraptions which were enumerated on the bill.

"The diners almost seem like an afterthought," Michael said, "but just for the record, Tommy Boy's date is named Marilyn Conwell. Interestingly enough, she works for the Mexican embassy."

"Married name or single?" Karen asked.

"Single," Michael answered. "She was married to a man named Phillips, but she kept her own name and (get this) he died six years ago."

"Anything else in her resumé that might raise eyebrows?" Gwen asked.

"Her embassy title is innocuous; in English it equates to 'assistant to the ambassador'. What's interesting is that she worked in the past for the governments of Colombia and, yes, China."

"Hired gun," Karen said.

"So it would seem," Michael said. "The embassies like to have a local or two as system navigators. In this case Ms. Conwell is fluent in Spanish, Mandarin and chemical engineering."

"Drugs and drug dealers," Gwen said.

"That would be my assumption," Michael said. "Little Tommy is probably wining and dining her to pick her brain on products, purveyors and international relationships."

"My guess is that she would be more than a match for him," Karen said. "Especially if she's been able to swim in those kinds of waters without being consumed by the large fishies with the sandpaper skin and multiple rows of teeth."

"Parents are both hedge fund managers," Michael said, "with sufficient resources to help her cruise through Middlebury for language study and MIT for science training. Can I make a suggestion?"

"Of course," Gwen said.

"I'd keep her under tight surveillance until we know whether or not she's a highly-paid consultant or a partner in the actual operations."

"Good idea," Karen said. "Where does she live?"

"At the intersection of Thirty-fourth and O," Michael said. "Large townhouse; just under 4 mil when she purchased it."

"Heart of Georgetown," Karen said. "I'll check the parking situation and see what I can do to tag her *Tesla*. And her putative salary at the embassy?"

"Hard to get that information," Michael said, "but the market would be mid to high five figures, not enough to spring for the townhouse."

"There are those rich parents…" Gwen said.

"Yes, but if she's getting an infinitesimal portion of the skim from a cartel operation, the 4 mil would be pocket change," Michael said.

"No doubt," Karen said. "Looks like a very naughty girl."

"Tommy's preferred pool," Gwen added.

CHAPTER SEVENTY-NINE

"I'll notify the Director," Gwen said.

"And I'll sit tight here and see if she stays the night," Karen answered.

Two hours later Karen received a message from Michael: "In case you're still up I did some more checking on Ms. Conwell's husband. Brad (yes, Brad) Phillips died under slightly suspicious circumstances. He skied into a thirty-foot pine tree at Vail. There was some thought that he may have strayed from the straight and narrow in their marriage (as well as on the mountain) because there were rumors that he was shot before he hurtled into the limbs and branches."

"Yes, I'm here," Karen typed. "Shot? They should have been able to prove that."

"Not with a gun or rifle," Mike replied. "The thought was that it may have been with a crossbow bolt."

"That would go right through him and be lost in a mountain of snow," Karen said.

"It would indeed," Michael said, "and the damage done by a blue spruce, Ponderosa pine, Douglas-fir or an Engelmann spruce would mask the effects of a bolt. He was skiing through the trees (Vail is known for those runs), so it was entirely plausible that he could fall off the beaten path and get shredded by the local flora."

"What do you call that," Karen asked, "a hard divorce?"

"Not sure," Michael said, "but it would certainly cut down on the paperwork and the endless negotiations."

"It would take some serious planning," Karen said, "or the help of a highly-skilled compadre."

"As we've been saying, those are the circles in which she is probably travelling."

"Another point," Karen said, "this is nothing exotic or traceable."

"You can buy them on *Amazon* for fifteen or twenty bucks," Michael said. "The crossbow will run you a couple hundred, but that would be a standard item in any serious assassin's arsenal. I figure they'd opt for the crossbow so that they're be no gunshot sound attracting unwanted attention. The soundless crossbow bolt would also remove any possibility (no matter how remote) of triggering an avalanche. Ms. Marilyn wouldn't want the scene to look like something out of a James Bond opening credits sequence. She'd go for the quiet shedding and impalement. The only sound would be a quiet crunch and a minute or so of whimpers."

"Thanks for the information, Mike. As always: great food for thought."

She sent a heavily-encrypted message to the Director who responded thirty minutes later. Everyone was working late that night.

"Thanks, Karen. The husband's murder was suspected but never proven, but we have a record of another event, a few years earlier. Our subject was in a posh hotel in Merida…"

"Mexico."

"*Si*. A man died of poisoning…"

"Bad tequila."

"Something like that. It could have been beer. He was drinking both. She was seated nearby and was interviewed by the municipal police. Her name popped on the INTERPOL report."

"Pretty heavy coverage for an event in a hotel bar."

"Indeed," the Director said, "but it seems that the deceased was an enforcer for the Jalisco cartel. That's somewhat odd because the Yucatan is one of the safer places in Mexico, but the cartel members vacation anywhere and everywhere. If you're in a nice place there are probably members nearby."

"Like the old British saying that if you're in London you're never more than six feet away from a rat," Karen said.

"Precisely," the Director said. "She was never charged. The bartender was taken in for questioning but eventually freed. Taking out a cartel member was probably viewed as a public service rather than a crime."

"So the bottom line is that she may have been a field operative before she was a puppet master."

"Exactly," the Director said. "Bad *mujer*."

"Female hombre?"

"Right," the Director answered.

"If she has the titular identification of an assistant to the Mexican ambassador, I hope we're keeping close eyes on their embassy."

"Obviously the observers could use some stronger lenses," the Director said. "Tell Michael we're in his debt. The more dots we connect the more interesting it becomes. Anyway, keep an eye on both of them and we'll see whether this is a partnership that's at the periphery of our principal operation or closer to its center."

"Will do, General," Karen said.

CHAPTER EIGHTY

Early the next morning Karen briefed Gwen. "I'll try to tag her car," Karen said, "and I'll set up some cameras by her home in Georgetown and at points of ingress and egress at the Mexican embassy."

"How far is that from the White House," Gwen asked, "three or four blocks?"

"Yes," Karen answered.

"Is that significant?"

"It could be," Karen responded.

Both Davis and Conwell hunkered down for the next eight days. Then Conwell booked a flight to San Diego that drew the instant interest of Michael's software.

"Interesting that she's flying commercial," Karen said, "considering the access she probably has to cartel money and her probable desire to travel incognito."

"Hiding in plain sight, perhaps," Gwen said. "If she's going to cross the border she'll be surrounded by hundreds of cars and can fade into the sand and cacti easily enough. It may be that she's actually on embassy business."

"Or using the embassy connection and the commercial flight as cover," Karen responded.

"Right. Whatever she's up to you can at least attempt to track her."

"I'll take an earlier flight," Karen said, "and be ready when she arrives."

"She's being picked up in a nondescript, black sedan, a *Buick*," Karen reported. "They're heading north rather than to the border."

"Did she get in the front seat or back seat?" Gwen asked.

"Back."

Thirty-five minutes later Karen called. "We're in La Jolla on Torrey Pines Road; the traffic is terrible."

"Posh neighborhood," Gwen said. "Are they at the beach?"

"No, they're not at the Cove; they're heading north into the La Jolla Shores area."

"By Scripps."

"Right."

"Nice beach there," Gwen said.

"Heading onto Inspiration Drive," Karen said.

"To be inspired is to be 'breathed into'; I would have thought Conwell's specialty was reversing the process."

Karen gave her the precise address.

"Give me a sec," Gwen said.

"Well, that's not surprising," Gwen said. "The property sold eight years ago to one Luis Aguilar. Modest price for the neighborhood: $24 mil. Let me check him out…"

"I'd try INTERPOL rather than the local Rotary Club," Karen said.

"You're reading my mind again," Gwen said.

"That was an easy guess," Karen said.

"OK. I'll give you the long and the short of it. The Sinaloa cartel had two leadership structures, one led by Ismael Zambada Garcia (aka El Mayo), a longstanding presence. El Mayo was betrayed and captured. The remaining structure is led by El Chapo's sons, the so-called 'Chapitos'. Luis Aguilar is an attorney for one of the sons, Ivan."

"Probably more like his consiglieri," Karen said.

"Right. So why is he receiving a visit from Ms. Conwell?"

"What do you think?"

"Well," Gwen said, "Jan Sol was linked (however tangentially) to the CJNG."

"The Jalisco New Generation cartel."

"Right. And assuming that the Boerlings have taken over Sol's operations they could be seeking some sort of partnership with the Sinaloans."

"Or threatening them," Karen said.

"Yes. 'There's a new sheriff in town' and he's got the juice of the vice-president of the U. S. of A, someone who can inflict serious damage on you and your operations, so stay the hell out of the way."

"Or perhaps something in between," Karen said. "The new sheriff has promised to provide you with a certain amount of hitherto unrealized protection; it will cost you X and that's our most-favored-nation-status rate."

"All possible," Gwen said, "but whatever the purpose of the meeting, the stench is palpable. This meeting is taking place between a serious cartel personage and an individual whose ties can be traced back to the residents of Number One Observatory Circle. Any way you slice it it's not a good look."

"There's a teensy bit of daylight between Davis' dinner table and a staff member of the Mexican embassy, but not enough that they'd all be comfortable seeing it as a lead story on tomorrow's edition of the WaPo."

"No," Gwen said, "but it's a nice piece of evidence for us. Another dot to connect. Another bit of information to raise the Director's comfort level if we need any more to justify our operation."

"That's interesting…" Karen said.

"What's that?"

"The meeting's over."

"It just started."

"Actually nineteen minutes ago," Karen said.

"Sounds more like an ultimatum meeting than a negotiation meeting."

Forty minutes later Conwell was back at the San Diego airport. An hour and fifteen minutes later she had fortified herself with a pastry and a $7.95 cup of coffee and boarded her return flight.

"Not even a single shot of tequila?" Gwen asked.

"She's cold," Karen said. "She's done all of these things before."

"Good work, as always," the Director said. "This is something that could be of use."

"Deflecting blame?" Gwen asked.

"If they're playing with that kind of fire it would not be implausible to assume that they were doing their best to avoid any serious burns."

"We'll keep up the surveillance and see if we can turn anything else," Gwen said.

"Gwen…"

"Yes, sir?"

"This is getting interesting."

VI

THE VOID

CHAPTER EIGHTY-ONE

For the next two weeks Gwen and Karen were forced to slog their way through the grit and puddles of blind alleys and ride in endless circles through box canyons. Sam suggested that the only thing holding up the wall separating their work stations was the fact that each was climbing their own side. Their diet now consisted largely of black coffee, which extended their workdays but exacerbated their frazzled nerves. Finally they received a call from Michael.

"News…" he said.

"We'll take anything you've got," Gwen said.

"I've got Scherl," he said, "or what is left of him. You know the Woodson woman…"

"Yes," Karen said, "the student type who was watching Scherl's house in the Boston suburbs. The one with links to our subject's wife."

"Well, I've been tracking her every few days. Don't ask me how I could get into each of her cell phone records, but, well, I did. She hasn't been in Concord for a week."

"Maybe Scherl's given her some time off," Gwen said.

"I don't think so," Michael said, "he's gone off to his eternal reward or, much more likely, the infernal regions."

"Scherl's dead?" Karen asked.

"He is no more. He is a late Scherl and he's no longer pining for the fjords."

"How? When?" Karen and Gwen said simultaneously.

"A week ago (in the formal records)," Michael answered. "He fell off a ladder, or so we're supposed to believe. No one filed an obituary. When Woodson left his house (his very posh house, the one that would have been nicer than anything she was likely to be able to afford) I just did some cursory checks. There was nothing in any of the local papers of Black Earth, Mazomanie or Madison but there was an official death record. It was short and sweet, called him Lawrence R., and listed the date of his death. I made some calls to local restaurants, identified myself as an old military buddy, and said that I had heard of his death but that there was no next of kin and I was just wondering what happened to old Bob. I called six places before I learned anything. One of the owners of a brew house had a brother in the city government. His assistant had written up the death, which was officially reported as accidental. You remember the garage next to his house?"

"Sure," Karen said. "It was metal, a pre-fab job."

"Well, apparently there was some kind of weather vane thingie on top that had broken loose in a heavy thunderstorm. There was a ladder leaning on the top of the garage near it. The right side of the ladder had sunk into moist soil and Scherl had fallen off and broken his neck when he landed. Fairly elaborate setup if he was murdered."

"I don't remember any weather vane on the garage," Karen said. "It was all very off-the-shelf and generic."

"They could have just put him in bed and have him eat his handgun," Gwen said, "or put him in a warm bath with a sharp razor blade. God knows he had plenty of guilt to justify killing himself…. On the other hand, the accident route would draw less attention and keep prying eyes fixed on the perils of living in a place where nearly every shower brings stormy weather with it. The Boerlings wouldn't want the public's attention being drawn to his criminal past."

"That's what I thought," Michael said.

"They're consolidating," Karen said. "Now that they've got Davis' sleazoid D.C. partner on the case they don't need Scherl for field work, especially when the field work involves liaison activities at a far higher pay grade with far higher stakes."

"If our instincts are right and the past is prologue, she'd also be available for wet work," Gwen said.

"One less person in the organization whose potentially loose lips could scuttle the overall operation," Karen said.

"No room now for crude operatives," Gwen said. "The pros are in place; they're few in number and they're dealing with the Sinaloa cartel, not some bit players who simply need to be intimidated. I'll let the Director know."

"I'm glad you called," he said. "I need to talk to you as soon as possible anyway."

CHAPTER EIGHTY-TWO

"We'll need some time on this one. I'll come earlier than usual and we can work into the night if we have to. Unfortunately, I can't be there until tomorrow. I have a dinner meeting with the AG and I don't want to raise any suspicions by cancelling it."

That was all that he said and both Karen and Gwen returned to fully-caffeinated mode, wondering what had happened, what dots had been connected, what plans had been laid, or what news or intelligence had surfaced.

The next day he arrived at 4:00 and they had a long discussion before dinner, fortified with some seriously-aged *Dalmore* single malt.

"As you know," he said, "I report to the DOJ but Homeland Security has its own cabinet position and they enjoy exercising their independence and authority. Fortunately, I have a back channel or two and can usually remain apprised of anything they would prefer to keep to themselves. Needless to say, what I have to tell you has to remain completely secure, not because it's earth-shaking but because I want to protect my informants.

"I say that it's not earth-shaking, but it is somewhat strange; that's why I bring it to you. The details are sketchy, presumably to protect the informants, but I think you'll see the importance of the event for us. As you know, the Sinaloa people don't compete with the coyotes. In their price range the life savings of a would-be immigrant from central America is budget dust. The drug trade brings in the wealth 'beyond the dreams of avarice' and if someone suggests a plan for a new revenue stream it takes a large pile of currency to get their attention."

"But someone has," Gwen said.

"So it would seem," the Director responded. "Six days ago a chopper landed in a mostly-deserted area in the north end of San Diego county. It contained a small number of individuals, probably around a dozen. They were all women in their teens or early twenties…"

"Sex trafficking," Karen said.

"High end," the Director answered. "Not desperate mothers with children in tow. My informants believe that they were taken against their will, possibly by the Corsican mafia, who then proceeded to market them throughout the world. The language of the kidnapped women is unfamiliar, by design. They don't kidnap English, French or Spanish-speaking women."

"Makes it harder for them to escape and harder for them to make contact with individuals in foreign communities," Gwen said. "I remember seeing clips from some old news report, where young girls were taken to world capitals and rented to low-end johns, more by the minute than by the hour. They couldn't communicate in the local languages and they were largely kept drugged, worked until they were burned out and then disposed of. Pure evil; the lowest of the low."

"Right," Karen said. "I remember that. It could well have been one of Sol's operations. The story took place in Paris, I think. Maybe on *60 Minutes?*"

"Yes," Gwen said. "We talked about operations like that earlier. Mike had some information on Sol; he's been in that particular kind of business. He may even have been the inspiration for this new franchise."

"Well…" the Director said, "this is apparently much more high end. My informants believe that the women were from Slovenia, but that hasn't been formally confirmed. The business model is more or less the same, but the prices are far higher and the value, per woman, makes it worth the cartel's time. That's not the end of the story…"

Gwen and Karen refilled their glasses along with the Director's.

"One of the women could speak English. Apparently she attempted to organize an escape. The cartel members had transferred the women from the chopper to a small bus, to take them up the 5 to L.A. and when they learned that she had tried to free the others they isolated her and made an example of her."

"I'm not sure I want to hear this," Gwen said.

"No, you probably shouldn't, but it's essential. They stripped her, beat her to death and nailed her to a set of parallel trees, in crucifixion fashion. They then drove the busload of remaining women past her."

"*Pour encourager les autres*," Gwen said.

"Yes," the Director said, "but they weren't entirely successful. One woman escaped in L.A. and was eventually debriefed by DHS. Unfortunately, my sources were not present for the discussions, but I believe that they are placed in sufficiently significant positions that we can have confidence in the broad outlines of the story."

"And the conclusions are plain," Karen asked. "The cartel feels it can take such risks within our country and they can utilize the terror and intimidation techniques—hanging people from bridges, and so on—that they regularly utilize in Mexico. Do you think they've been greenlighted in some way?"

"So it would seem," the Director said. "The woman who escaped and was interrogated by the DHS agents reported seeing an Anglo woman speaking to the bus driver in L.A. DHS doesn't know who she is, because she was wrapped in scarves and wore large sunglasses in order to frustrate their facial rec software…"

"But she would be unable to conceal her height, weight, possible age and, perhaps, some wisps of hair color…"

"Yes," the Director said, "and those correspond with the general description of your Ms. Conwell."

"The person authorized to give the cartel the green light," Karen said.

"Quite possibly," the Director said. "I would not characterize this as indisputable evidence, the sort that would stand up to scrutiny in a court of law, but it's the kind of evidence that I am happy to have for our prospective operation. It's horrific, to be sure, but what we are proposing to do is equally serious, at least in the larger scheme of things. Of course, I keep returning to my original premise: someone has attempted to kill one of my senior agents. I don't like that and I don't care who attempted to do it…"

"A criminal is a criminal, no matter how large his or her desk and office," Karen said.

"Still a tad dicey," Gwen said, smiling. "When I was in college my roommate was close friends with a woman from rural North Carolina. Her uncle had been imprisoned for murder after he drove into a gas station, walked up to a man pumping gas and proceeded to pump four 9mm rounds into his upper torso. The uncle reported that the man had threatened to kill him a month earlier, so he pled self-defense. The jury did not agree with his plea."

The Director laughed quietly and took a sip of his scotch. "Awkward," he said, "but if I recall, your assassins took it a step further. "And there's the matter of Peggy O'Connor and Maryellen Blanchard. Disgusting. And they doubtless took out Grayson, Scherl, et al., but killing innocent women and crucifying an innocent woman…prostituting innocent women…Gwen, you're a soldier; Karen, you're a soldier. If anyone tries to hurt you I'm going to defend you to the death, but this kind of callous, vicious, evil behavior…the attack on civilians…that brings up the primal urges. What are we doing if we're not here to defend the defenseless? This is simply intolerable and there is no way that we can stand down."

"I don't think you need to convince us, General," Karen said. "We're just waiting for our orders."

CHAPTER EIGHTY-THREE

"Time to go operational," the Director said. "This will require significant planning."

"And possibly some external cooperation, but we would have to keep that to an absolute minimum," Gwen said.

"We should get Boerling's daily schedule," Karen said. "We have to find some patterns that will help us to be able to plan. Unfortunately, that was far easier back when Barack Obama was president; he saw the release of his and Biden's schedules as an indicator of transparency, but they're much more cautious now. They'll list the big things, leak things to the press when they consider it politically advantageous, but they withhold a lot of the things in which we would be interested."

"Your associate in Salt Lake might be of help here," the Director said.

"We'll check with him first," Gwen said. "At the least he might be able to hack into Eleanor's schedule; the word on the street has always been that she plays a far greater role in her husband's shadowy activities than anyone would assume."

"She's the money," Karen said. "She's always been the money and if there's anything that secures Carlton's attention it's green and carried in thick, banded stacks."

"But let's remember our amateur psychologizing," the Director said. "Securing his own money—through any means necessary and possible— is the way he proves his manhood."

"So we have thought," Gwen said. "And our assumption concerning their fatal flaw probably still holds: for each of them…there's never enough."

"Her parents had always been flush," the Director said, "but so were those of most of her classmates at Mt. Holyoke. Have you heard the story of Tricia Bates?"

Both Karen and Gwen shook their heads No.

"Tricia was a classmate of Ellie's. Her father was an investment banker in Manhattan and he was sued for a number of shady practices. The lawyer who handled the case against him in the civil trial was Tommy Turner, at Skadden, Arps."

"Ellie's daddy," Gwen said.

"Yep," the Director said. "Turner was a shark and after he sunk his teeth in he turned Bobby Bates every way but loose. Tricia made it her goal to make Ellie's life a living hell. They got rid of sororities at Mt. Holyoke over a hundred years ago, but there are a number of fashionable clubs. Tricia did her best to block Ellie from ever achieving what Ellie thought was her natural right to popularity and prominence, accusing her of everything from cheating on exams to sleeping with blue-collar dining hall staff of the female persuasion."

"And what was Ellie's response?" Karen asked.

"It was never proven that Ellie was part of the action, but Tricia was crippled in a cross-country race. She had to leave school for a semester of rehab and returned with a permanent brace, a cane and the realization that she had been bested—for now and for the future."

"I've never heard that story," Gwen said.

"The press has always been friendly to the Boerlings," the Director said, "even back in the day, and Ellie has always been the nastiest bit of the family businesses. If your friend in Salt Lake can identify a time in which both of the Boerlings are scheduled to walk into the common line of fire that could constitute a second public-spirited act, not a case of collateral damage."

Both Gwen and Karen held their expressions.

"Seriously," Gwen said. There was an implied question mark in the statement.

"Absolutely," the Director said. "Whatever Carlton is doing to turn his office into an instrument of self-gain, Ellie is there for the ride, and I wouldn't doubt for a moment that she is directing the operations behind the scenes."

"That complicates things a bit," Gwen said, "but it also serves as additional motivation."

"I thought you might come to see that," the Director said. "Remember, the decision to have two snipers do their very best to snuff out your life was probably made with her approval."

After a series of cups of strong coffee the Director wished them a good night and returned to his home in McLean. The moment he had left the SCIF Karen turned to Gwen and said, "He's serious about this."

"He is, indeed," Gwen said, "and I think he's also trying to suppress any personal involvement he has with the case. You know about his son…"

"The soldier?"

"Yes. Walter Jr. He was wounded in an action in the Middle East that Boerling had supported, at least according to the few investigative reporters that had covered the story. The president was waffling and Boerling came on all hawkish. The operation was a debacle and Major Gradison's military career came to an end, along with the use of his legs. Dad kept his powder dry and played the good soldier, as did Walter Jr., but he has a long memory and a notable thirst for justice…"

"Something we share," Karen said.

"Indeed," Gwen responded.

CHAPTER EIGHTY-FOUR

Karen called Michael and asked him to make this search his highest priority.

"Not to worry," he said. "I'll also check the schedules of both Davis and Conwell and see what surfaces. I can also try to get into the devices of the other staff around them, especially the junior staff. The farther they are down the food chain the more careless they can be. Young lips sink ships, especially young lips that are ignorant, preoccupied and arrogant as well. What we're actually doing here is not searching for a single fact; we're creating a crossword puzzle, but we're doing it without seeing the actual puzzle."

"And you're a *New York Times* puzzle expert," Gwen said. "What is that called?"

"A cruciverbalist," Michael said, "but the serious solvers don't use that term. Too pretentious."

"Any way you slice it, we're counting on you, Michael," Karen said.

"I always give you two my best work," Michael said. "It's as close as I get to having a romantic relationship."

Both Karen and Gwen smiled. Karen said, "We know the feeling."

"Bureau love," Gwen added.

"Let's get the bastards," Michael said.

"This will be difficult," Gwen said, "but not impossible. We will have to be involved; this can't be farmed out. However, we'll have the distinct advantage that Scherl has been taken off the board. Both he and his partner Grayson would have recognized me, but the Boerlings assume that I'm dead and probably wouldn't be able to identify me if I bumped into them on the street."

"And I'm a ghost," Karen said. "Presumably we'll deal with them in an indirect way; this won't be Vito Corleone confronting Don Fanucci alone in an apartment building."

"Ships passing in the night," Gwen said. "Make that heavily-armed ships."

"Works for me," Karen said, "but it will be more 'run silent, run deep'. We don't want to attract attention."

"Like the grand prix drivers going into a turn," Gwen said, "in slow and out fast."

"You're already planning this," Karen said.

"As a matter of fact, I have been giving it some thought," Gwen answered.

"Ready to share?"

"Not just yet. There are a lot of details to cover, but let me have a little more time to work on those."

"Want a nightcap?"

"I'll have another sip of that *Dalmore* if you will," Gwen said.

"I'll have two fingers of it and two ice cubes," Karen said.

"Works for me," Gwen responded.

For the first time that evening they actually put their feet up on the coffee table and sipped their drinks. Karen was finally off duty, at least for five or ten minutes, while Gwen looked as if she had been rejuvenated and was ready to reach for her *Sig* and shoulder rig, leave the rehab facility and walk onto the battlefield. There was a distant look in her eyes, but it was a reflective look, one that recalled the dead innocents and the weeks spent with tubes and needles in her arm and shoulder with glowing monitors at her back. If she still wasn't quite at 100 percent she was close enough for the drive and the adrenalin to carry her over the line.

"How are you feeling?" Karen asked.

"Ready to go to work," Gwen answered.

CHAPTER EIGHTY-FIVE

Michael called in three days. "As Karen knows, Conwell paid a visit to the Naval Observatory this morning. Davis was not there, but neither was Eleanor. This was a quick check-in, a meeting in a secure location that was probably little more than a signal of fealty to Boerling."

"A vassal or evil servant, licking his boots and slobbering over his ego," Gwen said.

"Exactly. Something like, 'Mission accomplished, sir. Is there anything else I can do for you?' With Boerling responding but not looking up from his desk: 'No, not at this time; just stay in touch.'"

"Any links between the two of them help solidify our case," Gwen said. "Karen had already noted it, but continue to pass along anything at all, no matter how remotely relevant you think it might be."

"Will do," Michael said. "I'm working on that Woodson woman…"

"Scherl's housesitter at his home in the Boston suburbs."

"Right. She's in D.C. now. Did you know that?"

"I didn't. Is she working for the Boerlings?"

"Yes," Michael said. "Low-level staffer. More of a gofer I would say."

"New kid in town; may not be as careful about the plans and protocols."

"Right, and if she knew about Scherl's untimely fall and who was behind it…well, it might give her a false sense of security, you know, the belief that someone at the top level is fully inoculated against prosecution…or even observation or investigation."

"Good idea. What's she been up to so far?"

"Nothing earth-shattering. She took Ellie's Beemer in for service yesterday. Simple check up and oil change, if it matters…"

"It matters that you can provide that level of detail, Mike. Thanks."

"Well, the only other thing was that she ran out for some breakfast sandwiches this morning. From *Loeb's Deli*. Must be a fave of the Boerlings. Eggs and cheese. Paid with her own credit card. Don't know if she was reimbursed. If I know them they probably stiffed her. They know how to choke the eagle."

"That they do," Gwen said. "Anyway, stay in touch, Mike. I appreciate your update."

Gwen checked in with Karen, who was working her surveillance cameras (nothing fresh to report) and had some lunch with Sam. Clam chowder and some salad with a crab cake resting atop the small hill of fresh, chilled lettuce.

"Very nice," Gwen said. "My compliments to Chef Julie."

"She does a great job," Sam said. "Glad we could get together. I wanted to tell you that the Director has asked me to keep some distance from your operation. I understand the general outline of what you're trying to do, but he wants me to have deniability. You know, keep the circle as small and tight as possible. I told him I'm here for you and if there's anything I can do to offer support…well, all you have to do is ask."

"Much appreciated," Gwen said. "I do have one question…"

"Sure…"

"I assume you have a full dispensary as part of the rehab center…"

"We do. I mean, we don't do transplants or anything super complicated, but anything that you could characterize as falling within the general bounds of tertiary care we do. Quaternary care? Not so much."

"There may come a time when I might ask for some medications."

"Ask and you shall receive," Sam said, "with no questions asked."

"Again, much appreciated," Gwen said.

"I also wanted to say, vis `a vis your general operation…I'm completely supportive."

"Thanks," Gwen said. "There's always a temptation to waffle, but we can't do that, not when thousands of our fellow citizens are dying of drug overdoses and innocent women are being tortured and prostituted…"

"And Bureau agents are targets for assassination…"

"Yes, that too," Gwen said.

"How about some dessert?" Sam asked. "Something served cold."

"I could do that," Gwen said.

CHAPTER EIGHTY-SIX

After lunch Gwen went back to her work station, fortified herself with some black coffee, and did a series of *Google* searches. She tried to find some information on Dana Woodson but the only thing that kept popping up was a graduation picture with Ellie Boerling standing in the foreground. 'Dana's not a shadowy figure who's a secret ninja warrior,' Gwen thought to herself. 'She's a bona fide nonentity who's been promoted into her current role for services rendered with regard to Scherl. How much does she really know? Probably next to nothing. Ellie's smart enough to keep their side hustles secret. The inner circle is now down to the Conwell woman and the weasel, Davis. And he may be circling the drain. The only problem is that he has enough of a D.C. presence to draw attention. Still, his clock may be ticking; with Conwell on the team they don't really need him anymore. Conwell can do it all: field work, wet work, language work.'

As she tapped away on her keyboard she started to feel some pain in her back, neck and shoulder and decided to try some stretching exercises, followed by a power nap on the nearby couch. She fell asleep instantly, even with the caffeine coursing through her veins, and awakened an hour and a half later. "I must have been more tired than I thought," she said aloud, and returned to her computer. Karen had checked in via a secure site, reporting on Davis.

"Nothing huge to report," Karen said. "He was briefly at the Observatory, but simply dropped off something to a Secret Service agent there. It looked like a book. Probably a gofer run."

"Interesting. I hadn't forgotten the fact entirely, but we will have to remember the Secret Service detail which will be accompanying the Boerlings."

"At least they're easily identified," Karen said.

"True," Gwen answered. "They look all burly and serious, but I've always wondered…with the gorilla appearances, why do they always seem to make more money than we do? Because they wear those earpieces so well? It can't be because they have a solid performance record. Back in the day they may have, but lately—not so much."

"Good question," Karen said. "Maybe because they've convinced someone that the work that they do is highly technical? They still do a little with counterfeiting but they spend more time on other stuff—credit card fraud, wire and bank fraud, computer network breaches, ransomware…cyber-enabled financial crime."

"More likely because they report to Homeland Security now, instead of Treasury, but I'm not going to worry about it," Gwen said. "We can work out the fact of their presence when we have a better sense of our setting. If we catch him in a private locale where he's not conducting any official business there probably won't be more than two or three agents along for the ride."

"The key is for us to be non-threatening and incognito," Karen said. "Let the agents chill with their coffee and sweet rolls while we do a workaround."

"Exactly," Gwen answered.

Karen and Gwen were eating dinner (pure Americana: steak, baked potatoes, green beans and strawberry shortcake) when the call came in from Michael. His opening words echoed the tones of Jane Lynch, "She *is* the weakest link."

"I presume you're talking about Ms. Woodson," Gwen said.

"The very same," Michael answered.

"What has she done?" Karen asked.

"She's made an electronic note to herself, forgetting that it's impossible to trace something composed with paper and pencil."

"Heavy duty information?" Gwen asked.

"Possibly," Michael answered. "She's made a note reminding herself that she has to arrange a dinner for the B's and MC."

"Celebratory, perhaps?" Karen asked. "A reward for her most recent crimes?"

"Can't say for sure," Michael said, "but it has that odor. People like the Boerlings…they consider it a great honor to allow an underling to be in their presence."

"No mention of Tommy Boy?" Karen asked.

"Not in the note; just the B's and MC."

"Hopefully they go off campus for the party," Gwen said. "With the house staff at the veep's residence there would be nothing to do in the way of arrangements except to say 'put out another plate for dinner and use the better china.'"

"Right," Karen said. "When is the event, Mike?"

"In two weeks."

"That will give us time to do our own planning," Gwen said.

"Give me deniability on the details," Michael said. "Brief me afterwards if you feel comfortable doing so."

"If things go according to plan you may be briefing us," Gwen said.

"I don't understand," Michael said.

"We plan to be in the wind," Gwen responded.

CHAPTER EIGHTY-SEVEN

"I have to put her in my full surveillance loop," Karen said. "She only surfaced recently so I'll touch base again with Mike and see where she's hanging her hat at night."

"Already got her address," he said. "It's a lovely one but the digs are modest. If you cross Chain Bridge and go up the hill into McLean on Dolley Madison you'll see a private road that goes off on the right. Black Jack Bouvier had a house there. Across the street is a lovely manse; she doesn't live there, but it has a small apartment over the garage…"

"Sounds like the kind of place you'd only know about via private connections. Very private," Gwen said.

"The owner is a lady who lunches," Michael said, "what you call your basic clubwoman; her clubs include major fundraisers for the Kennedy Center and the political party of the Boerlings."

"Close enough for me," Karen said. "This is Ellie pulling some strings. I'd bet serious money on it. Let me assemble some gear; I'll check it all out in the evening, when I won't draw as much attention."

"And you'll keep an eye out for any devices designed to detect uninvited visitors?" Michael asked.

"Absolutely. I've got better night goggles than the Army's PVS-14's."

"I thought you might," Michael said.

"As always, we're in your debt," Gwen said.

"I live to serve," Michael answered.

When Karen returned in the early morning Gwen greeted her with a carafe of hot coffee and some blueberry muffins.

"Mission accomplished," Karen said. "It was a tiny, efficiency apartment. I was actually able to install a listening device outside of her window along with a couple of cameras. The former may be of much better use than the latter. More important, perhaps, is the fact that I was able to put one of those pinpricks on her car. They're not allowing her to park in the garage; that's reserved for the owner's *Mercedes*, *Beemer* and *Range Rover*. Her clunker still had its Massachusetts license plate. Not a challenge to identify."

"Score a big one for the A team," Gwen said. "If she drives around town scouting possible locations for the attagirl dinner we'll know where as well as when. The more time we have to plan, the better. I'm sure Ellie will want to put her seal of approval on the final details; they're not going to get in a large black SUV and tell the driver to take them to the nearest *Burger King*. Their security detail will want as much planning time as we will, but another few days would always be welcome."

"Exactly," Karen said. "I'll also let the Director know that we're making progress. Can I help you with your planning?"

"I'm still working on the general outline; it'll depend ultimately on our setting. And I want you to be able to focus on your surveillance. I'm turning over possibilities in my head. Lots of churning. Maybe I should cut back on the caffeine and sketch with a pencil and paper. Help myself focus, reduce distractions and crackling neurons."

"OK," Karen said, "if I can do anything just let me know."

"Will do."

Karen returned to her computer station with a plate of muffins and a steaming refill in her coffee mug, while Gwen sat down on the couch with a yellow legal pad and a freshly-sharpened pencil. As she scribbled she thought about Michael's comment to the effect that he was constructing a crossword puzzle without the puzzle's actual outlines. 'So am I,' she thought to herself, but the basic principles were clear. She and Karen would need access to their targets without drawing attention or raising suspicions. They would have to work around the security detail, accomplish their mission and bid them all a silent sayonara. The method would need to be relatively inconspicuous; they weren't going to bludgeon their targets with spiked maces. Finally, they would need to limit the attention of the press and reduce the ultimate realities for the eyes of the president and a few members of her inner circle. Ideally the press would be kept in the dark entirely, but there was another alternative: accomplish the mission in such a way that the compliant press would suppress any embarassing information that they might be able to obtain. In slow and out fast, with no one asking about the masked woman and her Indian companion. 'This is going to be tricky,' she thought, as she continued to scribble.

CHAPTER EIGHTY-EIGHT

Karen's pinpricks worked well but the information that they yielded was unexceptional. Davis did his usual high end shopping and joined his parents for dinner at their Washington home in Georgetown. There was no face to face contact with the Boerlings. Conwell took a few days off and rented an *Airbnb* on the eastern shore at a modest $595/night. Woodson drove to and from the Naval Observatory faithfully, leaving each morning at 7:15 and returning 12 hours later. The Boerlings were hard taskmasters. Her go-to nearby restaurant in McLean was *Rocco's*, a vinyl, red-checkered tablecloth place with reliable food and modest prices that were easy on her limited budget.

Gwen continued to write and draw and scribble on her legal pad, asked Sam about the availability of certain drugs, switched from coffee to reduced sugar orange juice and checked in regularly with Michael, whose skills were exceeded only by his patience. On the third day he called in.

"The weakest link has done us a solid."

"We've been hoping for that," Gwen said

"She's been keeping notes in her phone again and just jotted something down for the evening of the attagirl dinner…"

"And it's…?" Karen asked.

"It's Q-DC-P."

"*Quaglino's*, Dupont Circle, on P," Gwen said.

"So it would seem," Michael said. "Returning to the scene of the original crime. Fine irony, don't you think?"

"Makes perfect sense," Gwen said. "The potential observers have been eliminated, or so Ellie believes. There's that nice private room on the mezzanine for cover and concealment. They can enter by the back door, position their security detail just below the stairs, out of earshot but close enough to protect them. They're not going to let the security staff listen in on their private conversations. All of that privacy and they'll still have room for a *Caprese* salad, some *Agnolotti in Brodo*, a *Bistecca alla Fiorentina* and a *canollo* for anyone who's left room."

"And a final sip of Anisette or Limoncello," Karen added, "the emphasis being on *final*."

"You're making my mouth water," Michael said.

"We'll treat you when you come to town," Karen said.

"And even let you finish your meal," Gwen added.

"I want to go back in," Karen said. "I still have the original blueprints, but I want to refresh my spatial memory and familiarize myself with some of the details."

"Give me a day to think this through," Gwen said. "I'll give you my list of things to check on."

"Done," Karen said.

Gwen was ready with her list in four hours.

"OK," Karen said, checking her notepad. "You want me to see where the hat check facility is and whether or not they have a rack for coats, hats and packages in the private dining room. You want me to see what they use to grate cheese and grind black pepper. You want me to see if there's a lock on the private dining room door. You want me to check on their brand of mineral water, both still and sparkling. You want me to see if there's a sink in the storage room and if they have a refrigerator there. You also want a list of the service staff, with their assigned duties and current addresses…"

"We've got the personal info. on the owner, don't we?"

Karen shuffled through the earlier pages of her notepad. "Clement

Wilburn…yes. Nice digs in Kalorama. Purchased for the floor space and remodeled to a fare-thee-well. Down to the studs, just like his Italian restaurant. Not far from Ivanka's place in the neighborhood."

"He has a couple other restaurants and some sort of wine bar thingie on Dewey Beach, as I remember," Gwen said.

"Yes. We wondered whether he was gay or not. Want me to check?"

"No, don't bother. He probably picked the site there and the site at Dupont Circle based on the level of prices he could charge for his food and drink."

"Anything else you want me to check on?" Karen asked.

"Yes, see if they have a supply of Naloxone at the restaurant. Probably marketed as *Narcan*. I think the *Evzio* brand has been discontinued in the U.S."

"You mean like in a box on the wall."

"Yes, you sometimes see them there. Sometimes they keep it behind the maître d's station by the front door. Oh, and one other thing…"

"What's that?" Karen asked.

"Check on the best ingress/egress routes if we find ourselves close to the security detail as they're racing up the stairs and peeing down their pantslegs."

"I think I see where you're going with all this," Karen said.

"Still need to polish some details," Gwen said. "Meanwhile I have to meet with Sam."

Sam was able to supply all of the materials that Gwen required and promised to begin the process immediately. When they got together later that evening for dinner they kept the conversation light and personal. Gwen told stories about her father's life as a lawyer and some of the oddball clients he had represented. Karen talked about her studies as an engineer at UCLA and how different the current climate there had become. Sam spoke of his own training as a lawyer: "I never practiced, of course. Never even took the bar exam. I had read that Edgar always recruited lawyers and accountants, so I figured that was my required road to success in the Bureau."

Then he added, "I take it that you two fine young ladies are about to go operational on the case of your lives."

"I don't know about the fine and young," Gwen said, "but we do have a job of work that we're going to perform in the not too distant future."

"I gathered as much," he said. "I got a call from the Director. He wants to meet for breakfast tomorrow morning. He doesn't usually do breakfast."

"He wants to keep us sober," Gwen said.

"I find that encouraging," Karen added.

CHAPTER EIGHTY-NINE

The Director arrived at 7:00 a.m. and requested some yogurt, rye toast and black coffee. Karen and Gwen followed his lead, even though they had been counting on something more substantial.

"I'm not going to whitewash this," he said. "You're opening yourself to considerable exposure. Necessary exposure, I believe, and in the most important of causes. If we neutralize these activities we reduce the death toll from drugs and the human suffering toll from trafficking to a noteworthy degree. And that is most likely our only option, since the pivotal figures are not subject to negotiation, bargaining or even naked threats. Their greed is exceeded only by their arrogance and ruthlessness. The bottom line is that this is ultimately a binary proposition: we can allow them to continue or we can stop them. Summarily. If we attempt to go through normal channels and expose them legally (the lawyers and paperwork route) they will drag us through the deep mud, reduce or destroy our effectiveness, challenge us to adduce precise evidence and, ultimately, have the time to develop new mechanisms and workarounds to continue their operations. The risks of a lethal operation are obvious. The task we have set ourselves may be a noble one, but it is also, shall we say…fraught."

"I believe that we both understand that, sir," Gwen said, "and we'll do our best to reduce exposure and risk. If it goes belly-up we'll deal with the consequences."

"With my help," Gradison said. "You can count on that."

"As you know, sir, part of the plan involves incentives to contain the details," Gwen said.

"You mean sweep them under a palace-sized Persian rug," Gradison said.

"Yes, sir, in a manner of speaking. We would disincent both the administration and their sympathetic press," Gwen answered.

"They do go hand in hand," Gradison said. "My guess is that the administration would leak just enough of the key information to insulate themselves later, when the full news of Boerling and his wife's activities begin to become public."

"In order to persuade the voters that his demise was in the public interest," Karen said.

"Yes. We do have some factors that can be leveraged. He's never been particularly popular and his wife even less so (to the extent that anyone knows her real personality and machinations). The drug and trafficking issues are both significant losers that no one supports. The shock will come from the realization of *his* involvement in them and the fact that it had gone largely unnoticed and completely unreported. The good thing is that this has all happened so suddenly; the timing is a significant point in our favor. Sol's death is recent and the belief that criminal opportunists quickly fill available vacuums will be an obvious media narrative. Sol has funded the party of the administration and he was not unknown to the vice president and his presumed better half. They are, in short, connected. And the cartels would not be expected to roll over and play dead. Suspicions concerning his removal could easily fall on a host of other bad actors."

"He was just getting started with his criminal activities and he was trying to punch above his weight. The cartels are ready for their closeup as the likeliest candidates to take the fall," Gwen said.

"Yes, far more than the criminal gangs."

"My plan would keep that possibility open," Gwen said.

"I'll want to know the precise details," Gradison said, "not to supersede them or second-guess you, but just for the opportunity to offer my input."

"Which we would welcome," Gwen said.

He offered both of them an avuncular smile and offered to refill their coffee cups. They each took a few sips and he began to speak again. "How about makeup? Does Sam have anyone here who could help with that?'

"You mean disguises, sir?" Gwen asked.

"Yes."

"I thought Karen and I would dye our hair, pencil our eyebrows and wear some glasses that would distract onlookers from focusing directly on our faces."

"Good start," Gradison said, "but I can secure some professional help for you. The trick is always to not overdo. We have a woman who was rescued from a life of sex slavery in the now distant past. She handles only the most sensitive cases and she is beyond reproach. I'll ask her to swing by on the morning of the operation and help you with your preparations. You should also prepare yourselves with names, addresses and backstories in the event that you're detained by the security detail. Practice your responses to their likely questions. Of course, I expect you to be able to elude them, but never forget the four P's…"

"Prior Planning/Proper Performance," Karen said.

"You see, I always said you were a soldier," Gradison said, as Karen smiled.

"I always thought there were 6 P's," Gwen said: "Prior Planning Precludes Piss-Poor Performance."

"Point, set and match," Gradison said. "Do you need any forged documentation?"

"Michael Liu will prepare the basics," Gwen said.

"Excellent. How about weapons?"

"I thought we'd leave them behind," Gwen said. "Their presence would be compromising if we had to interact with the security detail."

"Exactly," Gradison said. "In a professional kitchen you could find a host of field expedients."

"So I thought," Gwen said.

"You'll have a car, of course."

"Yes," Karen said.

"If you can't simply drive away you might consider taking along some cigarettes. When people are under stress they try to get to a place that's most like home. In this case that would be a personal vehicle. Puffing on cigarettes is common with restaurant staffs, just as it's common for anyone seeking the primal lollipop that will relax them. Sitting in a car, smoking, says 'we couldn't take the stress anymore, but obviously we're innocent because we're not in a rush to leave the scene.'"

"Excellent advice, sir," Gwen said.

"Scoping out and utilizing criminal behaviors is my long suit," Gradison said, smiling.

"I do have a question," Karen said.

"Shoot."

"We were planning to include the Conwell woman in the action…"

"I think she's earned it and fully deserves it," Gradison said.

"We hoped you would say that," Gwen said.

"And if anyone else should join them? Davis, for example…"

Karen and Gwen waited for his next statement.

"In for a dime, in for a dollar. He's colluded with Conwell; Conwell is the embodiment of evil-for-hire."

The women both nodded their approval.

"I've got to get back to my day job," the Director said. "Fill me in on the details as they develop. Don't hesitate to seek my help. And don't forget the dimensions of your mission…you're truly doing the Lord's work in the Devil's town."

CHAPTER NINETY

"That was helpful," Karen said.

"And reassuring," Gwen said. "Ready to go into protective custody or the witness protection plan for a decade or two?"

"I don't believe that will happen," Karen said. "I've got faith in you. You're the Bureau's premier tracker. You've run this bastard to ground and it's time for him to face the reckoning."

"And wifey too, along with the hired help," Gwen added.

That evening Karen replicated her last trip to *Quaglino's*. As she was driving back to the rehab facility she called Gwen on a secure line. "I'll work my way down from what I remember on your list, but I want to keep my eyes on the Shirley Highway drivers. They're as dangerous as we are…"

Gwen smiled. "I've got my checklist."

"OK. For still mineral water they do *Acqua Panna* and for sparkling they do *San Pellegrino*."

"Generic enough," Gwen said.

"Right, and no *Narcan* on site. I even checked Wilburn's office."

"That's helpful," Gwen said. "How about the hat check situation?"

"There's a room downstairs, but also a very nice, solid mahogany set-up in the private dining room. I can't see the security detail permitting any use of the public space on the first level."

"Me either," Gwen said. "Cheese graters and pepper mills?"

"They use those old *Mouli* jobbies for cheese," Karen said. "Most of them are now plastic, but you can get stainless versions on *Amazon* for 20 bucks."

"The thing with the turning knob on the side and the arm on top that holds the cheese in place over the circular grater."

"Exactly. And for pepper mills…strictly generic. Black wood, 9 inch. Available anywhere."

"Lock on the private dining room?"

"Perfunctory," Karen said, "but with the wait staff coming and going I doubt that anyone would ever use it. And while we're on the subject…I've got the names, addresses and phone numbers of the staff. They were all on top of Wilburn's desk and they were all written in pencil."

"Hard to get good help (and keep them) these days," Gwen said.

"Right. And I have the name of the external company he uses for payroll, fringe benefits and so on. It looks like the sous chef handles the day-to-day work assignments."

"That leaves us with the storage room."

"Yes," Karen said, "filled with glassware, china, starched table cloths and linen napkins. Like last time there were some cooking staples, principally large cans of olive oil. Actually, there were fewer this time; business must be good; it's time to reorder. There is a sink. Tiny. Like the kind in the galley of a cheap boat, but with hot and cold running water…"

"Excellent," Gwen said. "How about refrigeration?"

"Again, tiny, one step up from the kind of box you'd have in your college dorm room."

"Functional?"

"Yes," Karen said, "and it was turned on. They keep most of the bottled water near the bar downstairs, but they use the mini-fridge as a backup for the private diners. There's a little freezer space in it (presumably for a quick chill of the red wine to bring it down to cellar temperature), but it's mostly filled with bottled water. By the way, I made sure that there were equal parts still and sparkling."

"God bless you," Gwen said.

"Just for the heck of it I checked the dining room table for dust. There was a tiny coating. I don't think that they use that room every night."

"No, and the security detail will want the room locked down after they make their checks…not that there's that much to check. No windows, no prominent nooks and crannies for IED's. It's basically just your enclosed room, at least the way I remember it."

"You remember correctly," Karen said.

"Oh no…" Gwen said, "that was stupid. What was I thinking?"

"Servers' uniforms? I brought us a couple," Karen said.

"You're the best," Gwen said.

"I don't like to brag, but…"

"It's not bragging if you always remember to do it," Gwen said.

CHAPTER NINETY-ONE

"How much time until we begin the serious rehearsals?" Karen asked.

"Two and a half days," Gwen answered. "In the meantime we should check on which of the wait staff are undocumented. If we tell them to stay home on the night of the operation they will be less likely to challenge the order, particularly if we indicate that there have been rumors of a sweep by the authorities. We can then tell the sous chef that we were called by a staffer from the vice president's office and asked to come in for the special event. With the right winks and nudges he'll perceive that this is all above his pay grade. If he balks we can show him our documentation from Michael, with a number to call if he still has doubts."

"How do we keep Wilburn out of his office?" Karen asked.

"We'll have some authoritative voice call him and tell him that his space has been locked down and that he's free to return the following morning. If he balks we can promise him a picture of the vice president dining at his establishment, complete with a one-line, signed rave review."

"Appeal to him as a businessman; I like it."

"Thanks, Gwen said.

"It all sounds great," Karen said. "Now we have to practice our craft as top-of-the line waitresses."

"I did some of that in college," Gwen said. "Back in beautiful downtown Gambier, Ohio. Remember: we'll have the advantage of their desire to be left alone. Boerling and his team will probably have the standard expectations of the arrogant; they'll expect subservience, relative invisibility and competence, probably in that order."

"The invisibility works to our advantage," Karen said, "not that they'll be filing any personnel reports or *Yelp* reviews after dinner."

"How about you? Ever done any waitressing?" Gwen asked.

"Very little, but it was in top Westwood establishments when I was at UCLA."

"We'll have to play a lot of this by ear," Gwen said, "but the basic plan is simple enough. I'd like to be finished before his security detail gets through their soup course."

"Have you briefed the Director fully on the plan?"

"Yes, while you were running your surveillance protocols. He's OK with all of the details. He insisted on having some agents in the shadows in case we get bottled up. Top people. People who will have ironclad but unrelated excuses for being in the area. He wouldn't disclose any details. He simply said that if things begin to go belly-up we should follow their lead. He referred to them as our guardian angels in gray suits."

"With something more kinetic than swords beneath their jackets," Karen added.

"I think that would be a roger," Gwen said.

The Director's so-called makeup artist was East European, with the highly-unlikely *nom de guerre* of 'Kathy'. Her motto was 'less is more' and she proceeded to explain how it was better to remove physical characteristics than to draw attention to false characteristics. "You want to draw blank expressions when they're asked to describe you. Think of nuns: you hide their hair and remove their makeup and they are no longer women. Blank faces. Nothing remaining of the (what do you call them?) 'secondary sex characteristics'. Glasses are fine, but glasses that are designed to obscure your actual appearance. No prescriptions, no heavy tinting, no bifocal lines, nothing that will interfere with your work. We'll also do a little white scarfy thing around your neck. No earrings, no necklaces, no rings or bracelets."

"How long have you been working with the Director, Kathy?" Gwen asked.

"Since he freed me."

"Freed you?" Gwen said.

"When he was in uniform?" Karen asked.

"When he was in the Army, yes," she answered. "I prefer not to say where, but one of his units liberated the city where his enemies were confining me and…selling my body. They attempted to escape, thinking that the Americans would be focused on the battle itself and the armed combatants. They got as far as the command center, where the General was sitting with his driver and issuing orders from their vehicle. He told them to halt (in their language, mind you) and they ran toward him, shooting and wounding his driver. The General personally operated the large machine gun attached to their vehicle and took them all down."

"A .50 caliber?" Karen asked.

"I am not sure of the precise details but it was very large," Kathy said.

"A .50 caliber would have cut them into bite-size pieces," Gwen said.

"Bite-size? That is very funny," Kathy said. "It was not funny at the time. One of them was dragging me with him, through the dirt. When I was able to free myself and I was clear of them the General shot them all. They did not make many sounds."

"There was probably not much left to make any sounds with," Karen said.

"How did you free yourself?" Gwen asked.

"I had a sharpened metal implement," Kathy said. "It found its way into his…"

"His private parts?" Karen said.

"Yes, the first time," Kathy said.

"And then?" Gwen asked.

"His right eye."

CHAPTER NINETY-TWO

When Kathy had completed her work Gwen and Karen paused for a late breakfast. They decided to skip lunch and any alcohol so that they would be completely fresh at the time of the operation. Their breakfast was French toast with sausages, juice and black coffee. They covered the toast in maple syrup and sat in silence as they ate. A few minutes later they received a message from Michael.

"This is probably nothing," Michael said, "since there's no way that they could know about your operation, but Conwell has been texting Dana Woodson. At first she said that she might have to cancel dinner this evening because of a mini-crisis at the Mexican embassy. Then she said that the problem had been resolved, but that she might be a little late. Finally she said that the original time would not be a problem and that she would be there at 7:30, as planned."

"Did you see anything that would confirm all that?" Gwen asked.

"At the Mexican embassy?"

"Yes."

"I was able to get into the scheduler's master calendar. Apparently some Chinese official was trying to reschedule a meeting, but the problem was resolved. He came in for lunch rather than for dinner."

"They're very chummy these days," Karen said, "what with the building of vast Chinese automobile plants in Mexico. With those kinds of items on the table I can see why they would be prepared to rearrange all of their schedules. The disgusting thing is that they can do a lot of their planning and scheming in our capital city, because all of the representatives of their respective countries are here."

"And why they would want to be sure that Conwell was available for the meeting," Gwen said. "She's worked for the Chinese in the past and she speaks Mandarin. That would give comfort to both sides. The Mexicans would trust her to monitor any translation issues and the Chinese would see a familiar face on the other side of the table. For that matter, she may still actually be working for the Chinese."

"True," Karen said.

"Anyway," Michael said, "I didn't want to discombobulate your plans or add to your concerns. Conwell's communications with Woodson seem to be on the up and up."

"We appreciate it, Mike," Gwen said. "Any time you see anything that could conceivably be of interest to us we want you to share it. Anything on Davis? Karen's monitoring his movements; he appears to be hunkered down at his condo."

"As far as I can see he's completely outside the loop on the dinner," Michael said. "Since Woodson knows about it I'm assuming that she's simply functioning in her gofer role and has no idea of what the meeting might involve. She's just the messenger."

"Our opinion as well," Karen said. "Thanks again."

Driving against rush-hour traffic on the Shirley Highway was still a challenge, because rush hour now encompassed lunchtime and late lunchtime. Sometimes you hit a seam; most of the time you don't. When they arrived at the restaurant they came in the back door and approached the sous chef, a youngish man who appeared to be a Filipino. He seemed a bit harried and told them he was glad to have their help. "We want our special guests to have a good experience. I'm sure you'll see to that."

"Of course," Karen said. "How many covers do you have tonight?"

"We're full for both services," he answered. "Only one service in the private dining room, of course."

"Have the private diners made any requests for special meals?" Gwen asked.

"No. The principal's wife comes here often and always orders from the menu. I suspect that she recommended us to her husband."

"And there will be three dining with us?" Gwen asked. "No further additions?"

"Just the three," the sous chef said. "The table's set. You'll probably want to check it out…"

"Yes, thanks," Karen said. "We'll be down again when they order."

At that moment two of the line cooks were trying to get the sous chef's attention. "I have to see to this…" he said.

Karen raised her hand, as if to say 'we'll let you go. Thanks.'

When they got to the private dining room the door was locked.

CHAPTER NINETY-THREE

When Gwen attempted to turn the knob they were approached by a tall, barrel-chested man who came from the direction of Wilburn's office and displayed his credentials. "We're locked down," he said.

"We can't serve dinner if we can't get into the dining room," Karen said.

"Of course not; my site team will be replaced by the normal security detail as soon as the principal and his party arrive. We'll open it then."

"We'd appreciate as much lead time as you can provide," Karen said. "We have to check the table settings; do the last-minute measurements, check the glassware, and so on."

"Everything should be fine," the security man said. "My partner and I checked it all out."

Karen gave him a polite, professional look.

"I get it," he said. "You want it all fancy/schmancy—keep the silverware and glassware in proper order and all that stuff."

"Special occasion; thanks for understanding," Karen said. "We have a few things we can do in the meantime. We'll get scrubbed and you can let us know when the room is available." She reached in her pocket and took out a bar of strong, gritty soap. "Diners don't want to be served by people wearing plastic gloves. It's too…institutional."

"Agreed," the agent said. "That's a good idea. What is that, *Boraxo*?"

"I don't think they make it in that form anymore," Karen said. "It's like that though, but with a strong antiseptic."

"Cool," he said. "They should be here in about fifteen minutes. I can let you in in ten."

"We appreciate that," Karen said.

When they went into the storage room they each breathed a sigh of relief. "I'm glad we weren't searched," Gwen said.

"Not sure if he'd search everywhere," Karen said.

"Right, and good job on taking the lead. Not that any of the security people or diners would recognize me, but it's better if I keep my head down and defer to you."

"The Boerlings kill so many people they would probably have trouble keeping them all straight," Karen said. "Grayson and Scherl were the most likely to be able to identify you and they've gone on to their eternal reward, such as it may be."

"I hope they've taken air conditioners with them," Gwen said, as she checked the mini-fridge for bottled water. "All in order," she said. "Plenty of backups."

"The sink is functional," Karen said.

"That's essential," Gwen said, smiling and checking her watch. "I suppose we should position ourselves like a pair of sentinels and wait for the agent to unlock the dining room door."

He was there four minutes later. "The principal's driver just drove up and the person joining the principal and his wife is sitting at the bar, waiting for them. I'll unlock the door now. Just one request…"

"Yes?" Karen said.

"Keep all of your contact with them to a minimum and keep the door closed whenever you can. Their security detail will be at the table at the bottom of the stairs, in case you need them."

"Thank you," Karen said. "Much appreciated."

The table was set for three with glassware for red wine, white wine, water and liqueurs. Someone had instructed the house staff to bring out the best china, which displayed a golden capital Q that matched the thick gold rim.

The table itself was round, with the chairs equidistant on the periphery. It was covered with thick cloth. The linen napkins carried an embroidered Q and the candle display in the center was seated on a polished, circular mirror that extended the glow from the flames of the ring of vigil lights.

Three minutes later the Boerlings appeared at the door. Ellie's expression was one of hauteur mixed with equal parts of disdain. She stared through Karen and Gwen as if their presence was evoking a look reserved for lipstick-rimmed glasses or baseboard mouse droppings. Gwen immediately responded with a look that suggested that she had been properly intimidated. When Karen greeted the group and expressed the hope that they would enjoy their dinner Ellie said, "We expect you to do your work, keep your contact with us to an absolute minimum and neither gawk nor stare nor speak unless it is absolutely necessary."

"Certainly," Karen said. "Connie will hang up your coats. Menus are at your places. Bottled water is complimentary. Tell us which you wish, still or sparkling. We will serve you water and bring bread as you read the menus." She then added a mini-bow.

"Water?" Ellie said to her husband and Marilyn Conwell.

"Still," Carlton replied.

"And for me," Conwell added.

"Three," she said to Karen. "Pour it and return in ten minutes with the bread."

"Of course," Karen said.

As Gwen filled the water goblets with ice cubes Karen followed her with two large, iced bottles of Acqua Panna. Placing the second bottle in the chilled wine bucket, she filled their glasses with the first. Again offering a mini-bow she and Gwen exited the room, closing it behind them. Ten minutes later they returned. Marilyn Conwell was sprawled on the floor, next to the Boerlings. There was no response to stimulation. Their pupils were constricted and their bodies were contorted as if they had labored to breathe but ultimately failed. Their skin was clammy and their lips and fingernails had a blue tinge.

"I wonder who's looking into those dead eyes," Gwen said, "Grayson? Scherl?"

"I think we can safely rule out St. Peter," Karen said.

CHAPTER NINETY-FOUR

They returned five minutes later with a tray of bread, butter and extra virgin olive oil. Spilling the contents of the tray across the table and floor they proceeded to drop the tray, exit the room, close the door, walk slowly down the stairs as if they were going to the kitchen to place orders and then slipped out the rear door, past the CCTV cameras which Karen had temporarily disabled.

Before they got on the road to Stafford they drove around the back streets and alleys of Georgetown and Northwest Washington, insuring that no one was following them. When they reached I-95 they called the Director.

"Operation completed," Gwen said.

"And was there a valediction?" he asked.

"No, sir, just a thin line of drool seeping from the side of his mouth and into the carpet."

"Superb. Full debrief in the morning. Your house. 7:30 A.M."

Breakfast was celebratory. Belgian waffles with bacon, hash browns and fresh berries with cream. "Happy to see that you're replenishing," the Director said. "I do like the real Vermont syrup and Irish butter. I'm not sure that my endocrinologist would approve, but sometimes we all need a little time away. How did you like Kathy?"

"The best," Gwen said. "She shared a little of your mutual history."

"She's not supposed to do that," the Director said, "but sometimes she can't resist. Now…down to business. I assume that everything went as planned."

"Yes," Gwen said. "Almost suspiciously so, but some days you actually consume the bear."

"And avoid the trichinosis," the Director said.

"There were four members of the security detail," Karen said, "but they were seated at the bottom of the stairs on the first level."

"Ellie trusts no one," Gwen said. "She's happy to see them take a bullet on their behalf but she doesn't want anyone within earshot when they're making plans and scheming schemes."

"Carlton's evil half," the Director said.

"Exactly," Karen said, "but her ruthlessness was also her fatal flaw. She was so contemptuous of the mere mortals around her that she failed utterly to engage with them. We could have been holding our *Sigs* in our hands and pulling back the slides and she wouldn't have noticed them. As for her husband…his mind seemed to be elsewhere entirely."

"Probably on the next trafficking operation that Conwell would direct for them and the position of the decimal point after its completion," Gwen said.

"So you simply walked out the back door, slowly and deliberately."

"Yes," Gwen said. "I looked at the security unit; they were picking out the mini-meatballs from their Italian wedding soup, probably happy to be away from the Boerlings for a precious hour or two."

"The media have been kept at bay," the Director said. "They know that something important is afoot because the dining room was cleared and everything inside and outside was locked down. One of the diners arriving for the second service was a stringer for the *Washington Examiner* and the moment she began to make calls and ask questions the rumors began to fly. So far the speculation has been that Boerling had a stroke or a heart attack but the press is lined up at the White House, badgering them with all manner of questions. We can be sure that the President and one or more of her top staffers are bouncing off the walls of the oval office, trying to plan next steps. They would have needed the time overnight to conduct autopsies and complete lab work. It will be very interesting to see what they leak to the WaPo."

"We trust that we have created a plausible story for them," Gwen said.

"I'm sure you did," the Director said. "And after this is all over and behind us…we'll regroup for some serious steaks and my favorite wine."

"Our calendars are open," Gwen said.

CHAPTER NINETY-FIVE

The President, Caroline Hopkins, and her Chief of Staff, Wilson Prentice, were huddled in the oval office. Normally they would sit on the more comfortable couch and chair arrangement at the front of the room but Hopkins was all business, sitting behind the Resolute desk. Prentice was seated next to her, their heads leaning forward in full conspiratorial posture.

"Full details, Will," she said.

"All three died of opioid overdoses--Carlton, Ellie, and that not-so-shadowy figure from the Mexican embassy, Conwell. The principal drug was oxycodone but it was laced with fentanyl. Carlton had a vial in his coat pocket. It appeared to be a bootleg formulation—no prescription labels, just a small white piece of tape with the letters 'O-X' written in ballpoint ink. As you know, there have been suspicions of Boerling's involvement with the cartels. It could be that they had given him a free sample of their wares…"

"Or that that Conwell woman was the go-between, passing it on to him after they had each had a sample, but not knowing the lethality of the dose."

"Yes. The larger scheme of things suggests that the likeliest possibility is that he overreached and (as one of your predecessors might have put it) misunderestimated his opponents. He attempted to secure a portion of the cartels' operations and they responded by making an example of him for anyone else who had similar aspirations. The Conwell woman was a not-so-innocent bystander or a pawn sacrifice."

"Damn bold of them, doing that in our city."

"They don't lack boldness, Ma'am."

"What about the servers? Any likelihood that they were involved?"

"There was a notation on a slip of paper on the owner of the restaurant's desk. Two names, just given names: Consuela and Guadalupe."

"How religious," the President said.

"Initially, at least, we doubt that they were involved. Our assumption is that the owner was hiring undocumented workers; hence the absence of last names. After they had poured the bottled water they returned with bread, butter, olive oil and little bowls in which to mix the oil with salt, pepper and Italian grated cheese. They dropped the tray, presumably because the Boerlings and Conwell were found sprawled across the floor. They then left the restaurant forthwith, probably because they were undocumented and didn't want to spend the night being incarcerated and interrogated by local police and a long line of representatives of federal agencies."

"So how were the opioids ingested? A tablet a day keeps the ho-hums away?"

"We're working on the assumption that either Boerling or Conwell (probably Boerling) had passed around the drugs as an appetizer. He failed to anticipate the possibility that they contained a lethal amount of fentanyl."

"The servers could have put the drugs in their water."

"Possibly, but the spare bottle in the wine bucket had not been opened and an empty bottle found in the recycling bin in the storage closet was clean. The glasses on the table had all been tipped over and there was no drug residue found in the glasses or on the table cloth. There was something else, however…"

"Don't keep me guessing, Will."

"Ellie had several containers of *Narcan* in her purse; each was full, the complete 4 mg."

"So they had traveled this road before."

"Yes, but this time the fentanyl hit them so hard that she was unable to reach the *Narcan* in time to save them."

"How long does it usually take to work?"

"It depends on several factors, of course, but…maybe, two minutes?"

"They thought that they could kick back, go for some *Gaja* Barolo and some *pasta e fagioli* and mellow out. Instead they got the blue lip special."

"Yes, Ma'am, in a manner of speaking."

"So what do we leak to the WaPo?"

"That's a tough one, Ma'am…"

"Your job, Will."

"Perhaps that there was a tragic accident, that the Boerlings and their dinner guest had mistakenly ingested lethal drugs whose source is under investigation…?"

"Damn harsh message, Will, but it's better than saying that they were killed by the very drug cartels whose operations they were attempting to take over and control."

"We should also anticipate the fact that many will shoot from the hip and call for airstrikes against the cartels' Mexican headquarters."

"Right. Tell one of your toadies at the *Post* that the full force of the investigatory arms of the government are on the case and that they won't rest until the criminals are brought to swift and stern justice, etc., etc., etc. Tell them also that we're working closely with the *Presidente* to see if there is any cartel involvement. You can call your counterpart at that end and play patty-cake. Meanwhile I'll think about a replacement for Boerling."

"If I may say so, Ma'am, I'm certain that you'll pick an improvement."

"I never really cared for the son-of-a-bitch, Will. You want my take on this?"

"Of course, Ma'am."

"That asshole Sol was up to his eyeballs in illegal operations. Boerling saw an opening, took out Sol and tried to step in. The fact that this has all happened so fast is our hole card. Boerling was new at the game and way over his head. He tried to step in and was crushed like a lost *cucaracha*. Before we could assemble evidence and take the steps to indict him he was already gone. That timeline provides us the distance from his activities that we need. It's all very sad and a tad embarrassing, etc., etc., etc., but the voters will remember that we were forced to take him on by that asswipe senator from Washington state. Now that the decks are clear we can bring in our own person, some Galahad or Maria Goretti. Do you smell the scent of roses in the air, Will?"

"I do, Ma'am. From the spray on top of his coffin to the stands around the podium when his replacement takes the oath."

"Make it happen, Will."

CHAPTER NINETY-SIX

A month later a new vice-president took the oath of office. The Massachusetts congressman (black, Marine veteran) wore his miniaturized silver star medal in the lapel of his gray business suit as his wife and four children smiled politely in front of a broad wall of red, white and blue bunting and American flags.

The WaPo's story line featured the putting aside of a recent, sordid past and its replacement with blue skies and sunny uplands. The president had quietly worked with the senate majority leader to strip the Washington state senator who had forced Boerling upon her administration of all of his key committee assignments. The official line was that 'such realignments are common practice as we continue to strive to serve the American people in the most effective and efficient manner possible' but the symbolism of the action echoed from Pennsylvania Avenue to the original *Starbucks* shop in Seattle. The cooperating press saw it as an indication that the queen bee was fully in charge once again. In the Puzzle Palace and the Company's HQ in Langley the old timers said that 'the old girl is kicking ass and taking names and she's not taking many names.'

Karen was working on some terrorist threats in San Diego and Gwen was temporarily riding a desk at the Hoover Building when they received invitations from the Director to reassemble. The rallying point was a private dining room at the *Inn at Little Washington*. The menu was Maryland crab soup, Wagyu beef, fingerling potatoes, corn off the cob and a chocolate mousse with whipped cream that was guaranteed to bring sweat just beneath the eyes. This was all to be washed down with some *Chassagne-Montrachet, Chateau Palmer* and an Armagnac with a frayed and faded label.

"I realize that the menu is not as chi-chi as the chef would usually present, but this is soldiers' food, victorious soldiers' food," the Director said. "I trust that you will enjoy the meal but also appreciate the symbolism."

"George Washington surveyed and laid out the town when he was a teenager," Karen said.

"In 1749," the Director said.

"And Peggy O'Connor and her friend Maryellen ate here before they were murdered," Gwen added.

"Yes," the Director said. "I don't believe in ghosts but I believe in spirits and I thought that this might somehow enable us to connect with theirs."

As they tasted their white burgundy the Director asked them what they thought of Boerling's replacement.

"From a satyr to Hyperion," Gwen said.

The Director smiled broadly. "You know that we read *Hamlet* when I was a West Point yearling…"

"No, sir, I didn't," Gwen said, but it's the sort of thing that I knew you would know."

Gradison tipped his glass to her. "There's one thing that I've forgotten to ask…"

"Yes, sir? Gwen said.

"The water glasses…I'd love to hear the how's and why's."

"That was Karen's idea," Gwen said. "We knew that they would be checked for residue so we rinsed them until the glass nearly melted. The luck came in the fact that they were never spilled on the table cloth, so we didn't have to go through the arduous task of replacing the cloth, pouring clean water on it, and so on. We could have simply switched out the glasses, but we wanted to preserve the diners' fingerprints on them on the off chance that someone checked for them. After we rinsed the glasses we got a fresh bottle of still water from the mini-fridge, put some in each of the glasses and then turned over Ellie's glass onto the cloth. This would indicate that she was served first, drank first and died first."

"But there was only one bottle in the recycling bin."

"That was the fresh bottle," Gwen said. "The bottle with the residue was rinsed multiple times and we took it with us."

"So I assumed," the Director said, "but how did you transport something so large without anyone noticing it?"

"Again, Karen's idea," Gwen said. "It was really very simple…"

"I had a waterproof fanny pack under my server's uniform," Karen said. "I slipped the bottle into the pack, zipped it up and broke the bottle into tiny shards that would collapse into the shape of the pack. I tightened the belt so that the fanny pack would function like a girdle, tucked into my stomach. If someone had had multiple, high-resolution photos of me before and after they might have been able to detect the difference, but that's why we disabled the CCTV system. That was the tricky part, our one potential vulnerability as it worked out…"

"The fact that it could be determined that the system was disabled," the Director said. "Very suspicious."

"It would have been," Karen said, "but remember that Wilburn had purchased a cheap security system. Dupont Circle…in the middle of the evening…with all of the internet traffic…I had their security system timed to go in and out several times that evening, so that the interruptions appeared to be normal occurrences."

"My engineer," the Director said.

"Pretty elementary," Karen said.

"All the pros say that," the Director responded.

As they completed their steaks the Director proposed a toast with the *Palmer*. "You probably know that one of the owners of the estate— the person for whom the estate is named—was an English general, Charles Palmer. I personally prefer the *Palmer* to the once-upon-a-time first growth, *Margaux*. I can't say why, exactly. Maybe it's that slight touch of violets…anyway, it's unique. General Palmer had good taste. It's sometimes said that the English are the great appreciators of claret (and, for that matter, other French wines)."

"It's exquisite," Karen said.

The Director smiled and refilled their glasses.

"Your toast," Gwen said, "to those who take the narrow road…"

"Yes," he said, "I was thinking, of course, of the old notion that the road to hell is broad and more easily taken, but I was thinking more particularly of one of my company commanders, a young man named Norb Johnson. On a hot and bloody day he ignored one of my direct orders, saved the lives of 90% of his men, turned the enemy flank and enabled us to win an important battle. 'What were you thinking?' I asked him. 'You ignored my order. That's not a criticism, son, but it's a rare and dangerous thing to do. You could end up at Leavenworth behind bars rather than at the Command and General Staff college there.' He apologized for his actions and said, 'I have the greatest respect for you, sir, and I thought you would prefer to see us succeed rather than fail and be slaughtered. You can call it a gut reaction, an instinctive response or the need to follow my heart for the ultimate, higher good. I would rather be court-martialed than live with the fact that I had ultimately betrayed myself and my beliefs.'"

"Moral ambiguity," Gwen said. "It's a monster, but we have to face it down and deal with it."

"It's where we ultimately live," the Director said. "The protocols are all in place to protect us. They're there to keep us on the putative straight and narrow, but they're also there to give us something to refer to when we fail to do what we know we must do. I wouldn't go so far as to use the word *excuse*, but it's very close to that. If you don't mind me going all philosophical on you…life occurs in the blink of an eye but that eternal stuff has its own demands and its own priorities. I understand the fact that there's always a temptation to justify our actions by deceiving ourselves, but taking out an evil man when no one else was likely to do so, a man responsible for endless human suffering, well, ultimately, that's an easy one."

"Are you worried that we may be experiencing some kind of buyer's remorse?" Gwen asked.

"No, I just…well…it's still not something that is easily forgotten."

"Sir," Gwen said, "put your mind at ease. Our only regret is that we never got the opportunity to kill the three of them with our bare hands."

"That would be an interesting image," the Director said. "I won't ask for any details."

Karen reached inside her jacket, removed her *SigSauer* pistol, placed it on the table, reached inside a second time, turned over her shoulder holster and removed a small device that resembled a miniature arrow with razor-sharp edged points and a handle with a cross-hatched pattern tooled into the surface of the metal to insure a strong grip.

Gradison looked at the weapon, smiled, and took a sip of his *Palmer* as Gwen unzipped her purse, removed her pistol, took out a black stiletto and reached in for a third time.

"That's enough," he said. "You've made your point. I'm going to need some reinforcements. He reached into his tote bag and took out a second bottle of the aged Armagnac, placing it on the table with a modest flourish.